The Ancestral Suitcase

The Ancestral Suitcase

Sylvia Fraser

KEY PORTER BOOKS

Canadian Cataloguing in Publication Data

Fraser, Sylvia

The ancestral suitcase

ISBN 1-55013-758-1

I. Title.

PS8561.R36A75 1996 C813'.54 C95-933291-X

PR9199.3.F73A75 1996

The publisher gratefully acknowledges the assistance of the Canada Council and the Ontario Arts Council. The author also wishes to acknowledge the support of the City of Toronto through the Toronto Arts Council.

Key Porter Books Limited

70 The Esplanade

Toronto, Ontario

Canada M5E 1R2

Printed and bound in Canada

96 97 98 99 6 5 4 3 2 1

You may cut flowers off the tree
You may cut leaves off the tree
You may cut branches off the tree
You may cut down the tree
But the roots of the tree
Grow deeper still
Than this.

FROM THE MAYAN

Acknowledgements

A huge thank you to Anna Porter, who once again took the leap of faith, and to Susan Renouf, who jumped with her. Thanks also to my editor, Jennifer Glossop; to my agent, Sterling Lord; and to my friends who read early drafts of this manuscript, especially Lily Poritz Miller.

Contents

The Ancestral Suitcase / 9
The Wolfe Inn Moon / 49
The Spiral / 175
The Cave / 201

THE ANCESTRAL SUITCASE

1

She had come home from church, seated herself at the walnut desk where she composed her Sunday-school lessons, printed "THINGS TO DO IN THE EVENT OF MY DEMISE" on a piece of notepaper, choked on her own breath, and died.

Nora stared at that stark page, trying to imagine her mother's last instructions. Had they been grandiose – "LOVE GOD," "REPENT YOUR SINS"? Or mundane – "EMPTY GARBAGE PAIL UNDER SINK," "CANCEL MY SUBSCRIPTION TO *THE HAMILTON SPECTATOR*"? Either would have been in character.

The desk calendar still read "JUNE 6," suggesting that her mother's death – like almost everything else in Ellen Locke's life – had been willed rather than random. Nora tore off that date – her own first day of life and her grandma Flora's last. That death and birth had occurred within the same hour, thirty-eight years ago. Unfortunately, Nora had never doubted which event her mother considered the important one.

She allowed long-repressed anger to surface through her grief: her birthdays had always had a baleful quality, like a fancy pink cake with black candles.

After crumpling another eleven calendar days to produce a neutral "JUNE 18," she picked up a silver-framed photo of herself in university graduation cap and gown. Her eyes, set wide over high, lightly freckled cheekbones, had been the right color – ice-blue like her grandmother's. It was her hair that had been her first failure – dark and straight, not red and curly like Grandmother Flora's Celtic locks, which her mother had described so vividly and so often that in her child's imagination they had turned the color of blood. Nora had slouched her way into university before she realized that fashion now favored what she was – a leggy and *sportif* girl-for-all-seasons rather than the compact, more rounded parlor model represented by the dressmaker's mannequin still in her mother's sewing room.

Nora pried her graduation picture from its frame – a simpering likeness she detested. Underneath, she was surprised to discover another photo, labeled in her mother's firm hand: "FIRST FOOTFALL, QUEBEC CITY, 1913." It showed her grandmother, a widow of seventeen, debarking from *The Empress of Ireland* with her infant in her arms. Flora Quarry Flowe – the woman for whom Nora had been named, except that high-flying "Fl" had been withheld and she'd been grounded with an "N."

Nora tried to peek under the straw hat obscuring all but a determined jaw, plus a few wisps of that legendary red hair. She vaguely remembered other pictures of Grandma Flora, liberally scattered about the house, always in high places, as befits a household god: when had all those photos disappeared, and why?

Impulsively, Nora began to sketch with her left hand on her mother's "THINGS TO DO" page, producing a buckled suitcase like Grandma Flora's, complete with steamer sticker. Dropping the pen, she stared at her drawing hand, hanging like a turkey foot from her wrist . . . *trussed behind her back, forcing her to use her right one. "You'll thank me some day."*

Feeling the early-warning signs of a migraine, Nora pushed back from her mother's desk and went into the kitchen to make tea.

It took several minutes of pawing through meticulously glued china for Nora to find one cup that was uncracked, unchipped and unmended. She remembered the time that she, as a Mother's Day surprise, had replaced Ellen Locke's worn and damaged "Purple Posy" china with an identical set purchased with babysitting money, wondering how long it would take for her to spot this miracle of regeneration.

Her mother had not been amused. "Your grandmother bought that set with her widow's compensation. Those dishes are all we have left of your grandad!"

The discarded china had been retrieved from the basement, and the new stuff returned to Mill's Hardware for a credit that her mother had never used.

Nora filled her cup with tea – not the British kind, with mysterious dark leaves from which Grandmother Flora had once conjured fortunes – but a reddish herbal blend Nora had bought in a health-food store. Startled, she watched the cup split along an unseen fault line, gushing Raspberry Zinger in a red puddle over the enamel table. As she mopped up, she remembered a question on a personality test she had taken as a college freshman: "What would you do if you found half a cup on a path in the woods? (a) Ignore it. (b) Kick it aside. (c) Examine it before discarding it. (d) Pick it up in case you find the other half."

Nora had been attracted to "(b) Kick it aside" but had settled on "(c) Examine it before discarding it." Now as she collected the pieces of this cup, she gave herself permission to trash it, along with her mother's cupboard of patchwork china.

Nora had filled two garbage bags, rejoicing in the clinks and clunks, when the doorbell rang. Dolly Dolby was expected at 9:00 A.M. and that was the exact time. Punctuality was a desirable thing in a real-estate agent. Her mother would have approved.

A strawberry blonde in an orange "Big, Bold and Beautiful" dress, Mrs. Dolby radiated a down-to-earth cheerfulness that Nora found reassuring. "Just call me Dolly. That Dolby is left over from my second husband, and he's long gone, thank goodness – the jerk!"

Fortunately, Dolly's comments about the real estate were far more positive. She was especially pleased with the size of the kitchen, though it required updating. "Which doesn't necessarily hurt a sale, dear. Get a party talking about how a place *could* look and sometimes it hooks them harder than if it were already done. They feel the house needs them."

At the top of the hall stairs, Nora ushered Dolly into the master bedroom, featuring an Italian provincial suite and two of her mother's paintings, *Spring* and *Autumn*, meticulously copied from greeting cards.

"Your mum was one neat housekeeper."

Nora's eye flew to the highboy that had once held a football trophy, a stud box and a 1944 wedding portrait. "She was a widow most of her life." Where had those mementos gone? Nora walked over to the highboy, yanked open the top drawer. "My father's things are missing!"

"How long has this house been vacant?" asked Dolly indignantly.

Nora struggled to remember that final conversation with her mother.

"You wouldn't believe the rats in this town! They read the obits and —"

"No! It's okay." But it wasn't. Bottling dismay, Nora strode into her mother's adjoining bedroom.

"Say, somebody sure liked purple!"

Nora forced her mind back to the present task. "This place does look a bit like Barney the dinosaur. It sort of crept up on my mother in her later years. Everything that wasn't purple got painted, papered or replaced." Pride edged out her distress. "My mother did her own decorating, right into her eightieth year."

"And with these high ceilings, too. I go into some of the new houses and the lid's so tight you'd think you were walking into a grave."

They entered a room containing an easel and a Singer sewing machine. "My grandmother used to run a tearoom here, where she told fortunes. This place still has all the old kitchen plumbing under the wallpaper if anyone's interested in renovating."

"A fortune-teller – fancy that!" Dolly began pacing.

"It's nine by twelve."

Dolly halted. "I didn't mean —" She sneezed. "Is there an air conditioner in here?"

Nora laughed. "My mother never got around to anything as modern as that. Wait'll you see her washing machine! I can open a window if —"

"Actually, I was feeling a draft." Dolly dabbed at her nose with an oversized white handkerchief. "I have a passel of allergies that act up at weird times." She gingerly poked the dressmaker's mannequin. "This is certainly an antique."

"My fabled grandmother!" Nora unknotted a cherry-print scarf from the mannequin's throat. "Mother tried to use this thing to sew for me too, though I was as flat as a bean and my knees came up to the armpits. We got some interesting results." She sniffed the scarf – a powerful scent of lavender – then deposited it in a sewing basket. "Watch these attic steps. Some of the linoleum treads are worn. My family lived in this house for eighty years."

Dolly heaved up into what had been Nora's bedroom, a hodgepodge of unmatched furniture with a lace-curtained window overlooking a decaying but respectable working-class street.

Nora wiped her fingers on her black spandex shorts. They still smelled of lavender. "This cubbyhole's been turned into a closet." She flung open the door: a scooped-neck cherry-print sundress hung from a hanger. "My mother must have made this for me!"

Deeply touched, Nora held up the dress against her "Save the Wolf" T-shirt, then viewed herself in the mirror. "There's a storage room behind that back door if —"

But Dolly was halfway down the steps.

Below ground, the agent grew more practical. "That oil furnace looks new, thank goodness." She peered into a former coal bin now piled with a pyramid of tin. "What's all this?"

"Soup cans. My mother washed, peeled and flattened them with an ax. She used to make me haul them back to London before Hamilton went in for recycling."

Dolly jabbed her Kewpie-doll finger toward a row of preserved pears. "With my mum it's quart sealers. My daughter's a hoarder too. Do you suppose genes jump a generation?"

A jar of pears exploded on the brick floor. Both women leapt back. "I didn't —" Falling to her knees, Dolly began picking up shards.

Nora pulled her to her feet. "Please. . . . " The sound still reverberated. "That isn't necessary. I'll do it later."

Dolly vigorously rubbed her palms, chiming her bangles. "Let's look at the bright side – that's one less quart sealer for my mum to worry about!"

Back on the main floor, Nora poured lemonade while Dolly made a few sharp-penciled calculations at the gate-legged dining table. "My philosophy is to choose the right price and more or less stay put." She reached for one of Ellen Locke's spangled Christmas shortbreads. "I'd list this one at $80,000 and expect to come in around $79,000."

"But Mrs. Johnson across the street has a much smaller yard and she got $86,000 just last week."

"You're right, and I was the one who got it for the lady. There were differences, dear, unseen differences." Dolly lay a placating hand on Nora's arm. "Can I be frank with you? Every house has its atmosphere and, truth to tell, there's something off about this one. I felt it soon as I set foot in that old tearoom – something defiant and high-spirited, especially around that mannequin. 'Well, what do we have here?' I asked myself. 'Hello there!' Then, when we went up into the attic, I was hit with that clammy, sad feeling and I knew that this was just One of Those Houses."

Nora crumbled the shortbread in her palm. "That seems very subjective!"

Dolly fixed her with a defiant stare. "I did *not* knock over those pears. I was a yard away."

Was the woman daft? "Surely that's not an issue."

"We both were!" Dolly stifled another sneeze. "Now don't take this personal, dear, but there's some sensitive folk I couldn't even show this place to. They'd run right out that back door. Others – the majority – would just start finding fault without knowing why. They'd go around turning on taps, hoping to find something wrong with the plumbing, or else they'd make a mountain out of the poky cupboards as if a cupboard big enough to go bowling in was the one thing they'd set their hearts on. I've seen some battle royals. *She* gets some feeling about a house. *He* can't figure it out because it looks exactly like what she said she wanted and the price is right."

Nora resisted an urge to grab the woman and shake her. "Perhaps if you feel that way —"

"You're right. Maybe I'm not the person for this place." Dolly reached for her lime-green purse. "I'd be happy to suggest another agent who —"

"No!" Nora gripped the seat of her cane chair. Sweat trickled under the arms of her T-shirt. "Sorry, I'm still frayed from the funeral."

"Of course, putting away a life is very draining, and I see a lot of that in these old neighborhoods. People bought together and now they're dropping out together. But we've got to keep chipper."

Dolly rose from the table, using both hands to ease the weight off her legs. "I'm sorry if I've disappointed you, but at $80,000 I can guarantee this place will go within a couple weeks because the people I'll be bringing through will be dealers. They'll have it on the market again before the ink's dry, and they'll be asking $2,000 more than Mrs. Johnson got, and they'll wait and wait."

"But can't we set some compromise price?" queried Nora, determined to make a point more important than those extra dollars.

"Perhaps I could try $83,000 – "

"Yes!"

"– but I hope you'll agree to come down fast. Didn't you tell me that you were going to England?"

"Tomorrow night, but I'll be available every day by phone. I promise I'll drop the price if necessary."

"I hope so." Dolly fanned herself with her notes as she pushed toward the door. "Because when a house is left unattended, the atmosphere takes over. Nothing's left to counteract it." She smiled a bit too brightly. "I'll give it my best shot."

As soon as the door closed, Nora burst into forced laughter, which she struggled to make real: *a pear-pitching poltergeist!* Perfect. She could imagine her mother, tucking a peppery strand into her hairnet while indignantly tapping her toe, and saying, "The very idea!"

As Nora scraped up preserves from the cellar floor, she converted Dolly Dolby into an anecdote – the kind she might tell to colleagues in the university faculty club. "Picture strawberry hair, orange dress, and lime purse . . . or was it lime hair and strawberry purse?" However, her throat felt dry and her left foot had gone numb. Plopping down on the cellar stairs, she removed her Nike shoe and massaged her arch, trying not to notice that her hands were still shaking. *I mustn't let this wallpaper mausoleum get to me.*

Nora's legal appointment with David Sullivan was for two o'clock. As she entered the elevator, she smiled at the tall, pleasant-faced woman in the gray shirtwaist, then realized it was herself reflected in the mirrored walls. She'd done that too often lately – failed to recognize her own image when it caught her off guard. Maybe it was her vintage – too old for the latest fashions and too young to go eccentric. She knew she was aging well: health foods and plenty of exercise were part of her common-sense approach to life. It was just that she was beginning to look stodgy, like a bread pudding without the raisins.

Fortunately, this was a slow elevator and David's office was on the ninth floor – time for a little damage control. Nora dabbed on neutral lipstick, then loosened the sides of her French roll. As a kid she'd hated it when her mother twisted her braids so tightly they pulled her eyes askew. Now she was doing it to herself.

As the elevator jolted to a halt, Nora smoothed her calf-length skirt, wishing she'd worn the festive cherry-print sundress that had mysteriously appeared in her closet. *I should have made more effort after all these years!* However, it was precisely to avoid disappointment that she hadn't: *what if it's just his secretary with papers to sign?*

David's office looked like Upper Canadian money – knotty-pine bookcases, a pine chest with a collection of toy soldiers, framed legal degrees, a Cornelius Krieghoff snow scene, a collection of horse brasses, a refectory table serving as a desk and, incongruously, a tatty recliner like the one used by his lawyer-grandfather on their front porch.

David met her at the door, one tweedy arm cordially extended, the other placed protectively around her shoulders. Gone was every vestige of the wannabe sixties' rebel and the seventies' rock-'n'-roll star.

"Your mother was a gem, always so independent. I was so sorry I couldn't get back in time for the funeral."

He steered her to a parson's chair drawn up to his desk, then took the recliner. On the wall, like a rainbow around his crisply cropped blond head and Muskoka-tanned face, were pictures of his family – Alison, the good-scout wife in tennis togs, with three *Brady Bunch* children wearing a fortune in designer sportswear. Nora was assessing these signs of well-staked social territory with the wry detachment of a visiting sociologist when she realized – in one of those stark, unbidden moments of clarity – that without her mother's ambitions to prod and program her, she had no discernible future.

"Are you all right?" David leaned forward in concern.

Nora found herself slumped against his desk, with her arm across her mother's file. "It's just . . . these papers."

David's voice grew avuncular. "Yes, legal documents seem so

final, so cut and dried. My clients often feel that way, whether it's death or divorce."

Their official business took approximately thirty seconds, as Nora had suspected. "Sign here and here and here." That left only the unofficial business, for which David had apparently scheduled time. After directing her to a horsehair couch, he plucked the stopper from a cut-glass decanter and, with the bouquet of expensive sherry mingling with that of wood and leather, filled two exquisite glass thimbles.

Though the thought of such sweetness on an empty stomach nauseated Nora, she obediently touched rims, then slid the amber liquid across her lips, remembering how they, as kids, had once raided his father's liquor cabinet.

David caught the downward tug of her mouth – what he used to call her upside-down smile. "You're laughing at me."

"At us. There was a time when we didn't mind passing the bottle."

Mirth spilled from his eyes and down his cheeks. His lean face was so transparent that she used to tease him: *You haven't any fat to hide your emotions.*

"*Crème de menthe!* My father's study. Ahh, there was a time when . . . there was a time," he finished lamely.

Setting aside the decanter, David produced an old Central Secondary School yearbook, its pages bristling like a dinosaur's spine with green markers. "I thought this might amuse you." Placing it on Nora's lap, he began flipping pages.

Who was that radiant, extroverted creature with the swingy hair and butterfly smile – playing volleyball, decorating the gym, practicing for the chorus line of the Fall Follies? Nora felt a stab of poignancy. Had she ever been that confident and carefree?

"Here's something a little more sobering." He handed her a photo of the two of them, arm in arm – she with bouffant hair and glittery gold elephant-foot pants, he in leather vest, gold medallion, sideburns and slick pompadour. "Elvis lives."

"And Eldora the witch!" She turned over the photograph, which Alison had titled in her private-school backhand, taking possession just as her mother would have done: "SPRING TONIC, MAY 1970."

"*I* thought we were beautiful." His voice turned butter soft. "So was the evening."

Nora shuffled through the other loose photos – herself and David skiing at Chedoke, hanging out in front of Roberts' Restaurant, at a Lake Erie cornroast – Siamese twins joined at the hands, the hips, the cheeks, the eyes. She remembered how often they had turned up accidentally wearing matching colors and styles. *"Same make and model!" their friends had teased.*

Though all the photos were ordinary, even innocuous, Nora found herself studying them like exotic images in a deck of Tarot cards. She arranged them in chronological order, according to Alison's neatly printed dates, like ties in a railway track leading to the place where the bridge had blown up – June 28, 1970, when a chasm had opened in her life and linear time had given way to a chaos of disconnected events and fragmented images.

David placed his hand over hers. "It was time missing from my life, too." He reached for the sherry, though both glasses were full – probably an excuse to withdraw his hand before the moment grew awkward. "Look, could we have lunch next week?"

Nora stood up, scattering the pictures. "I'm leaving for England tomorrow. I should be packing now . . . a sabbatical."

Hastily retrieving the photos, David handed her the packet. "I made these copies for you." He straightened, matching her inch for inch plus one. "More D.H. Lawrence research?"

"How did you know that?"

"Your mother kept me informed. She was always so proud of you."

Nora thought with embarrassment of the plaques and medals and diplomas that her mother had forced friends, and especially foes, to admire. "She was determined that I would teach."

He scooped up her left hand and turned it palm up. "Not paint?"

Withdrawing it, she hid it behind her back. "Or play the guitar?"

Grinning, he ruffled his polished, corporate hair. "*You* had talent."

He escorted her to the elevator, then seemed reluctant to push the button. "Let's not make it so long next time, eh, Nora?"

Stepping into the mirrored cage, she waved the photos, intending to say a breezy thank-you. Instead, she blurted: "You didn't call!"

Catching the elevator doors, he responded from the exact place in their joint biography. "Yes, I did – right till the day I left for college. Your mother wouldn't let me near you. I guess she held me responsible."

"But I was the one who —"

"No. I was driving." The elevator door bucked against his hand. "I was hurt at first – I thought breaking off was what you wanted." The right side of his mouth turned up, the left down, in an expression she knew meant: *Help me out here, Nora.* When she didn't respond, he released the doors.

Nora watched David's face disappear through the slit as it once had done from her life, leaving only a Cheshire grin. The walls continued to contract. Panicking, she got off at the next floor, then fled down eight flights. . . . *Speeding along York Boulevard in David's father's Buick, through an ethereal lunar fog. Two high-spirited teenagers heading for Snake Road to park. Suddenly, inexplicably, she seizes the wheel with both hands. Jamming her left foot on the gas, she swerves the car, full speed, into the black-iron fence surrounding Hamilton Cemetery.*

Nora hit the lobby at top speed, then kept on going. It took the squeal of brakes as she bolted James Street to slow her forward plunge. Leaning against the base of Gore Park's famed statue of Queen Victoria, she forced herself to breathe deeply, to return to present time.

She strolled through what remained of that modest square after urban designers had replaced its happenstance greenery with concrete flower beds and iron hedges, surrendering to the beautiful June day. It was a long time since she'd taken a good look at Hamilton – something more than an impatient glance as she sped back to her English professor's job at the University of Western Ontario. Across King Street was the former Right House department store where she'd run an elevator one summer, now transformed into a mall of boutiques, and the Pagoda Restaurant where kids used to congregate after movies, and the boarded-up hulk of Woodhouse & Jones, the import–export firm where her mother had worked as a bookkeeper for fifteen years. Small shops known to her under staunchly British names like Stewart and Crawford and Wilkinson had been reborn as Caribbean restaurants, Vietnamese variety stores and East Indian health-food marts. Even in Hamilton.

She stopped at a Chinese herbalist's featuring dried octopi, recalling Grandma Flora's hand-me-down "old country" remedies – garlic necklaces, raw onions sliced under the bed, mustard plasters, horsetail tea. Nora stared at a pickled ginseng root, like a tiny, contorted ghost trying to escape its bottle . . . *not just the accident. For a year she'd been plagued with fainting fits, high fevers, even paralysis that no doctor could diagnose. Then, on June 28, 1971, the first anniversary of the accident, the symptoms mysteriously disappeared, leaving her with an intermittently numb left foot, splintering migraines and a troubling gap in memory.*

Nora found she had been staring into the window with hands and face pressed against the glass. The Chinese herbalist was staring back as if expecting a holdup. Embarrassed, she darted into the gourmet shop next door and bought the first thing she snatched from the shelf – a jar of pears! With an ironic laugh, she stashed it in her shoulder bag: *how silly of Dolly Dolby to cover up for herself – as if knocking down a jar of fruit had mattered.*

Ahead, Nora could see Central Street. She recalled when most of its wage-earners, like her father, had worked shifts at The Steel Company of Canada or Dofasco or Westinghouse. Unfortunately, as Dolly had pointed out, this was now a neighborhood of widows. Even the maples were dropping one by one like worn-out teeth, killed by new sewers, hydro lines, gasoline fumes.

Nora's eyes slid to the home-free chestnut tree on the lawn of David's stately old house, now a triplex, where a renewable gang of kids had once played hide-'n'-seek. With her father's early encouragement, she'd grown up as a tomboy, always pushing at the edges of her mother's authority. Even after his death she'd held her ground, abetted by David. The break with that lively spirit had come with the accident. Through its frightening aftermath, her mother had been an ever-present guardian angel, and then Nora had had to work twice as hard to catch up to her classmates. Scholarship became a habit, along with struggling to please her mother. One strong-willed parent and one child grateful to be alive. *Is it David I've yearned for all these years, or for the unfettered girl he knew?*

With a sudden queasy feeling, Nora realized that she had chosen the same route home her mother had taken on the last day of her life. Despite the unseasonal heat, Ellen Locke had attended Ryerson United Church, then stood for twenty minutes at the door, greeting friends, remarking on new hats, assuring everyone with characteristic certitude that tomorrow would be cooler. Though offered a ride home, she'd opted to deliver the altar flowers to a friend undergoing cancer treatment at St. Joseph's Hospital. "Who knows? This may be the last opportunity Grace and I ever have to visit in this world."

By the time she'd left the hospital, the temperature had edged close to ninety on the old Fahrenheit scale, but her mother was never one to waste money on taxis, which she considered a last resort of the disabled and dying. Though her gait slowed during the trek from her bus stop, she had refused to rest. "I've got my shades drawn and my doors closed. It's amazing how cool you can keep a house if you put your mind to it."

Ellen Locke had taken pride in her independence, supported by her network of aging church friends, glued together – like her chinaware – by eternal faith. Only reluctantly had she given up cutting grass, and she still refused a cane. "Wait until I'm ninety."

Despite this bravado, what relief she must have felt, as she turned the corner, to see her house with its promise of cool, dark air, like a refreshing draft of ice tea. Nora rounded the same corner, took two steps, then gagged: a woman wearing her mother's polka-dot navy dress waved from the steps of Nora's natal home. "Yoohoo!"

As Nora's knees buckled, Aunt Millie Baxter swept her up in arms of surprising strength. "You poor lamb! That's right, let it all come pouring out."

Nora heard a choking sound in her throat like a clogged drain that's about to back up. Struggling free, she slumped onto her mother's veranda steps and sniffled like a child onto the back of her arm.

Aunt Millie handed her a hanky plucked from her bosom, smelling of bread dough. "That's a lot healthier than those glassy eyes you took to your mum's funeral."

Aunt Millie's cluttered kitchen was just as Nora remembered: frilly dotted-swiss curtains, yellow oilcloth table covering, three graduated flying ducks and pots of African violets – a fifties' time warp like a Norman Rockwell painting.

Her hostess cleared balls of pink wool from a rocker. "I'm afraid this kitchen's not much like your mum's. I don't know how that woman kept up – polished every day and vacuumed. Once I asked, 'Land sakes, Ellen, how many specks of dust do you suppose you collected this time?' and she answered, sharp as a tack, 'As many as were sitting waiting for me.'"

Nora laughed. "That sounds like Mother!" As she watched Aunt Millie prepare her Brown Betty pot for tea, she wondered how she could have mistaken this elderly neighbor for Ellen Locke, even wearing the same dress. Where her mother's hair was severely rolled, Aunt Millie's stood on end like an electrified cat's; where her mother's features were thin and decisive, Aunt Millie's sank into fleshly folds and whirlpools; where her mother stood arch-backed in black oxfords, Aunt Millie shuffled in canvas slip-ons.

Feeling Nora's scrutiny, her hostess smoothed her polka-dot pleats. "Your mum insisted I take this dress. Said she was tired of it, but now I think maybe she had an inkling."

Nora dabbed away the last of her tears. "I'm sure there are other things of hers that you might enjoy. You know how she hated throwing anything out."

"Thanks, but to be frank I do like a bit of color. Your mum was all for blacks and grays and browns. This dress was the most cheerful one she owned. I complimented her on it so often that I guess she began to think I wanted it.... How do you take your tea?"

"No sugar," shrieked a voice from the pantry.

Aunt Millie set down her teapot. "Well, guess who's looking to join us!" Opening the pantry, she wheeled out an iron cage, then lifted a faded curtain to reveal green feathers and yellow-disc eyes. "I'm sure you remember Billy Boy."

"No sug-ar, Millie," insisted the parrot.

"Ellen used to say that, regular as clockwork – as if I was in danger of forgetting after fifty-five years!"

Was it just Nora's imagination, or had the damned parrot also got the intonation and tilt of her mother's head? As she cast about for a change of subject, she remembered Dolly Dolby. Setting the scene in a few deft strokes, Nora lay a confiding hand on Aunt Millie's arm as she dramatized: "'Can I be frank with you, dear? There's something *off* about this place. I knew as soon as I put my foot in the attic that it was just One of Those Houses!'"

"My, my, she said that?" Aunt Millie cut a banana cake into careful squares. "Just goes to show how sensitive some people can be."

"Just One of Those Houses," mimicked the parrot.

Aunt Millie shook a warning finger at the cage. "I guess he recognizes Ellen in your voice."

"Poo-or Ellen," whimpered the bird, rubbing his head against the bars.

Aunt Millie again raised her finger to admonish him, but stroked his neck instead. "These last couple of years *were* hard for your mum, no getting around it." Aunt Millie cocked her head as if deciding how much to say. Billy Boy tilted his the same way. "Some days she'd just sit on her veranda steps not wanting to go inside. She said the house had started talking to her."

Nora gulped her tea, scalding her tongue. "She never mentioned anything like that to me!"

"There's a trick to living alone. I sometimes wonder how well I'd do if I didn't have Billy Boy here to rattle on with."

Nora squeezed the remains of her banana cake into a sticky ball. "But we chatted for an hour on the phone at least once a week. All she ever talked about was whether she'd done her washing that day and who was sick or had died."

"Well, you know how folks are. If they feel the boat tipping too far in one direction, they put everything they've got on the other side. Though your mum fought against it, she was like your grandma Flora in that regard – both had second sight."

Nora was incredulous. "Mother?"

"I suppose you knew she sometimes went to that Spiritualist Church down on Cannon Street?"

Nora experienced a deepening sense of betrayal. "I most certainly did not! As far as I knew, she considered the occult to be religious pornography. When someone gave me an Ouija board, she burned it."

Aunt Millie eased her feet out of her canvas shoes with holes cut for bunions. "Well . . . Flora was steeped in all that. I guess your mother needed to put some distance between the two of them after her death. Your grandma left a note – one of those confessional things full of stuff best left unspoken. Your mother burned that, too." The older woman sighed, recollecting. "My, but that Flora was a livewire! No one imagined she had a bad ticker till she died of it."

"An hour before I was born."

"True enough. Flora took to her bed about the same time as your mum did. She said she'd never live to see you born. That was Flora all over – Flora and her premonitions. Right as rain one minute and dead the next. She should have been running an army, she was that strong-willed, but all she had was your mum. Ellen took a long time getting over that death."

"And my birth," reminded Nora.

"Well, births and deaths are like portals, don't you think? An awful lot comes tumbling through, as if it's just been waiting for its chance." Kicking aside her shoes, she curled her bare toes in her sheepskin rug like a child in mud. Billy Boy kneaded his perch with his claws. "Your mum took me up into that attic of yours a couple of times, and I have to admit I felt it, too – a cold clammy feeling and that oversweet perfumy smell. Gave me the goose-bumps, but then I'd been what you might call infected by your mother's mood."

Nora released the shivers in her spine with a shrill laugh. "Are you saying our house is haunted?"

Aunt Millie brought her snub-nosed face close to Nora's "I guess I'm telling you that your mum was, and that I felt it, too, though I didn't think it was something likely to strike strangers." The older woman lay her palms flat on the table. "I told Ellen that she should sell the darn place, maybe even move in here with me, but she wasn't ready for that. I guess she decided to let nature take its course and it has."

"This is incredible!"

Aunt Millie drained her cup. "That it is." She wiped her lips with a "Happy Birthday" serviette. "I guess all families have their secrets, if you're willing to dig deep enough."

2

Nora stood in the archway of her mother's living room, trying to view it with a demolition expert's calculating eye: a seventies' TV, worth less than the forties' radio console beside it; a wicker tea wagon loaded with miniature cacti; a frilly window lamp lit each evening to blind nosy neighbors; two more of her mother's gilt-framed oils, *Summer* and *Winter*; assorted end tables with their shiny veneers generously iced in the doilies that had fallen like perpetual snow from her mother's nimble fingers.

Nora plunked onto the oversized, rolled-arm chesterfield, which heaved under her weight with the same gushy breaking of wind that had mortified a long line of Avon ladies. About the year Nora had started Stinson Street Public School, her mother had discovered something called leatherette paint, which was how the chintz chesterfield had acquired its pea-green color, along with its plastic texture and mischievous ways. By the time Nora was an English major at McMaster University, the chesterfield's wire innards had fallen out and a handyman had glued slats across its bottom – an event fixed in Nora's mind by the fact that her aging cat had somehow become trapped inside and had had to be rescued by crowbar. *Dear old Ginger . . .*

She picked up a nickel-plated, "Souvenir of Buffalo" ashtray that her father had once used for cigar butts.

"You will not smoke in my house! I won't have that filth brought in here."

Now the ashtray rested beside her mother's bible, polished like the Holy Grail – a treasured trophy of a war that her mother had won. As Nora replaced it, she suddenly remembered what had happened to Grandma Flora's photos.

"That bloody woman causes more trouble dead than alive!"

"Don't you dare speak that way about my mother, and don't blaspheme!"

Her father had burned those pictures, nearly taking the house down with them, which was why their place had a stoop at the back instead of a porch like Aunt Millie's.

Nora massaged her head – right temporal lobe, just above the ear, feeling her migraine ripen. It always developed through the same stages: first, a vague sense of expectation – not unpleasant, which was why she sometimes missed that signal; then, a snuffling sound, like an animal rooting around a tent deciding whether or not to invade; next, a gentle kneading like a cat preparing a cushion before settling down; after that, the claws would dig in, and the creature – now revealed as a rodent – would gnaw and gnaw and gnaw. Nora was at the kneading stage, one stop before the point of no return.

She checked her Timex watch: almost 6:00 P.M. Through the living-room curtains, she glimpsed a truck marked "LORENZINI & SONS" pulling away from the curb, and bolted to the door, wondering how she'd missed the bell. Too late, she remembered her mother's brass plate: "PEDDLERS USE BACK ENTRANCE."

Waving from the steps, Nora shouted, "Yoohoo!" exactly as her mother would have done, exactly as Aunt Millie had done.

Luigi Lorenzini was her third and final prospect. Two other secondhand dealers had insisted on an itemized account before on-site inspection and then had declined to venture. Nora had high hopes for Lorenzini since the word *antique* or *estate* had never passed his lips; he called himself a junk man, and he couldn't meet with her until after five because of his day job.

She was further reassured when she shook his hand – a craggy giant in spattered overalls, bent like the tower of Pisa. He bowed even lower. "Luigi, ma'am."

The downside was that Luigi took a very long time to decide while consuming at least two dozen chocolate-chip cookies from her mother's Christmas-cake tin. Small matter. By now Nora suspected she'd be lucky not to have to pay someone to cart off most of this stuff, which was why the deal came down to the two-ton, wood-reinforced chesterfield. With arms outstretched to keep its cushions from huffing like camel humps, Nora had pleaded for "this artifact" as if it were the patriarch of a family that must be adopted together. "It's color-coordinated with the chair and drapes and rug. They belong together." *So true. Too true.* "It's one-stop shopping for some family." *The Addams family.*

By the look on Luigi's face, Nora knew she was driving a hard bargain. He seemed such a decent fellow she would have relented, save for that "& SONS" on his pickup truck. She hoped he had at least two as big as himself. She also hoped they would not find any dead rats embalmed in dust behind or betwixt the artifact's slats and coils.

"Okay, okay." Luigi's giant paw swiped up the last three cookies. "I take, I take." A deal was struck for $390, with removal timed to the sale of the house.

Though Nora had worked hard to close the transaction, no sooner had Luigi left than she wanted him back. The slamming of the door had seemed to collapse the wood-and-wallpaper edifice down upon her like a water-soaked tent. With no one to shield or distract her, it was creepy how easily she reverted to the routines associated with this house. For supper nothing would do but one of her mother's omelets made with chives "fresh from the garden," though she hadn't thought of such a thing in a dozen years. It had been a noontime treat the year of her illness, followed by episodes of *Guiding Light, Secret Storm, General Hospital* and all those other TV soaps her mother watched on her days off for the sheer pleasure of criticizing their characters' morals. More than once Nora had heard her mother exclaim while thumping her iron for emphasis: "That woman made her bed, now let her lie in it!"

Her mother's chive patch was beside her rose garden. *So many beautiful blooms and no one left to care for them.* As Nora cut a few for Aunt Millie, the ache in her chest reminded her of the last time she'd been overwhelmed by the scent of roses . . . her mother tidily packed in her ivory-satin coffin, her ringless hands folded over her best black dress; her thin nose slightly dented where rimless reading glasses once perched; her rusty, gray-streaked hair tightly secured with a net; her still-taut skin finely etched like the tissue she'd pressed every Christmas for reuse.

For two days at the funeral parlor, people had lined up to tell Nora what a saint her mother had been, and in many ways they were right. No one was faster with a casserole when a friend was sick, or more dutiful in fulfilling an obligation. Yet, as Nora had stood in the lying-in room saying her last anguished good-byes, she'd been shocked by a child's sudden, furious desire to take the corpse by the shoulders and shake it. *Why couldn't you ever see me?* Now, twisting roses in her hands, she thought of her mother hunched like a wet cat on her veranda steps, afraid to enter her own house, and tears gushed. *Why couldn't I ever see you?*

As Nora trudged back up the yard, she noted that Dolly Dolby had been right about one thing: without inhabitants, a house did rapidly deteriorate. Since her mother's death, Nora's natal home seemed to have acquired a vacant stare and a leftward list. It was already becoming a Halloween house, the sort children dared each other to visit.

Pausing with her foot on the stoop from which her mother had hung her wash, Nora guiltily recalled the many times she'd driven the 125 kilometers back to London through driving rain and piling snow to avoid spending the night in this house. Her mother had stopped complaining when Nora's excuses became so threadbare they embarrassed them both. Now, as she entered the back door, she asked herself: could a place acquire an infected atmosphere, as Dolly Dolby also had maintained? Could depression or tragedy stain its walls, seep between its floorboards, taint its air, cloud its mirrors, creep like lichen through its drawers and cupboards?

Nora's thumb throbbed. A thorn had pierced the flesh. Squeezing the wound, she watched the blood ooze . . . *the color of Grandma Flora's hair.*

After supper Nora sorted her mother's personal effects into two piles – throwaway and giveaway. As she emptied hangers onto her mother's purple chenille bedspread, she saw that Aunt Millie had been correct: nothing jollier than the occasional white-and-black print. She held up a granny dress with gored skirt, V-neck and housewife sleeves, convinced she'd seen models like this attending her seminars in early-twentieth-century literature. Had her mother's decades-old wardrobe, sewn from worn-out Simplicity patterns, become a timeless fashion statement? She imagined her students' delighted appreciation: "Awesome!"

As Nora filled garbage bags for Goodwill, she caught her reflection in the vanity mirror and wondered how, in principle, her own wardrobe, running the gamut from black to gray to navy, differed from her mother's. Dowdy dress had once been a wise career move – protective covering at a time when "female professor" seemed like an oxymoron. However, her no-choice wardrobe had proven so habit-forming, like eating granola every morning, that she'd forgotten it was supposed to be a disguise.

Nora felt a lump in her mother's bed and investigated: yet another Harlequin Romance. Sighing, she tossed it into the Goodwill box, along with the dozens of others she'd found stashed, like pot, down cushions, lacing blankets and lining drawers. Then she tackled her mother's bureau.

Here, still in their original cellophane wrappers, Nora found the expensive nightgowns and slips and cardigans that she'd given her mother during the past ten years, stacked like planes over J.F. Kennedy airport, waiting for her darned, mended, patched and threadbare items to *really* wear out. Was there no end to her mother's pack-rat legacy, spawned by Depression, war and widowhood? Broken Christmas ornaments; balls of knotted string from every parcel that had entered this house; bundles of pencils and jars of rotten elastics; yet nothing, nothing at all to suggest the emotions of the people who had lived here. No old letters or postcards, no family photos or marriage certificates or death notices. Like a crime scene vacated by a meticulous felon, the place had been wiped clean of fingerprints – especially those of her father.

Collapsing on what had once been the parental bed, Nora tried to conjure him up, as if this setting might provide one last chance. She saw a lanky frame like her own, topped by a gaunt, handsome face; curly dark hair; a laughing mouth and sad, gone-away eyes. Though barely nine when he'd died, she vividly remembered sitting with him on the turtle fountain at Gage Park, eating butterscotch-ripple ice cream at the Stoney Creek Dairy, riding the Ferris wheel at Burlington Beach. Mostly she remembered smells – kisses of cloves, hugs of Sunlight soap, whisker-rubs against an Old Spice cheek, the clog of talcum in the bathroom, a trail of cigar smoke wafting from the front porch. He alone had provided her with a physical universe, someone who defined her body by holding her, by hoisting her onto his shoulders, by squeezing her hand, someone solid and secure and dependable . . . or so she had thought.

It was only during the last month of her mother's life that Nora had discovered how he had really died. It had been one of those consequential tales her mother had taken to dropping as casually as a Kleenex between comments on the weather. In this case, they had been discussing a relative's wedding anniversary when her mother had announced: "I remember that date exactly because it was the day before your father took off with his floozie."

Though Nora's stomach had seized, she kept her tone offhand as she continued to pile radish rosettes onto a serving dish. "What do you mean by 'floozie'?"

"Muriel Gant, a cheap Woolworth's girl!" Her mother tapped the kitchen window with her wooden spoon. "She lived across that alley, right under my nose. Next I heard the police had fished their bodies out of the Burlington canal. Of course, they were all liquored up. That was to be expected. Fortunately, your father's lawyer – old Andrew Sullivan – managed to keep the mess out of the paper."

Nora's voice retained its unnatural calm as she responded: "I thought daddy drowned while rescuing a child from the canal."

Her mother's mouth had puckered and prickled like the pincushion cactus on her teawagon, while her hand beat time with her spoon. "Well, would you have wanted the truth?"

Yes, Nora had wished to shriek back through time, *if it would have helped me understand you!* Instead, she'd made an awkward attempt to put her arm around her mother, only to have it dislodged by an unnecessary move to the stove.

"Your father was a weak and sinful man. Your grandma Flora was right about that. We were better off without him."

Though Nora had promised herself to be in bed by ten, she felt too keyed up to sleep. Returning to this place had taken a higher psychological toll than she'd expected. Everything she'd attempted to throw out had had a story to tell. Even soap dishes had turned loquacious.

Despite the lateness of the hour, Nora decided to call Dolly Dolby to instruct her to drop the house price to $80,000, but all she got was a singing answering machine. "Hello, Dolly. Yes, it's your Dolly. And tomorrow I'll be back where I belong."

After pouring herself some homemade elderberry juice, Nora sat down to watch TV, wishing her glass contained something far stronger. Her mother had been staunchly temperance, and even now Nora felt too brainwashed to bring "spirits" into this house.

With the remote control under her all-powerful thumb, she watched the picture widen to fill the screen, then shrink, then widen, then shrink, like a shy genie reluctant to leave his bottle. At last it stabilized, but so out of focus she could have been gazing at fish circling in a dirty aquarium. Nora switched channels, or tried to. The controls were jammed.

With increasing fascination, she watched the set's one ghostly offering – a documentary on past lives hosted by a reconstituted, once-famous actor who'd seen quite a few of those himself.

Reincarnation and the laws of karma appealed to Nora's rational mind: what you sowed in one life you reaped in another. Even her mother, fervently committed to the goat-versus-lamb, winner-take-all Christian universe, couldn't fault that logic. *Just like tin cans, Ma. You peel off their contents labels, then cleanse, flatten and recycle them for relabeling and reuse.*

While a Celtic priestess explained to viewers the widely held belief that people reincarnate together, generation after generation, to fulfill a group destiny, Nora suddenly remembered Aunt Millie's comments about her mother and the Spiritualist Church. She also remembered the Harlequin Romances. In death, her predictable, straitlaced mother was becoming as mysterious to her as her father had done.

Of its own volition, the TV switched channels. Now Nora was watching a woman in old-fashioned dress walk down a cobbled street, carrying a buckled leather suitcase. The camera focused on an inn sign featuring a wolf howling at the moon. Before Nora could read the inn's name, the TV image exploded like a nova, shrank to a white dwarf, then disappeared down a black hole. Nora *click-clicked* but could get no image. *Done. Like clocks that die when their owners do.*

She yawned, trying to convince herself she was tired, reluctantly noting that her migraine was beginning to sharpen its claws. Then she switched off the lights and started upstairs.

On the sixth step, Nora paused, returned to the hall, flipped on its chandelier of electrified candles, then ascended the way she used to as a child, manipulating switches so as to reach her attic eyrie on an almost-continuous carpet of light. The break came at the attic staircase, which had no overhead fixture, forcing her to grope the last fourteen steps in the dark. On number eight she heard a loud creak and, with a screech, flew upward for the switch.

Light flooded her childhood room, plucking familiar objects from the darkness – an old iron bed, standard dormitory issue; an orange-crate toy trunk later used for out-of-season clothes; a vanity with fold-in mirror matching the suite in the master bedroom; a highboy with sticky drawers purchased secondhand from the Salvation Army.

Nora glanced down the shadowy staircase. Perhaps the earlier call to Dolly Dolby had been a mistake, for though she had begun her journey humming the agent's giddy phone message, by the time she reached the attic it was Dolly's cautionary voice that buzzed like a gnat through the soft places in her head. *"Every house has its atmosphere and, truth to tell, there's something off about this one."*

After undressing, Nora repacked her Nike shoes in the expensive leather suitcase she had purchased on impulse for the trip to England. She donned a ruffled granny gown, also slated for the journey, then creamed her face before her vanity mirror. *". . . something defiant and high-spirited, especially around that mannequin. 'Well, what do we have here?' I asked myself."* Nora angled her mirror to reflect an infinity of quicksilver selves, then waved, *"Hello, there!"* intending to mock but sounding frail and frightened. *". . . and then, when we went up into the attic, I was hit with that clammy, sad feeling and I knew that this was just One of Those Houses."*

A breeze billowed Nora's nightgown, though no leaf was stirring outside her window. Switching off the lights, she dived into the bed and pulled the covers over her head. Now she felt ridiculous. Reemerging, she systematically (a) retucked the sheet she had pulled out; (b) wound her mother's alarm clock, an old-fashioned bonger known as Big Ben; (c) closed her eyes; (d) folded her hands over Grandma Flora's handmade patchwork quilt and waited for sleep.

And waited.

Her fingers traced the quilt's irregular swatches of cotton, linen, silk and seersucker like a dog sniffing from backyard to backyard, looking for bones. She remembered inventing stories about each scrap – what outfit it had come from, who had worn it, and where. Since the quilt had immigrated with Grandma Flora, she guessed that many of these pieces must have been from her clothes, and since nothing was ever thrown out in this house, she supposed that she was also sleeping in Grandma Flora's bed – the one in which she'd died, age fifty-nine, of heart failure.

Detecting the scent of lavender, Nora fearfully pressed the quilt's blue-gingham backing to her nose. When was it that the Lavender Lady had become a persistent part of her childhood? Was it after her father's death when the odor of tobacco and talcum and cloves had begun to fade from the house? At first she had thought of the wispy lavender presence as someone to play with on rainy days as she dressed up in the exotic contents of cubbyhole boxes. After she'd started school, her secret companion had more or less retreated into the shadows until . . . *the year of her accident and illness, age fifteen . . . lying in a fever-cradle, waiting for the footsteps from the past to begin . . . aimless at first as they shuffled through the far cubbyhole, then growing more substantial as they padded across the storage-room linoleum. A long pause, followed by a creak as the door opened a crack, and then halfway. Another pause, during which the scent of lavender intensified while the footsteps paced toward her bed . . .*

As Nora cringed under the patchwork quilt, she acknowledged that she had had more reasons than her mother's prohibition to renounce her attraction to things psychic. Her reality in the years before the accident had been too dangerous, too lacking in boundaries, too – Nora awoke with a jolt. Though all was silent, her muscles were bunched as if for the hundred-yard dash. She listened for a few seconds, but could hear nothing beyond Big Ben with his no-nonsense tick and his large open face proclaiming 2:30 A.M. She buried her head under the pillow, and was again sliding down the sleep chute when her ears pricked and twisted like a cat's tricorner radar set: a scuttling sound from the far cubbyhole. She sighed in relief. *Ginger, catching mice.* She froze. *Ginger?*

For several minutes Nora stuck to her bed like a corpse on a mortuary slab. The air in the room seemed rigid and still, as if the whole house were holding its breath. Sweat oozed through her pores, drenching her scalp and armpits. If only she could move some part of her anatomy, she might survive. She focused all her energy on her right index finger, willing it to lift. At last, it broke free, unlocking her other muscles. Gulping air, she swung her legs onto the floor, then rushed across the room to switch on the overhead light. She groped inside the storage-room door for the next switch, and flipped it, to no effect: a burned-out bulb. She remembered the flashlight already packed in her shoulder bag. Guided by its unwavering beam, she crossed the linoleum to the far cubbyhole. Its door was warped. She pried it open, then shone her light into the dusty wedges. Flashing red eyes and a rusty swish – a terrified squirrel scooted out a hole in the shingles!

Nora rocked back on her haunches, laughing explosively. Yes, this was just One of Those Houses. As she cast about for something to plug the gap, her beam caught a cadaverous lump wrapped in a sheet. She yanked the sheet by its ragged hem, uncovering an old suitcase. It was stamped with a once-gaudy Canadian Pacific Steamlines sticker – "LIVERPOOL, 1913."

Nora unbuckled the rotting straps. Inside she found a handful of sepia portraits with the spines of their human subjects as stiff as the cardboard on which they were mounted. She examined the long gowns, the high-necked shirts. Who had had time to iron all those ruffles? To starch all those collars? To wax all those mustaches? And not a smile in the bunch. When had "cheese" become part of the photographer's art?

Nora flipped them. No dates or identification. She switched her attention to a red-fringed shawl with its once-vibrant colors muted to the tones of an ancient tapestry; an embroidered cotton chemise, a pair of buttoned knickers and a leg harness which, she knew from her research, shortened a woman's stride to keep her from ripping her hobble skirt. A side pocket also contained a heart-shaped silver necklace, part of a transatlantic-steamer ticket, a building-fund brochure for a church and a half-dozen pawn tickets for jewelry.

Wadding the suitcase's dust cover, Nora leaned deep into the cubbyhole to plug the eaves. Her hand touched what she thought to be leaves. She yanked – a nest of newspaper. Carrying the bundle into her bedroom, Nora pieced and patched with the grim determination of a scholar researching the Dead Sea scrolls, wondering if she, too, might have inherited the gene that addicted her mother to broken china and Grandma Flora to patchwork quilts.

She found she had assembled a copy of *The Barrow Times*, dated June 23, 1913, featuring an amusing story about a pilot who had been forced to land in a local pasture. Why had her grandmother preserved this paper above all others? Was June 23 the day she'd left Barrow – a last souvenir of her home town?

In a crumpled envelope Nora discovered several clippings headlined "MINING DISASTER KILLS EIGHT." Eagerly, she studied photos of the victims, looking for Grandpa Flowe who, according to family legend, had died down the mines on the eve of his slated departure to Canada. She checked the names in the copy: Judd, Mellon, Wilson, Hall, Emery, Bradley, Sutton, and a nine-year-old named Tommy Ross pictured in choir surplice. No Grandpa Flowe. She didn't even know his first name.

Nora inspected the envelope, rank with squirrel droppings. Though almost unreadable, it appeared to have been addressed to Mrs. F. Flowe in this house on Central Street. She checked the date of the clippings – June 24 – suggesting that a friend had sent them to Grandma Flora after her departure from Barrow.

It was now 4:00 A.M. Switching off the lights, Nora pulled the covers over her head, then fell into a troubled sleep.

She is sitting on the ancestral suitcase, wearing a T-shirt with "AGE 15" inscribed on one side and "JUNE 28" on the other. Everything in the room is sepia-toned, as in old photographs. Clothes seep like porridge through the cracks of the case even as she frantically struggles to close it. Every time she buckles one strap, the other breaks. Suddenly, the suitcase explodes, swooshing her out her bedroom window.

When Nora opened her eyes, daylight illuminated the room, and Big Ben's reproving hands pointed to eleven o'clock.

She donned her navy pant suit for the flight, then repacked the items she had borrowed from her travel suitcase. On impulse, she added the cherry-print sundress she'd found in her closet, still surprised by its scooped, bosom-enhancing neckline: to her mother, breasts had been like lumps in a bed – something to be smoothed out before company arrived.

After toting her luggage downstairs, Nora checked her must-do list. She'd already ordered her cab for four o'clock. That knock at the door meant the Goodwill truck had arrived as promised. Nora supervised to insure no one carted off her travel suitcase, or the personal mementos, which Luigi Lorenzini had agreed to store if/when the house was sold.

Now well down her list, Nora dragged her garbage to curbside – including four extra cartons she'd found in the basement: every report card she'd ever received, every prize for Sunday-school attendance. Her mind shifted to the academic papers in her own basement. *Years of labor, for what? A footnoted article in a literary journal that a hundred people might read, half competing for the same turf.*

Hurrying back to the house, she charged upstairs to the attic. It was just past three. She packed her passport, plane ticket and travelers' checks in her shoulder bag, along with the first draft of "The

Impact of Socioeconomic Conditions on the Work of D.H. Lawrence."

As Nora descended the attic stairs with the battered suitcase, she reminded herself to inspect it for artifacts useful to her British research. *Maybe a side trip to Barrow?* After all, Grandma Flora's birthplace wasn't far from D.H. Lawrence's, and her topic lent itself to exploring a second Midlands mining community.

While crossing what had been Grandma Flora's tearoom, she remembered that she would likely never see this place again, forcing herself to notice shadows where pictures used to hang and footprints worn in the linoleum, but finding herself drained of nostalgia. *Grandma Flora's mannequin looks more animated than I feel!*

Shifting the heavy suitcase to her left hand, Nora descended the second flight of stairs. As she rounded the curve, she noticed something that amazed her: aside from its 1913 sticker and buckled straps, the suitcase was identical to the one she'd purchased for this trip!

Nora's left foot went numb, pitching her headfirst down the stairwell.

3

She is floating over a staircase, looking down at the crumpled body of a woman with an oddly twisted neck. A man crouches over her, sweat glistening from his balding head. She hears words:

"Are you okay, lady?"

An olive-skinned man with frightened eyes stared down at Nora, his jowls pressed so close that she suspected he was about to start mouth-to-mouth resuscitation. His mustache twitched like a sooty moth as his lips repeated: "Are you okay?"

Beyond his head, Nora saw bunches of wallpaper grapes and an antler coat rack, identifying her mother's hallway. She wiggled her fingers and toes, then gingerly rolled her neck. Despite the pain shooting down her spine, everything seemed connected.

"I rang and rang. Then I seen you through the glass. The way your neck was twisted, I thought for sure it was busted."

Nora attempted to rise, using the banister. She made it to the crouched position, then slumped onto the stairs, head spinning like the rings of Saturn.

"Should I drive you to the hospital?"

Nora began to weep. Fumbling for a suitable reason, she

explained: "My mother died. This was her house." Wiping her eyes, she forced herself to stand. "I'm fine."

"You sure?"

"I'm fine." To prove her point, she grabbed her shoulder bag from the rack, then limped out to the taxi. As her head sank into the seat cushions, she heard the driver open his trunk, then fling in her luggage.

"How many bags?" he called.

"Just the one."

"D'ya want to lock up your house?"

Bad enough that it bore a FOR SALE sign advertising vacancy.

The driver reached for Nora's key. "I'll do it."

Willing her eyes to focus, Nora checked her Timex watch: 4:15. Fortunately, she always built in time when flying.

The cab hugged the Hamilton escarpment past the center of the city, then plunged north down Bay Street. She watched buildings undulate like reflections in water as the driver's voice also rose and fell. "Christ, lady, I don't mind saying you had me scared. I took a first-aid course once. Passed it with flying colors because I was motivated, d'ya see? When you're a cabby, you never know what's going to happen next."

Struggling to appear normal, she rehearsed her response, then punched the words as if into a computer. "I appreciate what you did, especially locking my mother's door."

The driver swiveled, still nervously checking her for damage. "I could see you were out to lunch. Now, don't get me wrong. Landing on your noggin like that, you had every right to be. Once I saved a guy from a hit-'n'-runner. Banged his head real bad on the curb, like you, but that kind of whack can work both ways. Do you get my drift?"

Though Nora wasn't up to conversation, she felt too grateful to refuse him. "I can't say that I do."

"One guy I seen on the television – a Dutch guy – fell off a ladder onto his head, and then he could tell the future. He helped the

Dutch Underground catch spies. There was another guy too . . . real famous. Edgar Something. Cayce! The wife reads all his books. He could tell doctors how to cure people, and you know how he got started? Go ahead, take a guess."

Nora massaged her right temporal lobe, trying to concentrate. "I suppose you'll say he fell."

"Close. He got zonked with a baseball."

As the cab turned north onto Highway 403, the driver switched his attention to the traffic. Next thing Nora knew, he was again staring into her face, with mustache twitching. "Are you sure you're okay?"

Nora smelled diesel fumes, heard the blare of horns: Pearson airport. "Absolutely."

He wasn't convinced. "Give me your ticket and I'll get someone to check you in." He pointed to a baggage handler, tall and thin like a date palm, with a thatch of white-blond hair. "Go inside to those seats by the phones and he'll bring you your boarding pass."

Though Nora attempted to tip the driver an extra ten dollars, he refused.

"I just like to do my bit, d'ya know?"

Taking an inside seat by the phones, Nora picked up a discarded *People* magazine and tried to read, but her hands were shaking too hard: she was thinking of what might have happened if she hadn't already ordered her taxi – an empty house with her body lying paralyzed at the bottom of the stairs while her friends imagined her in England.

"Your boarding pass, ma'am." It was the blond date palm.

No delays, no problems with her ticket. By the time Nora's flight was called, she felt almost normal, but still the trip got off to a bumpy start. It happened as soon as her seatmate – a gangly youth with limbs too long for his tweedy suit – turned to her and grinned: "I'm Howie Hampton."

As Nora's fingers crunched in his knuckly hand, she idly wondered why so many people with "H" surnames chose to replicate:

Hubert Humphrey. Howard Hawkes. Henry Hudson. Hal Holbrook. Howard Hughes. Herman Hesse. Hedda Hopper. Harry Houdini. Hugh Hefner. Holly Hunter. Helen Hunt.

"Imagine, we've never met, and now we've got the whole night to get acquainted."

Long-winded people on endless voyages had a way of sniffing out Nora. Going into radical defensive action, she replied: "It's wonderful to meet you, Howie, but I'm terrified of flying. I've taken a couple of pills to knock me out, and if I'm not asleep before take-off, I'm likely to throw up over both of us." Beaming a wonderful smile, she donned her earphones, switched to a dead channel, closed her eyes, and drifted into oblivion.

As Howie had so unnecessarily warned her, it was an all-night trip. Over dinner, he shyly apologized: "I know I came on strong but, gosh, my first trip to Europe, and my first airplane ever."

Regretting her rudeness, Nora compensated by drawing him out.

"I'm a clerk in the Registrar General's office in Thunder Bay. At first it was so depressing, sending out death certificates, but then I got interested in family trees. Trouble is, everyone waits until the relative they're closest to dies, only to find that was the person with all the answers."

Nora remembered studying her mother's corpse in a way she'd never have dared stare into her living countenance. "I guess death gives us permission to pry, Howie. Perhaps in life we need those boundaries."

"Like people on subways!" He cubed his steak into bite-sized pieces. "My grandpa is helping me. His great-grandfather died in the battle of Stoney Creek, and when my grandpa and I stood on that hill outside Hamilton, I got all goose-pimply. I could practically hear the cannon. It's like a piece of me had been there, fighting and dying, you know?"

Nora remembered her two identical suitcases and felt her own flesh marble. "I guess it was, Howie – your DNA. Genetic memory."

"Gosh, you mean this stuff's got a name? I thought it was just me."

Nora quoted from one of the unsolicited journals that washed like tidal debris against her office door: "Since our genes pass on learned biological information, who's to say they don't pass on personal experience as well?"

"You feel it too, don't you? Like, it's mystical! I don't usually tell people in Thunder Bay, but sometimes my grandpa will be reminiscing, and I'll start feeling real weird, like I did at Stoney Creek, and I'll add bits he hasn't gotten to yet."

Nora shifted uneasily: was everyone flying New Age? "I suppose you're going to England to look up your ancestors."

"To St. Catherine's House in London. That's where they keep the records for everyone in England. Births in red books, marriages in green and deaths in black." Reaching into his duffel bag, he handed her a brochure: *How to Trace Your Family Tree* by Howard A. Hampton. "I'm working on the sequel."

By the time their 747 had landed at Manchester, Howie's ingenuousness had won Nora's heart. However, since he was continuing on to London, she found herself alone at the immigration desk, and then at the luggage carousel. By now most passengers from Nora's flight had sailed off with full carts. One set of golf clubs had passed her a dozen times. No more bags were sliding down the chute. She experienced that familiar clench of fear that her bag would be one of the strays winging to Tokyo. Squeezing her shoulder purse, she encountered the hard lump made by her Lawrence manuscript – *at least that's safe!* Instead of relief, she felt her migraine begin to gnaw.

An invisible hand switched off the rolling carpet. The golf bag froze like a video image on hold. Nora prepared for the worst, convinced her expensive suitcase was exactly the kind thieves would pinch, lured by its false promise of Parisian perfume and designer labels. Why hadn't she settled for kick-me luggage like everyone else's? An attendant began clearing the ramp.

"Please, sir . . . " Nora's voice sounded supplicating and reedy like an orphan's in the chorus of *Oliver Twist.* "I've lost my bag."

The handler scrutinized her claim check, upside down and without shifting his eyes. Could he read? As Nora reached for the stub, he burst into a gap-toothed grin. "More bags. Another place." He pointed to a bench. "You sit. I fix."

Minutes passed. Nora was growing anxious all over again when the handler reappeared wheeling a cart. On it he carried a single battered case, like a turd on a shiny silver fork.

"That's not mine."

"Yours," insisted the handler. He read aloud each digit of her stub. Though he reversed their order, the numbers matched, as Nora knew they would, for by now she'd seen the 1913 Canadian Pacific Steamlines sticker glued to the side.

She did an instant replay: *falling down the stairs carrying her ancestral suitcase. The cabby loading the trunk while she sat in the car.*

"How many bags?"

"Just the one."

Then at the airport a handler had checked her in while she'd waited like the dowager queen for her boarding pass, never thinking to inspect the suitcase.

Nora felt the irrepressible urge to laugh. *How absurd!* As she picked up the old bag and headed for the exit, she experienced an unexpected surge of freedom: Barrow came two stops before Nottingham, the gateway to D.H. Lawrence country. Patting the suitcase like a friendly mongrel, she remarked: "I guess you just wanted to go home."

THE WOLFE INN MOON

4

The British Midlands, spread in Cinemascope outside Nora's train window, made her soul sing: soaring fells flocked with sheep and their pestering lambs; foaming hedges of hawthorn rippling in dark waves across the dales; villages nestled amid white-flowering chestnuts poked through by a single church spire; shimmering fields of golden rapeseed, of barley, of clover, stitched together by miles of old stone walls, like one of her grandmother's patchwork quilts.

Where were the smokestacks and slag heaps and Stygian pits of Britain's industrial heartland? She'd spent so long pouring over archival photos of cramped row houses and miners down holes chipping coal that she'd forgotten these sweeping green fields with their toothy upthrusts of limestone.

Barrow train station proved a disappointment, like a bad movie after spectacular credits. Of glass and yellow brick, it was a commercial replacement for the arched and turreted structure Nora had glimpsed in one of the old *Barrow Times* photos. Yet, as she debarked she reminded herself that the fissured alders edging the Barrow River might be the same ones Grandma Flora saw as she departed her birthplace with her infant in her arms. Did she take a horse-wagon or a taxi to the station? Was it a grim occasion or a hopeful one? So many questions for which her mother probably possessed some answers. Nora had been so stuck on library research that she'd failed to consider that she might have had a living oracle close at hand. Now all that ancestral knowledge was lost forever, or were such experiences encoded in the genes, as she had speculated with Howie Hampton?

Nora approached a glass cage containing a youthful ticket-seller studying a tattoo catalogue. His arms were already plastered with dragons and eagles and sailing ships. "I was wondering . . . what happened to the old station?"

"Well, I've nowt got it, now 'ave I?" Even his shaved head was inked with a green parrot.

Nora trudged around the building. No taxis waited in the dusty parking lot. She was halfway up the hill before she remembered she hadn't inquired about accommodations. Never mind. She didn't fancy a room over a tattoo parlor, and just ahead was a street of shops.

At first glance there was nothing quaint about the town of Barrow. Turning right on Station Road, Nora passed red-brick stores, chockablock with polyester blouses, matronly underwear, and packages of gloves lightly layered in grit. Since she had to outfit herself from the skin out, she noted prices with more than casual interest. Shapeless dresses were in the £80 range – around $180 Canadian; boring shoes were £35; pantyhose were £3.

Nora was about to inquire for accommodations at a corner video store when she spotted an intriguing sign down a side street. Of carved and painted wood, it featured a wolf howling at a full moon. That image seemed familiar. Remembering her "Save the Wolf" T-shirt, she approached the two-story, blood-brick inn with its single peaked tower and row of iron-trimmed gables: WOLFE INN MOON.

Though well-maintained, the place possessed such an attitude of deadness that Nora wondered if it was open. As she rested her suitcase, an orange and white cat ambled from the inn's doorway, then stretched its forelegs on the cobbles before continuing on its way. It seemed so amply satisfied that Nora retraced its pawsteps through the red-pillared archway.

She stood in a lobby so dense with dark brocades, plants on tripods, somber oils buried in gilt frames, overstuffed settees and black wicker chairs that she felt she'd wandered into the props and flats department for a Merchant–Ivory movie.

Though the ebony reception desk was empty, a middle-aged woman in a long black gown stood on a burgundy staircase, staring up at a candle chandelier hung on chains. Her pitchy hair was slicked back from a profile so sharp it seemed to cut the air. Turning, she registered surprise, then flowed down the steps and across the black-and-white foyer without seeming to use her legs. That movement, plus an oversized head set on a featureless body, made her look like a black queen gliding across a chessboard.

She settled, hands folded, behind a brass nameplate identifying her as Mrs. Wolfe, before offering a stiff welcoming smile.

"Do you have a room with a bath?"

Flourishing a price list, Mrs. Wolfe underlined the appropriate item: single B & B, sixteen.

As Nora was about to sign the vintage leather registry, her niggling academic eye caught an error: "This page is dated June 23 and it's only June 22."

The hotelier's right brow arched up toward her widow's peak. "We weren't expecting you – or anyone – until tomorrow." She added mysteriously: "And we still aren't."

Shrugging, Nora scratched her name onto the blank page with the proffered straight pen, while Mrs. Wolfe clanged a bell like those once used to stern effect by schoolmistresses.

A girl with gingham dust cap tossed by a storm of dark waves, tumbled from behind a curtain, her face groggy as if she had just awakened from a deep sleep. Despite an over-lush figure and air of untidiness, her beauty was startling, including full lips pressed open like a pink butterfly, and swampy blue eyes tilted as if they might spill.

Mrs. Wolfe reached under the counter for a ring of heavy keys. "Eleanora, escort our guest up to Number Two." She pointed to the wagon-wheel chandelier. "And trim those candles. You know they should have been done before breakfast."

Trailing hems like a harem girl her veils, Eleanora undulated up the burgundy staircase, wafting lavender from a nosegay tucked in her cap. With a key fished from her ankle-length pinafore, she opened a heavy door onto a cheerful surprise – a brass four-poster overhung by a Coronation picture of George v and Queen Mary; a cast-iron fireplace bracketed by chintz wing chairs; assorted Victorian lamps on tables with barley-sugar legs; a mahogany high-boy, armoire and vanity set against exuberantly flowered wallpaper; a Queen Anne desk with needlepoint chair; a dark-stained floor scattered with rag rugs; a back window overlooking a garden and a side one framing a cobbled stable yard.

As Eleanora placed Nora's suitcase on its rack, the white-bibbed orange cat leapt up from the patchwork quilt, then bolted back out the window.

"I had one just like her!" Nora laughed. "Same girth and mottlings." She hunted for change, but found only an old coin of indiscriminate value, apparently left over from her train ticket. Handing it to the maid, she apologized: "When I get change I'll —"

"Nowt for me, mum!" Snatching the coin, Eleanora bobbed out the door as if on coil springs. "Oh, thank yer, mum. Thank yer."

Was the girl unspoiled or just cheeky? Well, what more could she have expected from someone toting an eighty-year-old suitcase?

Anxious to see the town, Nora entered her relentlessly antique bathroom to freshen up. She twisted the brass tap over its deep marble bowl and was drenched in a rusty gush. How long since the damned plumbing had been used? The water's brackish smell was not reassuring.

According to the street signs, the Wolfe Inn Moon was at the corner of Backwater Lane and Edge Road, the last street before the plunge into the valley. A sharp dogleg right took Nora into Market Street, yet another cobbled passageway lined with red-brick shops. Though most were turn-of-the-century, their false fronts gave them the gaudy, nondescript appearance of stores in any modern town.

A steeply pitched building, constructed in what Nora called the Methodist style, bore a discreet sign: "Barrow Town Library." Smelling maps, Nora entered.

With her strawberry hair, blowsy figure and Kewpie-doll smile, the librarian reminded Nora of Dolly Dolby. "You're probably wanting our local-history section."

"Does the accent show before I open my mouth?"

"I can always tell. Something about a person's face says, 'Lead me to my ancestors.'"

Escorting Nora to an alcove, the librarian selected a book with a faded green cover. "You may enjoy this one. *Barrow: Our Heritage, 1800–1913.* It's by John Slater, *my* ancestor. He was editor of *The Barrow Times.*"

Nora leafed through the lavishly illustrated history with its appendix of maps charting Barrow's evolution from poky farm village into bustling coal-mining town *circa* 1913. Though confusing to a tourist, the town's layout seemed eminently logical when viewed from above. Like a straw hat tossed on a billiard table, it was ringed with roads crisscrossed by verticals that left the crown open as a common for sheep.

"I'll make out a visitor's card," offered the librarian. She printed her name – "PAMELA SLATER" – on a bookmark. "If I can be of any help."

One of the history book's 1913 photos had been shot from the library steps. Though "Miss Jepson's Millinery" had become a stationery store, the gold-lettered window next door still proclaimed "Thomas Ball & Sons, Chemists." "Alcott the Wheelwright" was now a hardware store, and "Wilson's Dry Goods" a variety shop with a Vietnamese proprietor. The handsome movie and theater hall beside it bore the inscription "PICTURE PALACE, 1910," but now advertised Monday-night bingo and Friday meetings of the Barrow Friendly Society.

With John Slater as her guide, Nora continued to peel away the modern skin of Barrow to view it as it had been when Grandma Flora had lived here. A working-class community, its peaked and lean row houses presented a solemn, unbroken facade to narrow streets, with their chimney pots marching up and down their roofs like crosses in a military cemetery. Where once there'd been a jail, she discovered a dental clinic. Where once there'd been a colliers' co-op, now she found a mining museum.

After purchasing a few toiletries to tide her over, Nora opted for fish and chips at Elmo's Diner, then wound her way back to the Wolfe Inn Moon. A cloud brooded like a hangover above its single turret, isolating it from its surroundings. The inn was odd in all sorts of indefinable ways – as if she had to wake it up before entering it. Still, in a day's meanderings, she'd seen no other hotel.

Nora unlocked her door with her oversized key. A globular lamp painted with blue butterflies had been lit and her quilt turned. As she tossed her nylon shoulder bag on the desk, she smelled lavender from half a dozen places and grew uneasy – Eleanora, she assured herself, marking pillows and coverlets like an affectionate cat.

Shedding clothes en route, Nora entered the bathroom. Her cast-iron tub with its seashell back reminded her of Botticelli's *Birth of Venus.* Standing well back, she tried the taps, and was rewarded with a cascade of fresh water.

Nora settled in for a long soak, with the heat penetrating her pores so she felt she was floating. As she soaped her small breasts and well-contoured arms, she remembered Eleanora, gracefully swaying up the burgundy staircase, so confident in her flesh that each pound seemed like a thousand pounds sterling in the bank. How long had it been since she'd thought of her body as an organ of pleasure, with needs and desires to explore and savor, instead of as a convenience to be trained, disciplined and controlled?

For a few years after college, getting engaged had become a hobby with Nora, a way of convincing herself that she was charging full steam ahead when she'd secretly applied the brakes. All her fiancés had been "safe" men – until you scratched the surface. With the last – a fellow English prof who wanted her to research so he could publish while she perished – wedding invitations had even gone out. Her mother, anticipating grandchildren to parade, had been furious at the breakup . . . *or had she?* Ellen Locke had also been an expert at running in one spot while convincing the world she was winning a marathon.

Nora rubbed herself down with a bath towel, enjoying its fleecy abrasions. After breaking off that engagement five years ago, she'd fallen into a state of accidental celibacy. Bit by bit, she'd become her career – an academic observing life through literary pince-nez instead of embracing it with her senses. After all, wasn't that last the message of David Herbert Lawrence, the randy, lyrical Pied Piper she'd elected to follow to Britain?

As she rinsed out her lone set of underwear, Nora pondered the happenstance that had caused her to choose D.H. Lawrence as her specialty: a death in the English department creating an early-twentieth-century window of opportunity that she'd competed to claim. She'd scarcely thought of her ancestral roots in the Midlands or – now that she explored further – the personal significance of Lawrence's theme of body versus mind, flesh versus spirit, instinct versus intellect, the natural versus the cultivated. In fact, she'd resisted this sabbatical, caught up in the scholarly mind-set that preferred dead authors to living ones, and archival research to anything that confused objectivity by talking back. Perhaps fate had targeted her for a message more relevant than she'd imagined: *my mind, my body . . . an adventure.*

Still naked, Nora examined herself in her vanity mirror, as Lawrence's Lady Chatterley had once done, finding her unloved flesh "grayish" and "sapless" with breasts "unripe and a little bitter" – and Lady C was only twenty-seven! Small wonder Nora had eschewed Lawrence's cock-and-cunt activism for socioeconomics in the coal-mining industry.

She continued to stare into the mirror, but no longer at herself. She was gawking at her four-poster with its turned quilt. Folded across the pillow was her ruffled granny gown garnished with a sprig of lavender. She examined it to make sure: the nail-polish spatter on the sleeve, the mended skirt where she'd stuck through her heel. How had this gown found its way into the ancestral suitcase?

That old case rested at the foot of her bed, with buckles unfastened. Nora flipped open the lid: empty. Her armoire door was ajar, the way maids leave things to prove they've been about their business. She nudged it open, revealing the skirt of her gray shirtwaist dress, the sleeve of her charcoal suit. She yanked the door the rest of the way – her wine pleated skirt and matching striped blouse, her cherry-print sundress.

Nora slumped into the wing chair by the fireplace, trying to remember where she'd last seen her new suitcase: in her mother's living room, while she'd fetched down the old one. She also remembered . . . *the driver's face pressed close to hers while she simultaneously floated overhead, staring down at his glistening bald head.* Had he really been trying to revive her, or had she come to while he was robbing her? She conjured up . . . *heavy jowls, a Velcro mustache, thinning dark hair parted left of center.* Had he transferred her clothes into the old case in order to steal the new one? Her rational mind rebelled: *crazy talk!* Why would anyone risk such an outrageous theft for so little? There had to be a reasonable explanation.

Nora's Timex watch said 8:15 P.M., which was 3:15 P.M. Eastern Daylight Saving Time – just fine for phoning home, if only her room possessed such a modern convenience. Yanking on her navy pantsuit, she headed toward the door. Whom could she call? Aunt

Millie? David? What could she tell them that wouldn't sound as if she'd lost her mind? She drew back, feeling too disoriented, too dizzy to trust her perceptions. *Tomorrow . . .*

Donning her nightgown, Nora slid between starchy sheets, comforting herself with one of her mother's cross-stitched homilies: "All problems look better in the clear light of morning."

5

When Nora awoke, the sun was shining through her window with brilliant optimism, but her spirit felt leaden and her head clogged with leftover dreams. *She is in a cage, banging against its bars – a bird cage sitting on a train platform beside the ancestral suitcase. An engine huffs into the station. Noise and confusion. People in old-fashioned dress crowd the platform, waving good-bye. A hand claims the suitcase. Clawing through her bars, she screams: "Stop! Don't leave me." Train and passengers disappear in a great exhalation of steam. She is left clutching a patch torn from a gypsy shawl and a hank of bleeding red hair.*

As Nora's head cleared of whistles and steam, she peered anxiously through the brass bars at the foot of her bed: her ancestral suitcase perched on its rack, somewhat sprightlier than she remembered, but unmistakable with its Canadian Pacific Steamlines sticker. Stubbornly closing her eyes, Nora counted to three, then opened them. Still there. She taunted herself: best out of five, then?

St. Michael's bell tower chimed eight. Nora glanced at her wrist but found only a ghostly imprint where her Timex should be. At eight Eastern Time, which would be one o'clock here in Barrow, she'd phone Aunt Millie or Dolly Dolby and ask her to check her mother's house for her new suitcase. If it was there, she'd consider the mixup some private aberration best forgotten. If not, she'd contact David and ask him to trace the cab driver.

Nora walked into the bathroom, searching for her watch. The gentle cooing of a pair of turtledoves lured her to the window. Beyond a stone wall, dripping with honeysuckle, tumbled a hillside pasture where yesterday she thought she'd noticed a park. She inhaled the dewy, meadowsweet air, feeling tension seep from her mind and body. The perfect tranquilizer: a post-breakfast stroll in the country.

Her toilet released a flood as noisy as Niagara. Surely the Wolfes should replace these abysmal antiques! She selected her cherry-print sundress from her armoire, and noticed the day's first anomaly: its neck was high-cut instead of scooped and – *My god!* – it had sleeves. Nora held it against her torso. Instead of capping her knees, the skirt hung to her ankles. Dropping the dress as if it were aflame, she pulled out her charcoal suit, her gray shirtwaist. Though the materials duplicated those she'd packed, the garments had been restyled with long skirts.

Nora stared at the chaotic swirl around her feet. *I'm mad. I've gone mad!* She was halfway to her door before she noticed she was still naked. Yanking open the drawers of her highboy, she discovered camisoles, whalebone corsets, knickers, chemises and petticoats. In eerie suspension, she donned what seemed necessary, encountering hooks and buttons and laces where she was accustomed to elastic and zippers. Everything fit, including a pair of ivory-colored lace-up boots – one of a half-dozen oddly styled sets lining her armoire. Avoiding the mirror, she dashed out the door and down the steps.

Mrs. Wolfe glanced up from her desk with a solicitous smile.

Struggling for control, Nora blurted: "Someone has taken my clothes."

"Theft?" The proprietress frowned. "That's a serious accusation." When Nora didn't recant, she clanged her bell.

Nora softened her stand. "Not theft. Not exactly." *What exactly?*

Mrs. Wolfe's nostrils flared. "Things *are* missing from your room?"

"Yes."

Breathless from the stairs, Eleanora burst through a basement door, wiping her hands on her apron. Seeing Nora, she erupted into smiles and bobbed three times.

"That's enough. Our guest has accused you of theft."

The maid's face crumbled. "Oh nowt me, mum, no, no, I niver. I swear I niver stole, mum, niver."

"Not theft," corrected Nora. "An exchange."

The irises of Mrs. Wolfe's eyes were the same color as her pupils – black discs that refused to reflect light. "Eleanora, did you handle our guest's clothes?"

"I put 'em straight, I did, mum – pressin' an' hangin' 'em. The lady ga'e me a shilling – a whole day's wages and —"

"Give me a list and a description, Miss Locke," demanded the hotelier, jabbing her pen into an ink pot.

"My clothes weren't stolen. They were . . . altered." Nora heard her voice babble idiotically. "It had to be someone skilled in sewing. They were very ordinary clothes." She plucked at her mutton-sleeved bodice. "Instead, I found this old-fashioned —" Her hostess was wearing a similar style but with the collar scraping her earlobes. "That is . . ."

Sheathing her pen, Mrs. Wolfe challenged Nora through thin lips that barely moved: "Would you care to withdraw the charge?"

Backing away from the counter, Nora escaped out the door and across the cobblestone stable yard. Though the inn's garden was a lovely tangle of honeysuckle, lilies and roses, their swooning fragrance seemed cloying and dangerous, like the poppies in *The Wizard of Oz.* Bolting through the gate, she flung herself face down onto an uneven patch of grass, then counted the rise and fall of her abdomen against the earth . . . *eighteen, nineteen, twenty.* Flipping over, she watched clouds scud by . . . *twenty-one, twenty-two.* Some possessed black faces. No. She was staring into a skittish ring of tar-faced sheep who'd given up munching to stare back. Nora tried to observe herself with their matter-of-fact sanity, beginning with her ivory boots, then moving up to her ankle-length skirt, but she remained too aberrant, too bizarre.

She searched again for a sensible explanation, but could construct no premise solid enough for the weight it had to bear. As her mind tumbled into freefall, her fingers clutched at grass: *I won't let them confuse me!* But who were "they," and why would they bother? Nora remembered Mrs. Wolfe's antique dress. *The owners of the Wolfe Inn Moon!* She reminded herself that the deception had begun at home with the exchange of suitcases. If only the fabrics of her missing clothes and their replacements hadn't been the same. Who had the resources for such an elaborate hoax? Using irony as crisis-management, she answered herself: *The CIA! The KGB!* As a thirty-eight-year-old, female, Canadian professor of English literature, she was naturally at the top of every international hit list. Perhaps Luigi Lorenzini had decided her mother was a nascent Grandma Moses, and was plotting to flood the black market with her purloined paintings copied from greeting cards. Certainly, that made as much sense as anything else. *Who is trying to drive me crazy?*

Am I crazy?

That was the obvious conclusion, but Nora wasn't prepared to accept it. The sun felt too real. The sheep smelled too much like sheep. Her mind was whirring too rationally – in fact, it had never seemed more crystalline as she sorted through the impossible possibilities like a child rifling a magician's cape, trying to discover how his tricks worked. She pinched her wrist to make sure she was awake – wasn't that accepted procedure? Though she almost drew blood, the pain did not alter the landscape around her.

St. Michael's tower chimed ten o'clock – far too early to call Dolly Dolby. She'd go for a walk to stabilize herself, then return to the inn for her telephone credit card. There had to be a plot that made sense. There had to be a motive. Sanity depended upon it.

As Nora hiked downhill, Barrow's cobbled streets gave way to unpaved alleys with boards spanning puddles, the fragrance of roses and lilies to the stench of pigsties and outdoor privies. She was in a jumble of sooty, slate-roofed hovels where women swept with handmade brooms, tossed slops to goats, haggled with tinkers bent low under pots and pans. All wore ankle-length dirndls, high-necked blouses, sacking aprons, bonnets and shawls in smoky or earth tones.

According to John Slater's map, this was The Bottoms, once housing Barrow's coal-mining families. The soil was gummy, the air acrid with a sulfurous yellow smoke. Faces seemed washed in sepia, *just as in archival photos.* A premise *was* forming in Nora's mind, but one too aberrant to allow into full consciousness. Stubbornly she recalled her student-exchange visit to East Berlin during the late seventies, through one of those periodic cracks in the Berlin Wall. There, too, shrouded women had crept amid bomb rubble and crumbling buildings still cratered by Second World War shrapnel, as if time had stopped.

The twisted laneways converged onto a square as jammed with horse-carts as those attached to the Last Gulp Saloon in any western movie. While women fetched water at a pump, men in thick-soled boots and coarse wool caps lounged on benches in front of the Leg 'o Mutton pub, puffing pipes. She could see a dry-goods shop selling grain from sacks, a butcher shop hung with carcasses buzzing with flies, a barber shop advertising tooth-pulling as a sideline, and a blacksmith shop where a horse was being shod at an open hearth. Despite the reek of burning hooves, Nora felt drawn by the smithy's clanging hammer as he anvilled the red-hot metal while an assistant nailed a shoe.

"Are ye lost, ducks?" A bowlegged man with a rusty mustache waved his gnarled stick, his tone challenging, his blue eyes cold and strangely opaque.

"What place is this?"

"This 'ere's Black Pit Square." He pointed with his pipe. "Pit's over there. Yer can see th' rigs."

Beyond the last row houses, Nora found a cindery wasteland of startling proportions, overhung by a gritty cloud: several brick buildings on a crisscross of railway lines, dozens of wood sheds dwarfed by a slag heap, three spidery rigs of wheels and pulleys, four fiery chimneys like toxic toadstools.

A gold-lettered sign informed her:

BLACK PIT COLLIERY
&
CHEMICAL WORKS
Founded 1888

Abruptly turning her back, Nora consulted her Timex watch, only to remember that it was not on her wrist. Panicking, she tried to zigzag back through the muddle of nameless alleys, with their murderous vapors, to Upper Barrow, but kept ending up in cul-de-sacs. By the time she'd finally climbed to Edge Road, every bell in Barrow was chiming eleven; it was another ten minutes before she reached the Wolfe Inn Moon lobby.

No one was behind the counter as she fled to her room. On the desk where she'd left her nylon shoulder bag, she found a handmade black suede satchel. She dumped its contents: a tortoise-shell comb, a lace handkerchief, a tin of hairpins, a change purse stuffed with old coins and . . . a fat billfold leaking pound notes. Nora counted: £8,000 – the exact amount she'd been carrying in travelers' checks. She rifled the pockets of her satchel: no travelers' checks. No credit cards. No driver's license. More seriously: no passport.

Battling hysteria, Nora ransacked her room. All her documentation was missing, along with her manuscript. She flung herself onto her bed, still trying to run a golden thread of common sense through the murky maze in which she was spinning. She'd phone Dolly Dolby to check her mother's house for the new suitcase, then cancel her credit cards, contact the Canadian embassy about her passport, and catch the next train to London.

Though Nora hoped to sneak out undetected, Mrs. Wolfe's imperious voice skewered her at the door: "Our guests pay *in advance*, Miss Locke."

Anxious to avoid conflict, Nora set a £50 note on the counter. "Last night and tonight."

Mrs. Wolfe methodically folded the money so that only the denomination showed. "What do you expect me to do with this?"

"Your quoted rate was sixteen for a single. I thought the Value Added Tax was always included in prices in Britain."

Mrs. Wolfe defensively shifted her shoulders in their narrow black cage. "Our rates are exactly as advertised." Pushing the price list toward Nora, she underlined with her fingernail: "Single bed and bath, including breakfast, sixteen shillings per week. You can hardly expect me to change a note of this size."

Nora gaped at the price list: sixteen *shillings*, not pounds, and *per week*, not per night. With shaking fingers she dumped her change purse onto the counter – a spill of gold and silver and bronze coins. Pecking through it like a chicken, Mrs. Wolfe clanked three crowns and a shilling into her cashbox. "If you're dissatisfied with our prices, Miss Locke, you'd best pay in advance for a month and claim our discount."

Nora's glance struck a copy of *The Barrow Times*, lying on the desk. Its headline was dauntingly familiar: "AIRSHIP LANDS IN LOCAL FIELD." She picked it up. It was dated Monday, June 23, 1913. *Calmly, calmly, now.* "This is my paper."

"Of course." An exasperated Mrs. Wolfe seized the other end. "Next we'll hear that someone has stolen *your* hotel."

"Agnes!" A male hand clasped Mrs. Wolfe's wrist. "Let it go."

Agnes Wolfe released her grip.

"I apologize, Miss Locke," soothed the male voice. "That paper is for our guests."

But by then Nora was out the door.

Nora raced up Market Street with *The Barrow Times* in her fist, feeling the sidewalk slide under her feet like a slicker of air, at last surrendering to the reality engulfing her. She was acutely aware of others jostling, shoving, elbowing, hustling, shouldering, bumping, pressing, swirling around her – women in ankle-length hobble skirts, with their heads festooned in feathers and flowers; men in flannels and herringbones and tweeds, with straw boaters and homburgs, swinging either walking sticks or furled umbrellas. The cobbled streets were a muddle of bicycles, spring wagons, dog-carts and pony-traps, challenged by the occasional antique car. Though the air rang with a cacophony of clomping hooves, jingling harnesses and tooting horns, each sound seemed to reach Nora several seconds late, like the thunderclap trailing the lightning of a distant storm.

She realized then that *everything* had slowed down. The lace handkerchief waved by a woman to a friend across the street was like a flag on a near-windless day. The arm of the window-cleaner, arching through Thomas Ball's gold lettering, traveled at the pace of an hour hand. Each joint of the wing of the pigeon, swooping from one chimney pot to the next, seemed to articulate separately in a long sinuous ripple.

During these overplump moments of time, it seemed to Nora that she could observe every detail in every shop window without bothering to angle her head – Miss Jepson's Millinery, featuring a navy bonnet ripe with cherries at 5s 5d, a jade turban with ostrich plume at 10s, a tulle wedding cake topped by nesting bluebirds; not only the next play at the Palace, but the cast, right down to the understudies. And the smells, *ahh, the smells* – not just the scent of lumber at Alcott the Wheelwright, but each plank of ash, oak and elm that Alcott's staff was sawing, planing or sanding into wagons and prams and wheelbarrows. At Godwin's Confectionery, she could distinguish the peppermints from the horehound drops, the ginger from the linseed cakes, the almonds from the maple buds.

Market Street splayed like a duck's foot into Market Place, where hawkers with stalls competed with peddlers pushing carts for ground and airspace. "Thread 'n' twine, thick 'n' fine!" "Pick o' th' piddle-pots fer thru'pence!" "Barrow BA-SKETS! Best BA-SKETS!" "Scissors 'n' knives, I'll give 'em a grind!"

As Nora wove through the aisles, the jumble of buckles and buckets and boots and pork pies and potted meats and candles and calico and sandalwood and sassafras and beeswax and brushes pouring from each booth and barrel proved too powerful an assault on her heightened senses. She escaped into a park, where children in pinafores and sailor suits played with marbles and hoops and tops. Flopping onto a bench, she was both relieved and disturbed to see that she looked just like the other women reading or jiggling prams, except that most wore upswept hair with hats, while hers was still in an unaccustomed tumble to her shoulders. Curiously she studied their elegant coils and waves and knots and twists, now functioning chiefly as rookeries for birds or nookeries for flowers. She examined patent pumps with buckles and calf boots with fabric uppers as they peeked from pleats of linen, flounces of cotton, draperies of silk. When a hand-knit red-and-yellow ball landed at her toe, she rolled it to its tiny owner, smothered in layers of muslin, anxious to see if she were "real" enough to raise an answering smile. When the muffin man trundled by with his cart, she purchased a scone to assure herself that she could eat, then delighted in the sweet explosion of raisins against her tongue and the freshly churned butter as rich as whipped cream.

Quitting the park, Nora turned onto High Street, where the frenzy of Market Place gave way to Georgian dignity. Here was a street of bankers and insurance companies and stockbrokers, where doors with gold lettering and brass bars forbade entrance; where clerks in high starched collars scratched into leather ledgers while phone operators in crisp shirtwaists plugged lines into switchboards; where glossy black toppers predominated over tweed caps, silver-headed canes over gnarled staffs, and antique cars over spring wagons; where gentlemen in frock coats escorted ladies in chapeaux spun with so much veiling Columbus could have sailed any one to America in place of *The Santa María*.

A stylish group of strollers clustered before a three-story Georgian building where a Grim Reaper with brass scythe bonged twelve o'clock. A display case labeled "TODAY'S NEWS" contained a mockup of the front page of *The Barrow Times.*

Joining the rest, Nora read:

AIRSHIP LANDS IN LOCAL FIELD

A monoplane, whose pilot was attempting to best the record for the Channel crossing, was forced down by fog in a pasture three furlongs north of Barrow. With the assist of a number of our citizens, the airship was brought to anchor for an hour of repairs to its rudder. For many Barrow residents, this was their first opportunity to view a flying craft whilst on the ground.

Though pilot Lt. Richard Colson agreed he was not likely to beat the 47 mph Dover–to–Calais record set in 1908, he told his well-wishers he'd had a "jolly good time" seeing more than he'd expected of the British countryside. As he called from his cockpit at 11:00 a.m., "Cheerio, chaps. Now, it's on to Paris!"

Other headlines announced: "MR. LLOYD GEORGE REPLIES TO CRITICS," "GERMANY ESTABLISHES AVIATION DEPOTS," and "NEW OUTBREAK 'TWIXT BULGARIA AND SERBIA." The paper in the glass case, like the one gripped in Nora's hand, carried the dateline Monday, June 23, 1913.

Nora scurried from the Times building, shoulders hunched, repeating that date like a mantra. As she turned onto Church Street she noticed the plume of a locomotive streaking like a jet stream as it sped across the Vale of Barrow. In her head, an image materialized the way foreground separates from background in a pointillist painting . . . *Grandma Flora.*

Picking up her gored skirt, Nora ran down High Street toward Barrow Railway Station. By the time she reached Church Street, she was racing head to head with the engine in the valley below. She watched in despair as each passenger car slid past, leaving her to chase the caboose as it rounded Barrow Hill.

Nora dashed down Station Road. Below stood the terminal, peaked and arched as she had once imagined it. The train was disgorging passengers, with baggage being claimed and kisses exchanged. Hitching her skirt, Nora scrambled downhill through dusty brambles, past a parking lot jammed with cars, carts and carriages.

All Barrow passengers had now debarked, with new ticket-holders being welcomed into the coaches. As Nora sprinted toward the platform, her left foot went numb, pitching her into a patch of thistles. By the time she recovered, the baggage-handlers were loading the last pieces of luggage – an iron bird cage and a buckled leather suitcase.

"Stop! Don't leave me," begged Nora. She pushed through well-wishers blowing kisses while the locomotive flexed its steel muscles, snorting like a racehorse at a starting gate. She felt the metallic surface of a closed door slide under her sweaty palms as the wheels began their forward thrust, then a workman's calloused fingers as he yanked her by the shoulders from the tracks.

Wrenching free, Nora limped beside the train, searching curious faces pressed against its windows as they glided past. She glimpsed *. . . a red-headed woman in a traveling suit and straw hat, cradling an infant in a colorful shawl.* Though the woman's eyes seemed puzzled, her lips parted as if she might speak. She raised her left hand, clasping a copy of *The Barrow Times,* and saluted Nora, who waved her own copy in return. Then, both woman and child disappeared in a grand exhalation of steam.

When Nora returned to the platform, it was empty. A sallow youth, wearing green celluloid cuff protectors, scratched with a straight pen inside the only ticket window still open. "Can I 'elp yer, missus?"

"When's the next train to Liverpool?"

He tugged at his spiky forelock. "Same time tomorrow, missus – twelve-fifteen noon, arrivin' Liverpool at twelve a.m."

"Do you happen to know when Canadian Pacific Steamlines sails from Liverpool to Canada?"

"Once a week – tomorrow evenin' at eight. I can sell yer a ticket fer th' train, but nowt fer th' steamer. That would be Thomas Cook's business on 'igh Street."

"Do you know if there's a faster way of getting to Liverpool?"

The youth was astonished: "There's niver a ve-hi-cle faster than th' train, missus!"

Nora thought of the cars she'd seen on the streets of Barrow – a loose assemblage of metal and rubber held together with paint and chewing gum. She thought of the downed pilot attempting to better the Dover–to–Calais record of forty-seven miles an hour, and acknowledged defeat.

"Would yer be th' lady that missed th' train?" asked the youth, assessing her jumbled hair and sweaty face.

"I . . . was just seeing someone off," hedged Nora. She forced herself to add: "A . . . relative who's sailing to Canada."

"Would yer be wantin' to send a telegram to th' ship, then? It's sixpence fer twelve words."

Closing her eyes, Nora composed:

WAIT DONT LEAVE EXCLAMATION UNBORN GRANDDAUGHTER AT BARROW STATION URGENTLY DESIRES CONTACT . . .

"I don't think so."

Nora fled the station into the Vale of Barrow, seeking solace in this timeless landscape where grass and trees looked the same, independent of numbers on a calendar, with her legs stretching from her body in slow motion and her feet never impacting the ground.

Had she tumbled, like Alice, into the Wonderland inside her own head? If this was a dreamscape, why were all the laws of physics so scrupulously obeyed? Why had she encountered no Mad Hatters or talking White Rabbits or other anomalies beyond her being here?

If not a dream, perhaps she lay paralyzed on her mother's staircase, or was wandering insanely from room to room, living out her years of D.H. Lawrence research, catalyzed by the emotional contents of the old suitcase. Perhaps Dolly Dolby was right about the power of houses to cast spells. Perhaps their conflicts could spin psychic spiderwebs, ensnaring hapless victims. Maybe her fall had thrown a neural switch in an obscure section of her brain, allowing her to replay genetic memory like a movie video.

Collapsing in a clump of poppies, Nora asked herself the dreaded question: *Am I dead?* Reluctantly, she recalled . . . *a woman with a twisted neck sprawled down a staircase with a balding man crouched over her.* Even now were friends filing past her casket, gazing into her closed eyes, solemnly telling each other how peaceful she looked? If she was lost in the twilight zone between death and waking, where was the celestial guide with archangel's wings whose job it was to judge her life and help her sort her options? Where was the tunnel of light and her welcoming ancestors? Why was Grandma Flora speeding toward Liverpool instead of beckoning from that silver-edged cloud? *If* she'd managed the impossible feat of spiraling back in time to confront her ancestral past, why wasn't that past here to greet her, instead of chasing her own birth in Canada?

The bells of Barrow's Norman church chimed three, along with those of other churches on other hills, filling the valley with stereophonic sound. Though Nora's costume was outdated, it felt and smelled as real as her own flesh. She seemed to be the same person, yet nothing made sense to her rational mind, which insisted on filing a minority report.

Rising unsteadily, she shook grass from her cherry-print skirt, then circled around Barrow Hill, her mind still churning. Perhaps linear time was just an illusion, as Plato and Einstein had opined, with so-called moments coexisting like cells in a honeycomb. If this landscape possessed a reality outside her own head, had she stumbled down a black hole, bumbled through a time warp, slid along a wormhole into a parallel universe?

Her granny gown, folded across her pillow last night, fit both eras. So had everything in the Wolfe Inn Moon, while The Bottoms had been *circa* 1913, though she'd refused to accept it. Was it coincidence that her two suitcases had been so much alike, or had they been two versions of the same suitcase – a space–time anomaly creating a portal into the past?

As Nora looked toward the town of Barrow, wound like a red-brick ribbon around Barrow Hill, she wondered when the rest of it had regressed, and where Grandma Flora had been while she herself was stubbornly adjusting to life in prewar England. While Nora had lain in bed, still unaware of her dilemma with time, perhaps Flora Flowe had been packing last-minute items, acutely attuned to the passage of each second. While Nora was plunging downhill to The Bottoms, perhaps Grandma Flora had been bidding a tearful good-bye to friends and relatives. Was it just a random accident that had caused Nora to trip, preventing her from catching the same train, or did some universal law prevent her from interacting with her progenitor in her own band of time? Would such a meeting have glitched Time's computer, interfering with her birth?

Church bells chimed four o'clock. Had an hour passed so quickly, or was that another trick of time? Could it possibly matter? *Yes!* To remain sane – if she were still sane – Nora had to believe some logic underlay what was happening to her. She squinted up at the sun – God's eternal timepiece – confirming the approximate hour, though of course not the year. Just ahead she could see a ragged line of miners plodding home from their shift at the smudge she knew to be Black Pit Colliery. As their paths converged, she slowed to let the weary silhouettes pass, separating each piece of their grimy clothing like a housewife sorting a wash: flannel vest, short-sleeved shirt, sweaty scarf, thick trousers, calico lunch bag. Though their blackened faces looked alike, their caps, worn at a variety of angles, hinted at the divergent personalities underneath. Nora drew close enough to hear their labored breathing punctuated by the *thwunk* of hobnailed boots, and to smell the stench of their corduroys, which acquired their khaki color and waxy gloss from boiling in dog excrement.

Scattered among the men were sooty children. While some seemed as worn out as their elders, a few played catch with their pit bottles. One lad drew Nora's attention, though she didn't know why. She imagined lifting his cap, taming a resistant cowlick, gently scrubbing his cheeks.

A freckled child with red ringlets came bouncing down the hill to meet him. Reaching up pudgy arms, she placed a kiss on his charcoal cheek, then handed him a bit of bread from her pinafore pocket. As the two fanned right toward The Bottoms, the lad stopped, turned to Nora, lifted his cap, and nodded gravely while his sister shyly curtsied.

Nora felt a surge of elation, as if she were being welcomed to this world once locked inside old histories, realizing that the same faith underlay everyone's life, even though most of us failed to acknowledge it. Every human worked, played, procreated, bought lottery tickets, emptied the garbage, assuming that it all added up to something. What protected anyone at any moment from a tumble into chaos was simply a refusal to examine reality too deeply, even to ostracize those who did. Despite inner terrors, she must trust that what was happening to her would prove life to have profounder meaning rather than none at all.

With its single tower tilted at a precarious angle, the Wolfe Inn Moon looked drunk and disorderly, like a tramp leaning against a lamp post.

Relieved to find the lobby empty, Nora climbed to her room, intending to enjoy a relaxing bath and then to snack on the savory pie she'd purchased from a street vendor. As the steam seeped into her pores, she found herself imagining a British dinner like her mother used to cook every Sunday: a sizzling leg of lamb with roast potatoes, two veggies and a ton of gravy.

Rising from the tub, Nora felt reassured: surely a ghost could not produce such a ferocious appetite.

In fact, now that she no longer blamed the inn's owners for her conundrum, Nora felt curious to meet its inhabitants. While high necks had been *de rigueur* for afternoon in Barrow, the dressier costumes in her armoire suggested that the women of 1913 adopted different tactics for evening. Nora selected a Wedgewood-blue, off-the-shoulder crêpe de chine with cinched waist, then filled in the neckline with a lace bib. She had already slicked back her hair into its accustomed roll, when she noticed a mother-of-pearl comb with blue ribbon exactly matching her dress. Remembering the luxuriant hairstyles she'd seen on the street that day, she looped and coiled her own to match.

Though she'd intended to give the cosmetics in antique pots short shrift as usual, the artist in her again seized control. With her left hand, she highlighted and contoured, like a child playing with paints. The result was stunning – not because of any skill at artifice, but because of the joy that radiated through her eyes and smile. Nora shook her head: nothing snuffled, pawed, clawed or gnawed. Her migraine had vanished!

As a parting gesture, she shed the lace bib. *When in Barrow . . .*

It was quarter after seven when Nora entered the Wolfe Inn Moon dining room. Its opulent gold-and-crimson damask walls contained ornate mahogany sideboards set with silver candlesticks, vases of peonies and bowls of fruit. Deeply buttoned burgundy chairs, the shape of plump dowagers, cozily clustered around tables set with white linen and cranberry glass. Bare shoulders, waxed mustaches, sleek coiffures, satin lapels, jeweled necklaces glowed in the gaslight.

With a strained smile reflecting their morning altercation, Agnes Wolfe ushered Nora to a table marked "No. 2." Her black satin hotelier's gown, its collar scraping her earlobes, resuscitated Nora's self-consciousness about her *décolletage.* Glancing covertly left and right, she caught smiling approval on the faces of several male diners, one of whom arose from an adjacent table.

Bowing low in frock coat and striped pants, he inquired: "Might

I coax you into dining with me this evening, Miss Locke? I'm your host, Nicholas Wolfe."

He was over six feet, in his early forties, with black curls framing a multiplaned, clean-shaven face. His plum waistcoat was hung with a gold pocketwatch, while his gray cravat was secured with a ruby stickpin matching his cufflinks. Still nervous over Encounters of the Third Kind, Nora was about to plead exhaustion when his voice twigged her memory. "You're the man who ended this morning's newspaper wars!"

His smile was broad and ingenuous. "And now I'm offering you a place at the captain's table."

As he seated Nora, Agnes Wolfe ill-humoredly transferred her place-setting. "I *say* I'm the captain but my wife runs a tight ship." Unfurling Nora's napkin, he graciously softened what otherwise might have seemed like husbandly criticism. "It's because Mrs. Wolfe is so efficient that I can dine with our guests."

Nora fingered the cutwork "W" on the linen, acutely aware of Agnes Wolfe's possessive eyes. "I see . . . good cop, bad cop."

Her companion seemed puzzled.

"That's Canadian slang."

"Then you must forgive me. We've never had a Canadian guest before. A small coal town, after all. Too far north, too far inland and not pretty enough. Our townsfolk move the other way. To the New World." Without turning, he signaled to a waitress in a crisp white-and-black uniform, expertly negotiating tables with chest thrust forward like a pilot ship avoiding ice pans.

Her cropped and curly red hair snapped and sizzled in the firelight – the region's famed Celtic locks. As she placed a decanter of red wine on their table, Nicholas Wolfe informed the maid: "Our new guest is from Canada." When the girl ignored this introduction, he deadpanned to Nora. "Flame and I used to be great friends till she heard about women in London demanding the vote. Now talking to her is like striking a match across flint."

Flame slapped down a plate of bread and cheese. "Canada?"

Her eyes flared a pyrotechnic blue. "Oh, this one's come from a lot farther than that . . . much, much farther, I'll guarantee it."

Nicholas brushed his hand across Nora's in apology. "Please forgive the rudeness of an unworldly girl. Our impressionable locals read radical newspapers and it spoils them for country life." Raising his goblet, he smiled. "To a long and enjoyable residency at the Wolfe Inn Moon."

The wine was palatable, but the toast was unsettling and the politics rankled. "Don't you approve of female equality, Mr. Wolfe?"

"Indeed I do! I find your sex so superior in every way that I welcome anything that redresses the balance." He flashed a disarming smile. "I like all women, but especially independent ones."

"And what is your experience of them?"

"A strong mother, a strong sister, a strong wife and now a strong dinner companion. What is your experience of strong men?"

"That, despite what they say, they don't like independent women any better than the other kind do."

As he leaned toward her, she caught the first clear view of his eyes over high cheekbones – topaz, almost yellow. "Then let us drink to those rare exceptions and to the women who inspire them."

Across her own left shoulder, Nora saw Agnes Wolfe leaning at a precarious angle, attempting to eavesdrop. Seeking a topic less personal, she traced the crest on their wine decanter – a wolf howling at the moon. "Where did your inn get its name?"

"A family legend – really more of an old wives' tale." Nicholas Wolfe paused to savor his wine. "It's said that when the moon is full, Wolfe eats Wolfe. One version tells of a Wolfe who slew and ate his brother, then swore the body had been devoured by wolves. Another claims that a scullery maid killed her master at full moon, then ate him to feed the little Wolfe she was carrying." Though his tone was offhand, he seemed to relish his tale. "That's the trouble with a name like ours. It attracts both the lunatics and the gullible, and of course our family – like every other – is no stranger to scandal." He drained his goblet and reached for the decanter in a single motion. "But I'm not much interested in the past, are you?"

Laughter bubbled in Nora's throat. "Since coming to Barrow it's been my whole life."

Again, her companion leaned toward her with flattering attentiveness. "What *did* lure you to Barrow?"

Before Nora could invent an answer, the voluptuous Eleanora arrived with bowls of sherry consommé. Flashing a dimpled smile, she bent to her task, spreading a puddle of silence as male patrons vied for the best view of her comely chest. All but Nicholas Wolfe, whose intense yellow eyes never strayed from Nora's face. "You were saying?"

As little as possible, she reminded herself. Gesturing toward a neighboring table, where Agnes Wolfe was chatting to diners, Nora inquired: "Are these people regulars?"

Nicholas Wolfe shrugged. "Mostly. We don't have many overnight guests since the turnpike opened on the other side of town, but" – another generous nod to his wife – "Mrs. Wolfe can still attract the dinner crowd. See that bearded fellow in the green waistcoat?" Again, he inclined his head without turning, as if possessed of compound vision. "He's our doctor. The one with his mutton chops pressed into our mutton chops owns a woolen factory. The bald chap with his mustache dripping into his soup is growing rich shipping coal by barge down the river. Most of our guests are from the new class of capitalists." Without apparent bitterness, he added: "The better folk have better things to do – which brings me back to my dinner guest."

Now rehearsed, Nora answered easily. "A great-aunt from Exeter left me a modest inheritance. I decided to see more of the country before returning home to my work as a schoolteacher."

Her host applied his large spoon to his small bowl. "May I ask what your priorities are whilst staying with us?"

"Just sightseeing. Maybe you and your wife can advise me."

He finished his soup with evident pleasure. "I will make that one of *my* priorities!"

Eleanora served their main course – roast lamb with potatoes, gravy, carrots and beets – in a room growing raucous with laughter. As the decibel level rose higher, Nora and her companion enthusiastically cleaned their plates. She had never known anyone to enjoy food as much as Nicholas Wolfe while remaining equally concentrated on his guest. Even more surprising was her matching appetite: from almost-vegetarian, she'd reverted to carnivore with a stake-pit stomach. She was similarly amazed at how willingly the checkered truths rolled from her agile tongue. The whole evening felt thrilling, like ad-libbing the heroine's role in a costume drama during an out-of-town tryout. Only Agnes Wolfe's sharp eyes thrust like fork tines into her back reminded her of a competing reality.

Nora had reached the bottom of her fourth glass of wine when a crash spun her head. Eleanora stood in the kitchen doorway, wringing her apron over an overturned plate. In two strides, Agnes Wolfe arrived at the disaster and was arching her hand like a serpent to strike when Nicholas intervened. The two Wolfes exchanged verbal volleys while Flame resentfully cleaned up the debris and Eleanora fled sobbing into the kitchen.

Nicholas returned to Nora, his fury netted like a fish in a jovial grin. "A domestic spat after a long day."

He reached for the decanter, but Nora placed her palm over her glass. "No more, please."

"Don't let a few seconds of strife spoil your appetite for our hospitality."

But it had. The Wolfes' violence had unnerved Nora, especially since she suspected she might be its secret trigger. Precisely refolding her napkin, she arose unsteadily. "Jet lag."

Frowning, Nicholas inquired: "Jet lag?"

"Jetty lag. Seasickness. More Canadian slang."

Nora was too keyed up to sleep. The Wolfe Inn Moon seemed gridded with live wires she was in peril of tripping over. Taking a sketchpad she'd purchased on impulse, she tried to draw some of the things she'd experienced that day. At first, her fingers were stiff and her hand felt heavy – like pushing a bag of wet sand . . . *trussed behind her back as a turkey foot. "You'll thank me some day."*

Defiantly, Nora switched her pencil to her left hand, then watched it fly about the page: Agnes and Nicholas Wolfe, heads jutted together like fists; the enigmatic, straw-hatted face in the train window; the sooty pit boy now incongruously outfitted in a choir surplice.

As Nora turned off the light, she felt a soft footfall on her coverlet. Lifting the corner of her patchwork quilt, she let the orange cat creep inside.

6

She is wandering through a garden riotous with color. Eleanora sits under an apple tree, cradling a baby in a patchwork shawl. Flame perches beside her, also in her gingham uniform, reading to the sooty-faced pit boy and his red-haired sister. Smiling, he tips his tweed cap at Nora, then reaches out to pick a rose for her. As his fingers clasp the pulpy bloom, it explodes in a spatter of blood and petals.

Nora jolted up in bed, clutching the patchwork quilt. Slowly the sights and sounds and smells of this time and place intensified around her – the open window with its floral potpourri, the gas lamp on the night table, the bureau stuffed like a goose with pre-war stage properties, the brass bedstead and, between its bars, her ancestral albatross.

She felt assaulted in mind and body – first, by last night's red wine, now like a rag muffler around her brain; second, by the red meat, with its full complement of hooves, lying undigested in her stomach.

After several false starts, she reached for the preposterous pieces of uniform she was supposed to assemble: muslin chemise and buttoned knickers; whalebone corsets laced at back and hooked in front, with suspenders for lisle stockings; an eyelet camisole and a petticoat trimmed with ribbons – *my fortune for kneehighs, for something in lycra, for briefs by Calvin Klein.* After simplifying as best she could, she secured her hair in its familiar French roll, and then – still doing penance – donned the backdated version of her gray shirtwaist. Though she was supposed to top it with a chapeau as extravagant as those in Cecil Beaton's *My Fair Lady*, she settled for a comb with a bow, then grimly studied her reflection, girded for battle *circa* 1913.

As Nora collected her suede satchel, she noticed last night's sketches on her bed table. Shuffling through them, she thoughtfully dropped the one of the pit boy into her bag.

The burgundy dining room, so grand by gaslight, now looked too stuffy, too dark, too heavy, too . . . burgundy. Though most tables were a welter of soiled napkins, greasy plates and half-filled cups, No. 2 was neatly set for one.

A mahogany sideboard decorated with carved wolves' heads was laden with breakfast foods tended by Flame, while Eleanora cleared tables, with the orange and white cat weaving languidly in and about her skirts, begging for tidbits. Though both women wore white pinafores over blue-gingham dirndls, each looked uniquely herself, like the miners who rose above their common pit dirt to make jaunty statements with their headgear. A voluptuous assemblage of hanging threads and missing buttons, Eleanora wore her cap with its sprig of lavender precariously perched on the back of her tousled sable curls, while the robust, angular-faced Flame wore hers stiffly centered and upright. Yet Nora suspected Flame's identity to be more accurately telegraphed by that foxy red hair.

As Nora picked through fried eggs, kippers, lambs' kidneys and porridge, she noticed the captain's table was occupied by a dandy still in evening dress. Despite the gloom of this cellar room, everything about him gleamed as if his valet had dipped him by his

Achilles heel into a vat of varnish before dispatching him into a starless night. His black hair was slicked like oil on a highway; his bloodshot eyes floated like broken eggs in a pan of skim milk. Since he bore a striking resemblance to Nicholas Wolfe, Nora guessed he was related – probably a brother. *As close to a vampire as I'll ever see.* Which was why she dubbed him "the Count." Rearranging her greasy food like a child who fears being scolded for waste, she felt his albumen eyes roll familiarly over her as if expecting her to speak: lascivious, or merely bored? She did not judge it in her best interests to glance up and find out.

Abandoning her still-life portrait – fried eggs for eyes, kipper mouth, kidney ears – Nora sought out Flame, just removing her pinafore to assume desk duties. "Do you know where I might make a phone call to Canada?"

Giggling, Flame replied: "I certainly do, mum. That'd be th' same switchboard from which yer'd make a call to Mars. Best take plenty o' quid. It's thru'pence fer three minutes and twenty-five miles."

Nora strode along Market Street in search of Thomas Cook & Sons. In retrospect, her behavior last night in the dining room embarrassed her: who was that coquette, with plunging neckline, who'd paced Nicholas Wolfe glass for glass and chop for chop, while his wife looked haplessly on? Fate hadn't catapulted her back in time to seduce a married man or – now that she thought about it – enliven her socioeconomic paper with on-site research. She'd missed Grandma Flora by barely five minutes at the train station – fifty-five minutes closer than their first missed connection in 1955, when she'd arrived on this planet just as Flora had departed it. Since her progenitor remained her only link with this band of time, then Nora must track her to Canada, and the sooner the better. Everything else was diversionary.

With that resolved, Nora allowed herself to respond to the vitality around her – a sooty chimney sweep gobbling a pork pie, a woman in hobble skirt pushing a perambulator as elegant as a coach, a poster advertising brick houses at £25 and rented ones for £5 a year. With £8,000 cash, she was practically an heiress.

By the time Nora hit High Street, she was no longer ogling people's hats or vacuuming up every button in every shop window. She marveled at the adaptability of the human species – how quickly the abnormal could become normal; how stoically soldiers conditioned themselves to muddy trenches, prisoners to barbed-wire fences, civilians to skies that rained bombs. In fact, the Barrow of 1913 was growing disconcertingly familiar, with walking sticks now appearing appropriate for frock coats and buggies for cab stands.

She was approaching Thomas Cook's when she noticed a pawnshop with a creaky sign shaped like a pocketwatch: TIME PAST. Its windows were packed with intriguing items: fiddles and accordions, ostrich fans and ornate helmets, military insignia and ivory pipes, all backed by a wall of clocks ticking in unison.

Nora entered. "I'd like to buy a watch."

The elderly proprietor – an engaging cross between Gepetto and Einstein – jumped down from his stool. "And I have such beautiful watches." After unfurling a piece of purple velvet, he began to display the contents of small boxes. Before opening the seventh, he tapped its side. "I have a feeling this will be for you."

Onto the velvet he placed an oval watch ringed in seed pearls, hung on a delicate gold chain.

Nora cupped the watch in her palm. It felt like a child's beating heart. She turned it over, saw the engraving of a butterfly, and felt an urgent need to possess it. "Yes, this is the one."

"It's the prettiest in the shop. I'd be happy with fifteen shillings."

Less than something featuring Ninja turtles.

Mistaking Nora's hesitation, the pawnbroker prompted: "Twelve shillings would be quite sufficient." He cocked his crested white head like a friendly woodpecker. "I want you to have it. It's one of a kind, like each one of us."

Nora smiled. "The first price was fine."

He rang up the sale on his immense brass register, as deftly as if playing Mozart on a pianoforte.

"No need to wrap it."

"But I must . . . a watch like this." He slipped it into a purple drawstring pouch. "Time is the one thing we own that we can never hold on to." He presented the pouch to Nora with a courtly bow. "Seeing it pass through a window onto eternity as lovely as this eases the sorrow of our loss."

Outside the pawnshop Nora slipped the watch around her neck. Then she joined the citizens clustered around *The Barrow Times* news board. Remembering yesterday's shock, she affected insouciance as she read:

The Folly of Playing with Fire

The spectre of our European leaders, rushing from conference to conference, collecting treaties with one neighbour to fight another, is indeed a sorry one. When did we, as a collection of civilized Nations, enjoying the highest standard of living since the beginning of Time, develop the notion that the way to keep the Peace was to prepare for War? Despite our superficial differences, the Nations of Europe are closer to being a single community than at any other time in our History. Our forms of government, from Constitutional Monarchy to Republicanism, share a common sense of decency and fair play. A man can travel from Liverpool to the borders of Russia without a Passport. Our currencies can be freely exchanged. Our various Religions are a source of personal comfort, rather than of International strife. Yet, as the spring of 1913 blossoms into summer, we note a developing political and military frenzy that flies in the face of our Common Blessings. Take care, Gentlemen, in whom we place our Trust, that in playing with fire, for the purpose of preventing fire, you do not bring about the Conflagration that you fear. With the modern weaponry at our command, War is not a solution but sheer Folly.

Though Nora still followed the lines, she'd ceased to absorb their meaning. Her eyes had clamped onto the name of the editor. *I have to talk to John Slater.* She strode toward the brass-filigree door of the Times building. *Talk to him about what?* She hadn't the foggiest idea. Nora stepped back, trampling a man's beige spats. Apologizing profusely, she hurried away, stopped, pivoted, then bolted back through the filigree door into the Times's marble lobby, vaulted like a cathedral. With muscles still tensed to flee, she spotted the elevator – a bird cage, brass arms empty and open. Remembering her summer as an elevator operator in Hamilton's Right House, she stepped inside, closed the door, spun the wheel, felt the cage lift. *("I'll bet this job has its ups and downs.")* The elevator jolted to a stop. *("And its jerks.")*

Nora stepped into a hall laid with blue-and-white tiles in an intricate geometric design. She veered left, into the intimidating gaze of founder Henry Slater, sternly posed in gilt frame with signet finger on vest. Ducking past, she targeted a paneled double door, then stepped through that into an oak-lined office. Sailing by a woman at an antiquated switchboard, she breached another paneled door, strode through another antechamber, then seized a third brass knob.

"Stop!" ordered a female voice behind her. "You can't go in there."

Nora entered a book-lined Georgian office, almost knocking over a trimly bearded man carrying a silk hat and walking stick.

"I tried to stop her, Mr. Slater!" huffed a secretary with furiously heaving chest.

John Slater politely inclined his frosty head, one hand on his dove-gray morning coat, just like the gilt-framed founder in the hall. "May I help you?"

Now, what? Nora had radar-locked onto her target like a smart bomb, but why?

More sternly: "Do you have business here?"

Nora's voice sounded distant and tinny as if played on a gramophone. "I have . . . something startling to tell you."

John Slater's courteous smile, ending in a mole, covered the impatience of a busy man. "Many people have promised me that. Very few have succeeded."

"I'm not from *here*."

Slater tapped his amber-headed stick against his gloved palm. "I dare say I guessed as much from your accent."

"You've written a book, *Barrow: Our Heritage, 1800–1913*."

Slater's bushy brows dipped down the bridge of his nose. "The title's not been confirmed."

"But it *has*, absolutely. It contains photographs, maps, graphs." Nora outlined the contents of John Slater's unpublished history as she had viewed it before her slide back in time.

"I don't know where you get your information, Mrs. – "

"Locke. Miss Locke."

" – but my book is not precisely a parliamentary secret and certainly not startling."

"But . . . I know other things!" Nora felt like a child trying to stretch a parent's attention to include a bedtime treat of cookies. What could she tell him that wouldn't sound too crazy? "Things that haven't happened but will."

Slater leaned away from her. "I'm sure you do, Miss Locke."

Nora rattled off a few random facts about life in Barrow. "The King is inviting Barrow's mayor to a garden party. The play *A Wrecker of Men* is on at the Palace . . . ahh, the rector of St. Michael's Church is holding a charity fête. The owner of the Leg o' Mutton is being fined for —"

"That's *yesterday's* newspaper, Miss Locke. My own."

Nora tried to think of something significant yet believable that was about to happen, but her head was abuzz with fabulous international history: moon landings, presidential assassinations, Winston Churchill . . .

"You were right," she blurted. "There'll be a war: 1914 to 1918."

"Miss Locke, I'm afraid —"

"Please believe me!"

"Believe *what*, Miss Locke?"

What, and why?

"Everyone has a political opinion, and I'm flattered you agree with mine." John Slater softened his dismissal with a teasing smile. "Now if only you could tell me something useful, like who will win today's Oxford–Hampshire cricket match or the steeplechase at Newmarket."

Eager to avoid further embarrassment, Nora allowed the publisher to escort her by his still-fuming secretary. "For the record, Miss Locke, your description of my book was entirely accurate. In fact, I've been toying with that exact title, but it's an obvious one, isn't it?"

Nora bolted past the open elevator, down two flights of stairs, almost knocking over a wiry little man in parakeet-green uniform on the trail of his missing cage. She reached ground zero drenched in humiliation. Surely her survival here depended on astute observation, not blurting prophecies equivalent to flying-saucer landings to skeptical strangers.

She darted across the street toward Thomas Cook & Sons, but stopped halfway, causing a horse to rear and a horn to hoot. *My sketch of the pit boy – the clippings mailed to Grandma Flora!*

Nora scrambled back to the curb just as John Slater emerged from the Times building, accompanied by a tow-haired young man in tweed jacket, cap and knickers.

"Mr. Slater, wait!"

He paused at the door of his sumptuous green Lanchester while the youth slid into the driver's seat. "Miss Locke, I'm certain that —"

"A mine explosion!" She tried to remember the dateline on the old clippings. *Today?* "Very soon." She waved the drawing from her satchel. "This boy . . ."

John Slater opened his car door. "Miss Locke, you must curb this desire for drama. Surely you see that —"

A shrill whistle cut his protest.

Nora's stomach seized. "Black Pit No. 8!"

Leaping into the Lanchester, Slater ordered his driver: "The colliery."

Nora opened the back door. "Take me."

Slater slammed the front door. "Impossible."

Nora climbed in. "You must take me."

"On the contrary. I must ask you to leave. *Now.*"

Nora handed him her drawing. "Eight people killed, including this child. See for yourself."

Slater weighed the time and trauma of evicting Nora against the nuisance of keeping her, then swallowed an angry retort. "Very well. But you must do everything I say. Is that clear?"

The people of The Bottoms were already pouring like slag down Barrow Hill as John Slater's car reached Black Pit Colliery.

"Park here," he ordered his driver, introduced to Nora as Daniel Slater, the son of his deceased sister whom he had adopted. "We're as close to the pit head as we can get."

While the youth sprinted off into the wailing confusion at a rugger's pace, Slater ordered Nora: "You stay in the car with the hood secured and the doors and windows closed."

"But —"

His frosty beard jutted forward. "Surely you can see that you've no role here."

Smoke plumed from a wooden rig, jetting cinders and flame several stories high. Wives and mothers huddled in shawls, as close to the calamity as sulfurous vapors allowed, while off-duty colliers rocked on their heels, separate and silent under sturdy caps. Few paid any attention to the green Lanchester till a bow-legged man with rusty mustache circled it. Whacking the rear tires with his oak staff, he peered into the window with steely blue eyes. Nora recognized the man who'd challenged her in Black Pit Square. Though she suspected he also recognized her, he gave no sign before loping off to rejoin the others.

She returned to the disaster, gazing through her window into smoke and hazard like a seer into a cloudy crystal, watching images clarify then dissolve, reciting what she could remember of *The Barrow Times* story that she'd read a few days ago in the eighty-year-old clippings.

MINING DISASTER KILLS EIGHT

At exactly 10:17 yesterday morning, the peaceful atmosphere of Barrow and environs was torn asunder by a gas explosion in Black Pit No. 8, killing seven men and one child. As smoke poured from the bowels of the earth, the people of The Bottoms rushed to the colliery yard to stand vigil. . . . Eyewitnesses attributed the accident to the build-up of noxious gases in the poorly ventilated stalls, ignited by lanterns utilizing naked flame.

John Slater returned with cinders stuck like pox to his face, oily mud smeared to his knees, his morning coat slung over his shoulder, and his shirt streaked with sweat. Deftly he reassembled himself, even producing a crease in his ruined striped pants, before ushering Nora into the passenger seat and grimly confirming: "Black Pit No. 8. Seven dead, one still missing."

As he assumed the driver's seat, Nora recited: "Judd, Mellon, Wilson, Hall, Emery, Bradley, Sutton . . . Tommy Ross, age nine."

Slater's grip tightened on the wood steering wheel as he inquired sardonically: "Does 'your source' say what caused the explosion?"

"Gas build-up ignited by lanterns utilizing naked flames," retorted Nora. She mentally consulted her Lawrence research. "But wasn't that usually the case before the invention of Davy safety lamps?"

John Slater started his engine. "It isn't the 'invention' of Davy lamps we're awaiting, Miss Locke, but mine owners willing to sacrifice a little profit for their use. The lifespan of a miner – "

" – is only forty-nine years," completed Nora. "Ten years less than the national average."

Slater glanced curiously toward his passenger as he navigated the gravel road to The Bottoms. "Most women of your station don't concern themselves with such matters."

His comfortable, all-knowing tone irritated Nora. "You have no understanding of my station. I'll ask you to stop patronizing me."

John Slater gave an unexpected chuckle. "Perhaps you mistake the beginnings of interest for its opposite."

They entered the deserted streets of The Bottoms. Though it was several more minutes before he spoke, he kept glancing toward her. "Would it offend you further if I inquired how you inform yourself?"

Nora chose the easiest answer. "Do you know the work of D.H. Lawrence?"

Slater steered around a heap of slops. "A local writer. From Eastwood, near Nottingham, I believe."

"He's the reason I came to the Midlands. I'm an academic researcher."

Slater's voice radiated its first real warmth. "My wife was also enthusiastic about his work . . . before her death. I had no idea he was so famous."

The shops of Black Pit Square were empty, some with their doors flung open. No women lined up at the village pump, where several buckets had been abandoned. Nora thought of Grandfather Flowe, killed in a mining mishap on the eve of his family's departure to Canada.

"When was the last fatal accident at Black Pit Colliery?" she asked.

"A year ago this September. Two pit boys were killed when some timbers collapsed."

"No adults?"

"None fatal, though limbs were lost."

The Lanchester lurched over the brow of Barrow Hill. "Where are you staying?"

"The Wolfe Inn Moon."

The editor's nostrils twitched as if scenting spoiled meat. "I didn't think they still took guests."

"I may be the only one." Nora recalled the repellent man in the breakfast room. "And a relative." As the green Lanchester sped along Edge Road, she demanded: "What's wrong with the Wolfe Inn Moon?"

John Slater parked to one side of the inn's entrance. "Everything, I dare say!"

As he opened Nora's door, she impulsively squeezed his arm. "Oxford University will beat Hampshire by an inning and twenty-five runs."

Exasperated, he demanded: "How do you know these futuristic things?"

"The scores?" Nora shook her head. "That part . . . I'm not sure."

7

She is playing tag with Flame and Eleanora in a cave of mirrors. All are wearing dust caps and gingham pinafores. She finds herself abandoned in a cul-de-sac ending at a mirrored door. Confused and frightened, she bangs upon it. "Let me in!" The door revolves, hurtling her through.

Eleanora and Flame are lying side by side on a mortuary slab with a dark-haired man, naked except for shiny black boots. "Look 'oo's 'ere," taunts Flame. "If it isn't Miss Mucky Muck wantin' 'er fair share!"

The man beckons with his cigar. He has no face. Nora slams the door. She hears their laughter – the women's high-pitched and hysterical, the man's sepulchral. As the sounds merge, the mirrored walls of the cave shake, then shatter, blasting Nora with shards of her own reflection.

Nora lay huddled inside her patchwork quilt, listening to Barrow come alive like a 1913 production of *Our Town*. OFFSTAGE *a rooster crows.* CUE *chirping sparrows and cooing doves.* SLAM *of door as maid collects laundry from the line.* CLATTER OF WHEELS *as milkman arrives.* LIGHTS UP *to simulate a beautiful dawn.*

A footfall outside Nora's door caused her to open it. On a silver tray she found *The Barrow Times* and a business card: "Compliments of John Slater."

Under the headline "MINE DISASTER KILLS EIGHT," Nora read the story by Daniel Slater that had been mailed to Grandma Flora in Canada. It was accompanied by portraits of the deceased: Judd, Mellon, Wilson, Hall, Emery, Bradley, Sutton and Tommy Ross. The first three were wedding photos; Hall was wearing a rugby uniform; Emery, Bradley and Sutton posed in studio portraits; nine-year-old Tom Ross smiled out from a choir surplice. Nora stared at the shiny face, wondering if the rules of the game into which she had been drafted would have allowed her to save this boy or whether she was prevented from interfering to preserve the historical record. Perhaps she was deluding herself into imagining any rules existed. If she jumped from this second-story window or off the lip of Barrow Hill, would she be killed, or would she sprout an umbrella like Mary Poppins, guaranteeing a soft landing in a mound of sheep dip? She wondered what, in her present circumstances, constituted a reality check. The bruise on her wrist where she'd pinched herself did not easily persuade her to leap out a window.

Nora returned to the photo of Tommy Ross in his choir surplice. Closing her eyes, she imagined him stretched thin and pale in some lace-curtained parlor in The Bottoms with a bruise on his temple where a boulder had struck, and not – as her head insisted – already reduced to dry bones under a gravestone with eighty years' moss on it. Cradling young Tom's portrait, she rocked on her bed, tears streaming down her cheeks, melting through those decades, watering that moss, seeing the lad as he had appeared yesterday on the trail to The Bottoms, with one hand clasping his sister's and the other raising his cap over his pinched face, knowing in her heart that time did not exist even while her head warned: *Be careful. Your plot line is all that connects you to your own time and place. Sever that, and you're like a space-drunk astronaut who cuts his oxygen line so he can fly like Daedalus into the sun.*

Nora wiped her eyes, shaken by the depth of her response. Aside from a warm relationship with her students, she'd kept her maternal feelings tightly bottled, along with a child's confused agonies about father-husbands who died too soon, leaving others to shoulder the grief and blame.

She turned Tommy Ross's picture face down on the bed. Spread with the cold detachment of all newspapers that bleat with sympathy or outrage on one page only to return to business as usual on the next, she found a plastering of cricket scores that had faintly bled through his forehead: Oxford over Hampshire by one inning and twenty-five runs. So, she hadn't just picked that figure out of the air. *There are rules!*

Encouraged, Nora reconfirmed yesterday's decision to follow Grandma Flora to Canada, feeling the potent tug of bloodlines. As she padded toward her armoire, her gaze caught the notebook on her desk, reminding her that it wasn't necessary to cross an ocean to make contact.

Tearing off a sheet, she attacked it with a straight pen:

Dear Mrs. Flora Flowe,

I hope that your transatlantic voyage was a comfortable one and that you have arrived safely in your new country, your new city and your new home.

I am a Canadian teacher related to you through a branch of the family that moved to Exeter. Recently I arrived in Barrow only to find you had departed by train for Liverpool.

Nora paused, debating whether she should mention seeing Grandma Flora through the train window, but decided to stick to polite clichés:

How disappointed I was to miss you! Of course, I am anxious to visit you on my return to Canada. Rather than impose on your hospitality, I will make reservations at the Royal Connaught Hotel in downtown Hamilton.

Hoping to see you soon,

Sincerely,

Nora Locke

She addressed the envelope to Mrs. F. Flowe on Central Street in Hamilton, then hesitated once more: how long had it taken Grandma Flora to sail the Atlantic and then to move into their Hamilton house? She printed across the bottom of the envelope: "PLEASE HOLD FOR ARRIVAL," underlining "PLEASE" several times. As she licked the envelope, she noticed *The Barrow Times* lying across her bed and, on impulse, enclosed clippings of the mine disaster.

It was ten minutes to nine. Deciding to skip Agnes Wolfe's greasy breakfast, Nora bathed and dressed, surprised at how well she was mastering the knack of buttoning, hooking, and lacing. Even the drag of a skirt around her ankles bothered her less. As she scanned her wardrobe, she recalled the retro costumes she'd eagerly adopted during the seventies in the name of fashion – the elephant-foot pants and platform soles, the maxi skirts and granny boots. Deciding on a pleated wine skirt with striped cotton shirtwaist, Nora checked her armoire for hiking shoes, intending to buy a steamer ticket at Thomas Cook's and then to tramp to The Bottoms to trace the elusive Grandpa Flowe.

A key turned in her lock and she caught a whiff of lavender.

Eleanora stood in the doorway with fresh linen over one arm and a hand held protectively to her throat. "I thowt yer'd be gone to breakfast, mum."

"I'm running a bit late." Nora selected a sturdy pair of oxblood slip-ons with high vamps and cleat heels.

As she tried them on, the maid watched from the doorway, playing with a heart-shaped silver pendant of the sort lovers exchange.

"Do you have a boyfriend, Eleanora . . . a beau?"

Girlish pride broke through the maid's shyness. "'e ga'e me this locket fer me last birthday, mum."

The oxblood shoes fit perfectly – handcrafted from calf. "How old were you?"

"Fifteen jus' turned, mum. On June 6."

"But that's *my* birthday!"

The maid pointed to the paper on Nora's desk. "'e works fer th' newspaper, mum. 'e wrote th' story about th' explosion."

"Daniel Slater?"

Eleanora nodded so vigorously she nearly dislodged the lavender sprig from her cap. "Me mither worked fer 'is. She did all th' Slaters' laundry and sewin', mum."

Nora wondered idly how the patrician John Slater viewed this humble match. "I met Daniel yesterday with his uncle. He seemed like a nice fellow and very attractive."

"Yes, mum. What's it like in Canada?" The girl inquired so eagerly it felt like a pounce.

"Well . . ." Nora mentally scanned old history books. "Big! Yes, the country's big, and I come from a big city – Hamilton on Lake Ontario." *What did Hamilton look like* circa *1913?* "The streets are much wider than in Barrow and there are lots more cars." *Had trams been invented yet?* "The tallest building in Hamilton is sixteen stories." Picking up her satchel, Nora strode toward the door.

Eleanora blocked her path. "Are yer goin' 'ome soon, mum?"

Nora considered the letter in her satchel: "I certainly hope so!"

The maid seemed reluctant to step aside. Her lavender perfume was causing Nora to sneeze. "I have to leave."

Eleanora jumped out of her way. "'ave yerself a nice walk then, mum."

Nora fled down the stairs, almost tripping over the orange cat, grooming itself under the chandelier.

It wasn't until she was safely trotting along the scythe-shaped path around Barrow Hill that she allowed herself to mull over her conversation with Eleanora. She should have made more effort to befriend the girl, to draw her out. If she couldn't interact with the people of Barrow instead of just observing them, what was the point of being here? Reluctantly, Nora confessed that Eleanora disturbed her. Her sensuality seemed so naked, both fascinating and unsettling. *June 6.* She shuddered. *Fifteen is such a terrifying age!*

A car swooped over the brow of the hill, whipping her around in a dusty tornado. The driver backed up, removed his leather cap and goggles.

"I'm sorry, Miss Locke. I truly am." Nicholas Wolfe grinned from the cream seat of his wine roadster. "No one from these parts walks along this road, but then – you're not from these parts, are you?"

"I was headed to High Street."

"You've forked down instead of up. Nothing urgent, I hope?" Alighting from the driver's seat, he strode around to the passenger door, graceful even in knickerbockers and Norfolk jacket. "Allow me. It's the least I can do."

Nora hesitated only slightly: a hot dusty hike back up the hill, or a spin in a jolly two-seater resembling a Victorian sleigh? She climbed into the roadster.

Nicholas reclaimed the driver's seat, then checked his gold pocketwatch. "How adventurous are you feeling? I've an hour or so before I'll be missed. I know a special place not in the guidebooks. Something quite extraordinary, if you have time."

Nora was still swiping dust from her skirt and tucking sweaty tendrils into her French roll. "These days, I've nothing but time." *Forty-two years before* I'm *missed!*

Nicholas gestured behind the seat. "I've something back there you can use."

Swiveling, she found a box from Miss Jepson's Millinery, containing a leather bonnet, swathed in veiling like a beekeeper's helmet, and a set of goggles.

He started the engine. "Our ladies find them helpful on our country roads. You're probably used to paving."

Nora tied her rakish headgear – nothing like Agnes Wolfe would wear, she was sure. "You're very well prepared."

He accelerated to twenty miles per hour. "This doesn't frighten you?"

She adjusted the goggles. "I can handle it."

From the obvious pleasure that Nicholas took in braking and

swerving, he could have been racing in the Grand Prix. He glanced toward Nora with approval. "Some ladies still don't trust the motorcar . . . but you're not *some ladies*, are you?"

Inspired by her companion's immersion in the moment, Nora slowed her thoughts to match the languorous crawl of the landscape past her window, and was rewarded by a return of the same rapt awareness that had enlivened the streets of Barrow: the heady sweetness of purple clover frothing out of gullies and ditches; the buzz of bees inviting her to share their secrets; the tang of the wind wafting from Barrow River; the tremolo of each nightingale's note as it hung forever in the pure air before sliding down a silvery chute to the next and the next.

As the roadster jounced along The Flats, a pothole jilted Nora from her sensuous trance. Reluctantly, she refocused on her driver: who was this man in leather cap and goggles, with whom she now shared space as intimately as two fish in a bowl? Someone who wore charm like a well-tailored suit – the kind of rogue male whom she usually avoided; someone who needed admiration like Narcissus needed his reflection, yet someone who was willing to work hard to get it. Her mother's face filled her consciousness, including the mouth like a pencil sharpened at both ends. Well, Nora knew what it was like to strive too hard to please. She switched channels – *kisses of cloves, hugs of Sunlight soap, whisker-rubs against an Old Spice cheek, the clog of talcum in the bathroom, a trail of cigar smoke wafting from the front porch.* Like her father, Nicholas Wolfe was a man who kicked at the traces. He was what he was.

Her companion lifted his goggles. "You're very quiet." In daylight his eyes were gray, not yellow – mutant eyes that changed to suit the environment.

Nora shifted back to the landscape. "I was just taking all this in."

He caressed the steering wheel, polishing its fine wood grain. "That's where we differ. I was taking only you in."

Nora's spirits lifted in a way that had nothing to do with that devil-may-care twenty miles per hour. To her surprise, she found that she enjoyed being with a man who made it clear with every glance that he was courting her. She hadn't swum in such frankly erotic waters since . . . *David and I, our hands glued to each other, unable to let go.* She thought of her spring-drunk students, giggling together in the cafeteria, bodies entwined under trees, sharing books and dreams, with sexual attraction as the fixative in every interaction, and wished she'd dressed less like a schoolmarm.

They were once again laboring uphill into a landscape vibrant with green and blue and gold. Nicholas gestured toward a hedgerow twined with primroses the color of the early summer sun. "When I was a boy, that was my favorite place for sparrowing. My sister and I used to sneak in there of a winter's night with a net on a pole, and in no time we'd have a dozen to sell for thru'pence."

It was clear from his lazy mouth and drawling voice that he wanted to take the elements of this glorious morning and to spin a spell around her. Pointing to a brook rimmed with water irises, Nora gave him the crossweave. "And I suppose that stream has fish in it?"

"They would leap into my hands before I could get my net into the water!"

She swept her hand toward a field strewn with buttercups.

"Rabbits. By the hundreds! I'd fix a burning candle on a toad's back and send it down a rabbit hole. When the rabbits came rushing out, I'd shoot them. . . . A gypsy taught me that. A gypsy woman. Be warned," he teased. "I'm on the side of the hunter, not the hunted."

"How about Wolves?"

"I make a clear exception for those. They aren't natural prey, though our high-minded landed gentry have hunted them so relentlessly they hardly exist anymore."

He swerved onto a trail that was little more than mud ruts. The view was exhilarating – majestic limestone crags swooping down to sheets of hyacinths so tightly massed they rippled like waves.

"My father owned this land. It should have been mine."

"What happened?"

"Nothing was written down. He died rather unexpectedly. A bullet to the brain – his own, or someone else's, who knows?"

"That must have been hard, losing your birthright."

His eyebrow shot up under a fall of jet hair. "Birthright? We're all born debtors to the past, not creditors, Miss Locke. A worldly woman like you should know that." He braked in a stand of ashes. "My father did the only sensible thing. He was a man who lived life as he chose until the pleasure ran out. He was a gambler."

Nora matched his bravado. "Like you?"

Nicholas stared through the windshield so long that she didn't think he would answer. "Both my father and I are risk-takers, Miss Locke, but I have different priorities and my own fatal enemies."

"Such as?"

He leapt from the car. "I've already told you. My land is the first priority."

"And your fatal enemies?"

"Gravel pits!" he growled. "They're like pits of gold with the new roads going in. They eat land."

By the time Nicholas arrived at Nora's door, his anger seemed vented. She remembered his quick mood switch at dinner – to fury and back again – like Dr. Jekyll trotting down to his lab to slip into something more comfortable.

Tucking Nora's hand under his arm, he guided her along a dry stone wall that spilled over dales and moors like the ribcage of a dinosaur. "Remarkable, isn't it?" He ran his fingers along the wall, admiring it with the same enthusiasm he'd put into his driving. "It's held together by its own weight, with the heavier stones at the top and the lighter ones at the base. See the spaces between for the wind and rain? That protects the wall from erosion. Far superior to mortar."

"There's a Chinese proverb that says, 'It's the spaces between the spokes that make a wheel.'"

He squeezed her hand. "You're a perceptive woman."

They were edging toward a limestone outcropping, one of many dotting the Peak District. Nora deliberately withdrew her arm to point. "That crag looks like a skull. Do you see?"

He squinted up into the sun. "I suppose it does."

"Those two bushy hollows are the eyes. The lower part thrusts forward like a Neanderthal jaw, and those striations are grinning teeth."

"I'm a pragmatic man. You have the eye of an artist."

Nora flexed the fingers of her left hand. "Once upon a time . . . I might have been."

They were now at the crag's base – what Nora saw as a prehistoric jaw. From behind a thistly mustache, Nicholas extracted a rock tooth. Reaching into the cavity, he withdrew a torch, a gasoline can and a tin of matches.

Nora was still staring up at the crag, overhung by a pale lunar ghost, and suffering an acute case of *déjà vu*. Had she seen a picture of this place before, or dreamed of it, or merely observed it from Barrow Hill?

Nicholas was waiting with his torch lit. "We'll be descending a steep grade for thirty yards, then a six-foot ladder."

Belatedly, she felt apprehension: what was she doing in this remote place with a man she barely knew?

He caught her hesitation and provided a reasonable out. "Are you really dressed for this?"

Nora kicked a stone with one oxblood toe. "My feet are." Her head was still ambivalent.

"We could come back another time." Lowering his torch, he prepared to extinguish it.

Nora gazed up into the crag's prehistoric face: her whole life had become such an act of faith that it seemed pointless to balk now. Trotting past Nicholas, she rounded the jawbone.

He pointed to a gap at the skull's right ear. "There's the entrance. The footing may be slippery but hold tightly to me and you'll be safe."

The rock exuded a cool, wet smell that was a relief after the dusty heat of the road. As Nicholas's torch set light and shadows dancing across the tunnel wall, Nora couldn't shake the ominous feeling that she was being initiated into the sort of mystery that clung to Stonehenge.

Nicholas swung his torch in an arc. "This natural passageway was enlarged when coal was discovered here in the seventies. Coal used to be so close to the surface around these parts that you could sometimes turn it by plow. . . . Here's the drop-off. I'll help you."

Lodging his torch in a crevice, he leapt down to a rock shelf, clasped her by the waist, and lifted. For a dizzying instant she felt like a child sailing higher and higher in a swing, never wanting to descend. She smelled the familiar bouquet of tobacco, trapped in the rough fibers of his jacket, and the spicy scent of cloves. He set her down. Even with her feet on rock, she seemed disoriented, without horizon lines to stabilize her.

Nicholas's voice was reassuring. "When the first colliers crawled in here, this seam was only four feet high. They chipped away the floor to make this cavern." He illuminated the roughly hewn twenty-foot dome. "Here are their pick marks and the soot from their candles. Farm hands worked this place in winter. Whatever a man mined, he got to keep, after paying a modest fee to my grandfather. You can see the grooves worn by the pulleys that were used to drag up the coal."

She felt the scene come alive through his excitement and then her own. It was, after all, the sort of rocky womb in which her grandfather had lost his life. "You know this place very well. Don't tell me you worked here."

"I handled the cash box at the end of the day. It ruined me for real labor, but this isn't what I brought you here to see." The farther they had crawled into the cave, the more correct Nicholas's behavior had become. "I know what ladies like." He shone his torch onto a low arch. "That's our path. I'll duck through, then help you. Just one step and you can stand. If you want the full effect, close your eyes."

Nora ducked, then looked.

She was in a soaring, blue-green cathedral, dripping in stalagmites and stalactites – like Niagara Falls on a winter's night with ice flung in every direction.

"This is the Cave of the Snow Queen." Nicholas vaulted from one ledge to another, illuminating sections with his torch. "See, here's the grand lady herself – here's her crown and her wand. Here's her castle, with its turrets, and the magical forest of giant mushrooms. And here, this dark and dirty section, is the wicked witch with her chiseled nose and topknot, and her patch of cabbages."

"I thought you said you were a pragmatic man."

"I am. That description is my sister's. It was she who found this place. We used to hide out here. It was our secret."

Unexpectedly, Nicholas dowsed his torch. The cave gleamed with a greenish phosphorescent light. He claimed her hand. "I appreciate that you came here with me, that you trusted me." His fingers were like magnetic currents, drawing her forward. "I've one more place to show you . . . a place very few people have seen."

Without relighting his torch, Nicholas guided her along the cave wall, through an arch of stalagmites and stalactites, well-concealed by the witch's cabbage garden. "The height's about the same, but the passage is longer."

Struggling against claustrophobia, Nora crawled into the tunnel. Nicholas's hand gripped hers. "Come, don't be frightened."

Though it was pitch black, she had the impression that they had emerged into a small, crypt-like cavern. Without warning, Nicholas dropped her hand: was he relighting the torch? She gripped a boulder and waited. The cave smelled dead, yet feral, like an abandoned animal den. She felt tension coalesce in an unknown shape over her head – a predator preparing to pounce?

Nicholas? Had Nora spoken his name aloud, or had the sound lodged in her throat. Her anxiety built in the imponderable, impenetrable silence. Pressing against the wall, she touched her throat, struggling to speak. *Nicholas!* Though her lips moved, her vocal cords had frozen.

Panicking, Nora scrambled toward the exit. Her hands found the torch, then groped for the matches. Still crouched, she lit it. Standing, Nora thrust the torch high.

She stared into the blackness. She screamed . . .

Nora scuttled back through the tunnel, stumbling among stalactites and stalagmites, cracking her skull and bruising her shins.

"Nora!" Nicholas was calling from behind, with the sound ricocheting from cavern to cavern: *Nora . . . Nora . . . Nora . . .*

At last, she could see the tunnel's entrance. Emerging into full sunlight, she slumped against the rock, gulping air. Her skirt was torn, her hands grimy, her blouse spattered with blood from a head wound. Hitching her hem into her waistband, she sprinted down the thorny embankment toward Barrow and the tower of St. Michael's.

Once safely in The Flats, she turned to look. Nicholas leaned against the skull, his hand shading his eyes, squinting after her.

She kept running.

8

She slips and slides along a slimy tunnel. Behind her she hears a metallic echo. Glancing back, she sees a pair of oxblood shoes pursuing her. The sides of the tunnel turn rubbery as it contracts. She is in the esophagus of a snake. Its coils encircle and squeeze. Ahead she sees a brass gate through which light filters. Diving, she seizes its bars, trying to resist the insistent tug of the snake's sinuous body. The shoes stamp on her knuckles, loosening her grip as the snake's oily vomit oozes over her as corrosive as acid, ingesting and digesting.

Nora awoke, gripping the brass bars of her bed. Her head was bloated with putrid images, and her mouth tasted like she'd swallowed a toad.

She heard a tap on the door, followed by the scrape of a key. Still in the sludgy grip of her dream, she dived back under the covers. From a peephole, she spied Eleanora bearing the breakfast tray she'd ordered the night before. The maid was dressed in black, reminding her that a bell was tolling: *Judd, Mellon, Wilson, Hall, Emery, Bradley, Sutton . . . Ross.* Today was the funeral of the victims of the Black Pit No. 8 disaster. In a guilty rush of sympathy, she threw back her covers.

"Eleanora, did you know any of the men who were killed?"

The maid sniffled into her sleeve. "Nowt so much th' men. Tommy Ross use ter 'elp our stable boy. Flame learnt 'im 'is ABCs." Bobbing, she retreated from the room.

As Nora nibbled toast and sipped tea, she refocused on her suitcase still curled like a homeless mutt at the foot of her bed. She'd wasted another day without buying a steamer ticket or gaining a single insight into her predicament here.

Reluctantly, she brooded over the events in the cave: an image played at the farthest reaches of her consciousness, but every time she thought she'd caught it, it slithered under a rock like some repulsive reptilian lifeform. Shuddering, she discarded her breakfast tray. The air felt gelatinous, despite the calendar's assurance that it was June 26, give or take a few decades.

Opening the curtain did not brighten her mood or the room. Fog pressed against the glass as thick as the stuff still roiling around in her head. Wiping a pane with her palm, she thought about T.S. Eliot's foggy yellow cat nudging around windowpanes, and recited aloud a stanza from *The Love Song of J. Alfred Prufrock*.

Hey, why not have John Slater publish that in The Barrow Times*?* Then she could sue T.S. when he brought out his version in 1917. Better yet, after she returned to her own time zone, she'd write a feminist tract accusing him of ripping off this obscure genius, Nora Locke, poet laureate of Barrow, 1913.

Swinging her feet onto the hand-braided rug, Nora sidled over to the fireplace, then probed behind the grate with an iron poker. What had possessed her to burn yesterday's clothes? All that remained of her wine skirt and striped blouse were scraps of blackened fabric. She hooked her oxblood shoes with the poker: their leather was badly charred and a left cleat was missing.

Catching Barrow's somber mood, Nora dressed in a charcoal suit with double-breasted jacket and pleated skirt. On a brass hook inside her armoire, she found a banker's umbrella, a felt fedora and a waterproof cape, as she had a hunch she might. Her valet, whoever he or she might be, was a veritable Jeeves. Each day she found more clothes in her closet, and always – within the constraints of historical accuracy – what she wanted.

Nora returned to the fireplace, finding it harder and harder to connect with yesterday's melodrama in the cave and what she now chose to believe was her overreaction to it. Eleanora would think her daft if she found the burned shoes in the wastebasket. Wrapping them in tissue from a hat box, she slipped them into her satchel.

Flame was behind the desk, hunched like a hedgehog over a book. Though she tried to conceal the cover, Nora recognized a first edition of Lawrence's *Sons and Lovers.*

Eagerly she approached the desk. "Are you enjoying your novel, Flame?"

The girl's nose rumpled in disgust. "'tis 'orribly depressin', if yer askin' me. Th' men split their days between pit and pub, whilst th' women 'ave children and seam stockings. If I wanted that, I could trot back down Barrow 'ill, now couldn't I?" She slid the book under her desk, adding resentfully: "A teacher give it to me – to inspire me, I suppose, but I'll surely be takin' me leave from this place as soon as I can. I 'ave me talents to develop, and Barrow's 'ardly th' spot fer it. I'm more fer adventure meself, not like th' dry sticks 'round 'ere."

The girl's eagerness for life was appealing, despite her air of massed fury lightly contained. "Do you have any place in mind?" inquired Nora.

Flame spun the antique globe on her desk. "Would yer mind showin' me where 'tis yer from?"

Nora pointed to the southerly tip of a large red mass, testifying that the sun did not yet set on the British Empire.

"'ow long fer yer boat to do its crossin'?"

Better to overshoot than establish a world record. "Two weeks."

"My, my, people sail from 'ere in five days!" Flame's voice grew sardonic: "Must be much farther goin' t'other way."

"We made a stop in New York," deadpanned Nora.

"What did yer say was th' name o' yer boat?"

Nora sidestepped. "Are you planning to emigrate, Flame?"

"Well, maybe not that far. I'd like to get me a little crumpet shop in London." She couldn't resist boasting: "I've practically got th' runnin' o' this 'otel, exceptin' for th' addin' and subtractin'. Since I like me independence, I've got ter think ahead, now don't I? 'tisn't as if me life is practically over, like yers."

Laughing, Nora retorted: "I sometimes feel as if my life hasn't yet begun!"

"Oh, don't I know what yer mean. There's time present an' time past, an' sometimes they gets all jumbled up – well, *yer* knows that!"

Nora shifted uneasily, wondering if Flame's comments were just a pastiche of lucky shots.

"Like at th' shop Time Past," continued the maid, with her face cupped in her hands, as innocent as a strawberry sundae. "Yer knows, th' one with th' sign like a pocketwatch? Things from all different times get mixed together.... My, that's a nice clock you've got round *yer* neck. I wouldn't mind one like that fer meself."

Clutching her pendant, Nora escaped toward the door. "Since I've so little time left in my life, I'd better not waste a moment more!"

"True enough, but mind yer don't get lost in th' fog. Like yer say, sometimes th' comin' takes more time than th' goin'!"

Market Street was deserted and all its shops closed, many with black ribbons on their doors. Though some of Upper Barrow's residents yearned to forget it, this was a mining town. Like so many others in the Midlands, its wealth flowed from its black veins to be converted into calico, crumpets and carriages. No point in visiting Thomas Cook & Sons. Nora's depression deepened: another lost day.

Unwilling to return to the inn, she trudged on to Market Place, with its abandoned stalls looking like shipwrecks in a muddy sea. Feeling foolish, she hid her charred shoes under a heap of moldy potato peels, then turned right on High Street into a section of

Barrow she hadn't yet explored. The rain was slackening, though the clouds still hung low and full like the udders of a gray cow. With determined optimism, Nora meandered through the empty streets, pretending she'd caught Barrow as it was supposed to be – as a quaint museum installation, missing only the discreet signs: "PLAYER PIANO in this window donated by the estate of . . ." or "ANTIQUE DRESS COLLECTION assembled by . . ."

She had traveled about six blocks when she began to suspect she was being followed. At first it had been only an ill-defined nervousness that had caused her to glance over her shoulder like a child evading her shadow. Then she'd heard footsteps – a faint echo, audible when she halted. She remembered the oxblood shoes from last night's dream, and found herself swiveling more frequently, sometimes catching movement – in shop windows, in puddles – though nothing she could identify.

Nora was circling back to the inn when she encountered a one-story, Romanesque building marked "Barrow Girls' School," framed in flowering chestnuts. Through a classroom window, she spied a primly dressed woman sorting papers. Her corseted rump slanted back while her chest thrust forward in the S-curve still favored by the older women of Barrow. Though her honey hair was lustrous in the gaslight, it was tightly twisted into a topknot and without ornament.

As Nora gazed at the shelves of reference books and annotated manuscripts, the stacks of blue-lined copypaper and folders, the paperclips and scissors, she experienced a wave of nostalgia for the orderly life she'd left behind. Drawing closer to the lighted window as if to a fire, she noticed that the school's oak door seemed unlocked, inviting her to shove against it.

Once inside, Nora knocked on the first frosted door.

"Hello, I'm Nora Locke from Canada. I'm researching for . . . the Hamilton Board of Education. Do you suppose I might look at some of your texts and lesson plans?"

The teacher peered over her pince-nez, attached by chain to a high-necked white shirtwaist. "It's strictly forbidden but" – a surprise smile – "I've just resigned, so I don't see what they could do to me now, do you?" She clasped Nora's hand. "I'm Pamela Birchwood. Take your time, but mind you don't mix the piles."

For the next hour Nora lost herself in lesson books, using factual information to soak up troublesome emotions as she had learned to do.

Recitation for Class I:

1. Beautiful Grapes.
2. The Two Kittens.
3. What the Birds Sang.

This afternoon Miss Pringle taught Sewing to Class II Girls. We are studying the Potholder, and many of the specimens proved very fair.

School closed due to an outbreak of influenza.

Miss Fielde gave a Lesson on the Trifle to Miss Revell's class.

For Nature Study, Class III dwelt on the Frog.

Scholar Elizabeth Halton, age ten, dead today of typhoid.

The Christmas plum pudding made by teachers and children was eaten amidst much merriment. Each child took home a card on which was a design, drawn and colored by hand, e.g., a sprig of mistletoe, an orange.

School was dismissed since the visit of Sanger's Circus has interfered abominably with attendance.

School closed to see His Majesty driving through the district.

Miss Bacon conducted instruction in Pence and Half-Pence to Class I, and the children enjoyed shopping.

Twenty-seven students absent, due to measles.

Miss Bird did not arrive until Thursday, owing to the Railway Strike.

Every child received a mug with a picture of King George V and Queen Mary as a memento of the Coronation, June 16, 1911.

❦

Nora remembered finding a souvenir like that holding teaspoons in her mother's china cabinet. She addressed the starchy figure, swishing between cupboards and wastebasket. "I think I may have relatives in Barrow. The men would be laborers or coal miners."

Miss Birchwood stopped in mid-swish. "Then most likely the children would attend The Bottoms school." She deposited her sheaf of papers. "That's quite a different kind of research. That school has the lowest rating in the Midlands. It isn't just the lack of qualified teachers, but the poor sanitation. The doors were shut fifty extra days last year for pestilence."

Miss Birchwood removed her pince-nez, then sat down at her desk, warming to her subject. "When I first moved to Barrow, oh the difference I was going to make. I would tutor a few promising girls from The Bottoms, and they would tutor other Bottoms children. Of course, I was naive then, and filled with my mission."

The softening of Pamela Birchwood's features as she grew more animated made Nora suspect that she might be considerably younger than she had guessed. "But your good years aren't over, Miss Birchwood."

The teacher flashed an amused smile – almost merry. "I certainly hope not!"

"I was wondering . . ." Nora closed her lesson book. "I think I still have a . . . cousin living in Barrow. Her name is Flora —"

"Quarry?" Miss Birchwood's mouth tightened. "A very bright student!" Standing, she dumped her files into the wastebasket. "We expected great things from that girl. Then she hitched up with an inferior sort of person and became as contrary as leaves on a gusty day." Miss Birchwood realized she'd trashed the wrong papers and began retrieving them. "I'm afraid Flora's harsh family experiences blinded her to the fact that *all* Upper Barrowers aren't here by merit!" Some of Miss Birchwood's papers again slipped from her agitated fingers. "*Now* look what you made me do!" She glared myopically at Nora. "Who did you say you were?"

"A teacher from Canada. I missed Cousin Flora at the train station and —"

"She's gone, then?" Miss Birchwood seemed crushed. "Not even a good-bye? Oh dear, oh dear." She looked as if she might cry. "She always talked about it, but . . . to London, I suppose?"

"To Liverpool. She's taking the boat to Canada."

"Canada! Whatever got into her head?" Miss Birchwood collapsed into the nearest chair. "She could have made such a contribution here! She's a natural teacher when she applies herself, one of our best, or used to be."

Nora pictured the woman in the train window, one arm raised in salute and the other cradling a child. "Perhaps with the baby she thought that a new start would —"

"What baby?" Miss Birchwood rose from her chair. "You've certainly got that wrong!" She scrutinized Nora's face. "If you've come here to gossip . . ." Reaching across the desk, she collected her lesson book. "I'm afraid, Miss Locke, I must ask you to leave." Gathering up Nora's rain clothes, she escorted her to the door.

"I'm sorry. I intended only to —"

"Not today, thank you!" Miss Birchwood thrust Nora's cape, hat, and umbrella into her arms.

Nora extended a placating hand. "At least let me wish you well on your retirement."

"Retirement?" Miss Birchwood gave a proud toss of her honey topknot. "I start my new job tomorrow." Her voice softened. "At The Bottoms."

It was still drizzling. Poking her umbrella into the dismal sky, Nora checked both ways. No Phantom Follower. No marauding oxblood shoes in search of their owner. In fact, quite a few pedestrians had ventured from their warm nests, giving the street an inhabited look.

Wiping all shadows from her mind, Nora hurried toward the Wolfe Inn Moon, musing over her conversation with Pamela

Birchwood. The teacher had seemed so surprised to hear Flora Quarry had left Barrow. Yet, the mine-explosion clippings had been mailed to Grandma Flora in Hamilton. Why send clippings to someone who hadn't yet departed? Perhaps two Flora Quarrys lived in Barrow, one with a baby and one without – maybe cousins named after a favorite aunt? She should have emphasized Flora's married name.

Nora determined to seek out Pamela Birchwood in another few days to clear up the mystery.

The church bells were tolling once more – or perhaps they'd never ceased. Not just one carillon but all of them, uphill and down, every church in Barrow. *Judd, Mellon, Wilson, Hall, Emery, Bradley, Sutton . . . Ross.* As Nora reached the brow, the official funeral party was descending into the churning yellow vapors of The Bottoms – the mayor and town councillors, quite a few Barrow merchants, the owner of the Black Pit Colliery who, according to caustic editorials in *The Barrow Times*, might have some explaining to do. At the same time, shrouded mourners from The Bottoms threaded their way to Black Pit Square, where a communal service was to be held. *Judd, Mellon, Wilson, Hall, Emery, Bradley, Sutton . . . Ross.* While the uphill gang huddled under slick umbrellas, The Bottoms folk perched like ravens in a line, neither expecting protection nor noticing they lacked it. Nora counted coffins, noting the small one containing the corpse of Tommy Ross. Had Grandpa Flowe's funeral been just like this?

As she shuffled along the brow she also tried to guess which of the cramped and grimy buildings in the steamy caldron might be The Bottoms School. She thought of young Flora Quarry, maneuvering around slops and shit, vowing not only to climb the hill but to sail an ocean. She hoped that her grandmother would have been proud of her – proof that only opportunity separated The Bottoms from Upper Barrow, not intelligence or drive. She also wondered how often during her forty years of voluntary exile her grandmother might have regretted her flight.

As Nora offered up a prayer of gratitude to the feisty adventurer, gritty tears scored her cheeks, the result of a soupy inversion that was forcing even Barrow's flintiest citizens to mourn the dead miners. By the time she reached Backwater Lane, her lisle stockings were soaked and she was sneezing. She stared at the Wolfe Inn Moon, with the rain pouring from every crease and cranny like water from an old boot, reluctant to go inside but too miserable not to.

The lobby was dark, except for a single candle on the desk. It illuminated the sketch of a boy in choir surplice, decorated with garlic. At first Nora thought it was her own portrait of Tommy Ross, but then she noticed the greater detail and the greater talent, along with the artist's initial – "F."

Nora left a black cortège of clothes from door to tub. Too depressed to face the dining room, she propped herself with pillows, then sketched Barrow Girls' School and the eight coffins in Black Pit Square. She was dozing off with the lights on when she heard a tap at her door.

"Come in."

Nicholas Wolfe entered, bearing a tray of hot broth, bread and cheese, fresh fruit and trifle. "I missed you at dinner and made inquiries." He left the door discreetly ajar. "Mrs. Wolfe and I were both concerned. She prepared this tray for you."

Nora expected him to deposit it and leave. Instead, he tucked a napkin under her chin and spooned broth into her mouth. Afterward he wiped her lips, then placed his hand on her brow as if testing for fever. "Now I can sleep, knowing you've been taken care of. I'll leave the tray by your bed so that you can help yourself."

Lifting Nora's hands, Nicholas laid each under the covers, with palms crossed over her breasts. He kissed her chastely on the forehead, exhaling the scent of cloves and tobacco, whispering so low she wasn't sure she had heard it: "You look like an angel."

As he tiptoed toward the door, Nora angrily challenged him: "Why did you abandon me in the cave?"

Nicholas spun around. "Abandon *you*? I bumped my head whilst straightening out of the tunnel. By the time I recovered, you'd snatched the torch and run off."

Confused, Nora studied his guileless face: how much time had elapsed between the moment he had dropped her hand and she had lit the torch? Alone in the dark, with terror escalating, the space between heartbeats had seemed unending.

"Don't be embarrassed, my dear." Reaching through the bedstead, Nicholas affectionately clasped her toes. "You aren't the first to panic down a mine. As you can see, I did manage to grope my way out, though not without a scraped shin or two." Again he paused, hand on doorknob, to gently chide her: "Hasn't anyone ever warned you not to go off with strangers? Next time you might not choose someone who's so fond of you."

As the door closed, Nora felt her nipples press into her palms ... *kisses of cloves, hugs of Sunlight soap*. She slid her hands between her thighs, imagining the bones and sinews of Nicholas Wolfe pressing down upon her. Every cell he had touched seemed to bear his imprint. She felt a sexual hunger alien to her – "a thing" with weight and girth occupying her bed. Why not Nicholas Wolfe? *Why not?* Why should she continue to deny herself what other women had, what she apparently wanted so much? Why should she adopt the ethics of another age just because she was confined to lace-up boots and corsets? What, after all, was the point of being marooned outside of time if she didn't seize it as a unique invitation to freedom? Maybe that was the purpose of her mission here – to grasp opportunities that fear and habit had closed to her.

Yet, a small voice inside Nora continued to warn that she must preserve her own identity, firmly rooted in her own history, or what would she have left? While trapped in time's backwater, she must chart a course somewhere between the British missionaries who imported woolies to Hawaii and the alcoholic minister in Maugham's *Rain*, who went bad in the tropics.

A pair of yellow eyes gazed at Nora from the windowsill. She scratched the patchwork quilt, inviting the orange cat to join her. Though it padded about, sniffing the room, it would not.

9

Nora and Eleanora are chasing butterflies across a meadow clumped with wildflowers. The ground heaves like waves on a roiling sea. It is a giant patchwork quilt stitched from swatches of cotton, linen, silk, seersucker. Her mother and father, Agnes Wolfe and Nicholas, each hold a corner. They toss the two women higher and higher. Eleanora tumbles over the edge. Nora screams.

Nora awakened with the scream still blossoming in her throat. She found the patchwork quilt gripped in her fists and thought for a giddy instant that she was home. Then she spotted the ancestral suitcase through the brass bedstead and burst into tears.

For six days she'd been running on adrenaline – a punctured tire that had maintained its pressure so long as it was spinning – secretly convinced that any second she would awaken from this dream, or close this book, and find herself back in her own time. Now that hope had collapsed and she grieved unabashedly – for her friends and colleagues, for every dandelion in her garden and for all the atrociously spelled student essays she'd ever had to mark – everything that had been her life before she'd fallen down Time's pothole. She thought of yesterday's shadow dogging her through the streets of Barrow. Was it some phantasm of her own mind, or adversaries more substantial? Noticing the tray beside her bed, she guiltily crossed her hands over her breasts, remembering Nicholas's visit and her own erotic response.

Instead of breakfast, Nora finished the bread on the tray, solemnly chewing each mouthful. What if her fingers should pass through its crust? What if she became invisible, or aged forty years in forty seconds? She examined her reflection for signs of decay, then took pains with her grooming – powder on her cheeks to patch any cracks, combs and hair pins to secure herself to this summer's day. Choosing an upbeat yellow seersucker dress with a flared skirt, she searched her armoire for comfortable shoes.

Nora's consciousness skipped like a flat stone over a glassy sea. The oxblood shoes occupied their customary place – either them, or duplicates. Gingerly she touched the left one, almost expecting her finger to burn. Charring showed through its fresh polish, and its cleat had been replaced.

Wrapping the shoes in newspaper, Nora again slipped them into her satchel before lacing on gray kid boots. She thought of yesterday's shadow, tracking her through the fog. Barrow was growing dangerous: *I must return home while I still can.*

She rushed from her room in search of Thomas Cook & Sons.

Flame was at the desk, sketching in a pad identical to Nora's. While she was still on the staircase, the maid hailed her: "My, but you've got a real eye for fashion, you 'ave! Those shoes look ever so comfy. So much nicer than th' 'eavy shoes you was wearin' t'other day. I'm glad you're feelin' better. Must 'ave got yer feet wet."

Again, Nora wondered if Flame had a natural talent for unsettling remarks, or if her forte was snooping and baiting. While she was gathering speed toward the door, the girl sang out: "As a lady o' fashion, would you mind castin' yer expert eye on these little things and lettin' me 'ave yer expert opinion?"

She extended her sketchpad, covered with well-executed fashion designs. Several were copied from Nora's own clothes, including a few she'd never worn, indicating the girl had been through her closets.

"They look . . . very professional." What was more disturbing, some had short skirts like those Nora had originally packed.

"I'm always lookin' to improve meself. Me mother was a seamstress – went blind with all them tiny stitches. She was dead ten years afore they put 'er underground, if yer wants me opinion."

Nora's hand seized the doorknob.

"Thomas Cook's again today, is it? Mind yer don't get mud on them nice new shoes! Next time you're feelin' poorly, I'd be happy to fix yer tray."

As the heavy door slammed behind Nora, she asked herself: was Flame her phantom stalker? The girl was as opaque as a lump of coal.

The merchants of Barrow were having a slow start. Nora felt relieved to see awnings unfurl like flags, outdoor bins fill with carrots and cabbages, even an organ-grinder groom his fez-wearing monkey for show time.

Thomas Cook & Sons had a window poster that gladdened her heart.

Weekly Sailings to Canada!

CANADIAN PACIFIC

invites you to board its

EMPRESS STEAMERS

4 dys. open sea / 21 knots speed

Sailing from Liverpool

Though Nora couldn't get a booking for the following Tuesday, she did secure passage for the week after: July 8, *The Empress of Ireland*, first class, Deck A, Suite 100 – *and why not?* Thanks to eighty years of inflation she probably could have rented the Royal yacht.

Her extravagance transformed the clerk from snot to suck. "Sign *h*ere and *h*ere, madame," he instructed, exaggerating his *h*'s with a heavy exhalation of breath.

He handed Nora a pen, with little finger extended, as if from a Crown Derby teacup.

Playing the game, Nora gave him a £1,000 note.

He fingered the bill as if it were the finest of lingerie. She thought he might weep.

Regretting her meanness, Nora tried to retrieve it. "I've made a mistake – "

But by then he was hopping about the office, paws in front of his chest like the Easter bunny, begging change from co-workers. Cash boxes were ransacked, and everyone ogled Nora now cringing behind the counter.

"I do have something smaller – "

But finding change had become Galahad's quest for the Grail. The clerk was dispatched, in silk hat and kid gloves, to Barclay & Co. two doors away.

Nora feared he might return with a wheelbarrow of shillings, trailing children and a popcorn vendor. But no, here he was bearing a briefcase stuffed with notes. He sorted them three times, thumping each onto the desk while the whole office counted with him.

He garnished the pile with Nora's ticket: "July 8. First class. Deck A. Suite 100. *H*ave a *bon voyage*, Miss Locke."

It was pure theater – probably better than the organ-grinder was providing over on Market Street. Now beyond embarrassment, Nora shoveled her loot into her satchel, feeling as if she'd pulled off an international heist.

"You'll need a passport, of course, but coming from Canada that's *h*all taken care of."

Thud. Reality stamped its cleated heel on Nora's delicate arch. As she left the shop, she sorted her options: how could she document a birth that wouldn't take place for forty-two years? Perhaps she could convince the Canadian embassy that her hospital records had been destroyed in a fire. She spotted a woman of her approximate size, age and coloring being helped from a carriage. Perhaps she could steal a passport, or buy a forged one – or did that happen only on TV?

By the time Nora reached Church Street, the sun had pecked like a fuzzy chick out of the eggshell sky. Ahead she spotted the Norman tower of St. Michael's, its hand-hewn stones warmly tinted with their accumulation of history. She entered the yard through its creaky iron gate, decorated with Crusaders' shields, then tugged the knob of its massive timbered door, finding it locked.

Nora strolled along the path, noting the swell of the graveyard against the building's 800-year-old walls, like a green tide against the prow of an ancient galleon. She'd read somewhere – perhaps in John Slater's yet-to-be-published history – that the older the cemetery the higher it rose, thanks to its centuries of layered corpses.

The earliest graves were marked by elaborately carved Anglo-Saxon crosses. Then came rows of Gothic headstones like slate nuns shuffling to vespers. One celebrated the long life of an Ezekiel Hudson, 1596–1701.

He lived one hundred and five,
Sanguine and strong.
And a hundred to five,
Ye don't live so long.

The newer tombs resembled granite tables. She found several representing the merchant families on Market Street, but no Flowes and no Quarrys. She remembered the building-fund pamphlet in her grandmother's suitcase, picturing a sooty, squat-towered church. Probably down in The Bottoms.

A large and distinguished planting of Slaters dominated the hill. Nora read the latest inscription on the base of a white-marble obelisk:

SARA SLATER
1874–1912
Beloved Wife of JOHN HENRY SLATER
"Too soon this passionate spirit laid to rest"

Passionate? She wouldn't have linked that word to John Slater. Perhaps it was the attraction of opposites. History and literature were replete with those, including Lawrence's Lady Chatterley and her gamy gameskeeper, Mellors!

Given John Slater's impeccable taste, the tomb of Henry Slater, founder of *The Barrow Times*, surprised Nora – a white-marble walk-in monstrosity with Corinthian columns like braces over an inflated chest. She gave it wide berth, still headed downhill, planning to reach The Bottoms by way of The Flats, idly wondering what sins old Henry might have committed to require all this special pleading.

Pastures ruffled around Nora like an opulent green skirt, curving down to a flounce of bluebells. With her steamer ticket safely in her pocket, she admitted that a case might be made for her having found a life since coming to Barrow rather than losing one. At the very least she'd raised her status from college professor facing recessionary cutbacks to membership in Britain's leisured class. And, given what might modestly be described as her feel for the future, that could be just the beginning: first, she'd redesign prewar underwear by replacing its laces and hooks and buttons with zippers, Velcro and elastic. After that, she'd invent Kleenex, Band-Aids, Yo-Yos, Hula Hoops, theme T-shirts and refrigerator magnets.

Even in her own field of expertise, she held title to a creative gold mine. As an English professor with assorted degrees, she had committed yards of yet-to-be published poetry to memory. *Prufrock* had just been a sample. To make it fun and sporting, she'd jump-stake only future poets she most disliked. Yes, she'd tie her theft to critical values – a literary Robin Hood who silences the bad to protect the good!

In a giddy rush, Nora raced downhill, hair and skirts flying, almost tumbling into a bog, woven with reeds and rushes. Amidst the densest growth, she pitched one charred oxblood shoe, watched it sink into muck, then pitched the other. Liberated, she skipped along the path.

A skylark was singing, its crystal notes fluty and thrilling.

"Hail to thee, blithe spirit!"

As she searched the sky for this exquisite musician in his modest brown plumage, she heard a gentle warbling through the sedge and parted a fringe of it.

Eleanora was standing in swamp, her gingham dirndl soaked to her knees, her lushly tangled beauty a natural part of the exquisite setting. Smiling, she extended her straw hat filled with cocoons and chrysalises. "I'm supposed ter be pickin' posies fer tomorrow's Flower Festival, but what I really come fer are th' butterflies."

Nora remembered the summer that she and David as children had haunted gullies and alleys and parks and vacant lots, catching and hatching caterpillars – fat green roly-polies, brown fuzzies, striped and tufted clowns.

"Come." Clasping Nora's hand, Eleanora led her down a ditch choked with scrub. She bowed a rusty branch, then let it fly. Its "bark" exploded in an amber funnel of moths, hundreds of them, spiralling upward.

For the next hour Nora trailed Eleanora through the lyme and sedge that formed the bog's uncertain border, seeking out its lepidopterological wonders: wall browns, red admirals, small blues, yellow skippers, sometimes on the wing and sometimes pupating in wax or silken houses. Afterward the two lay in a mound of grass tinkling with bluebells, watching a willow warbler and then a kingfisher, with Eleanora mimicking each in turn.

Nora saw the silver locket lying in the hollow of her young companion's throat, and wondered if she should mention their unfinished conversation, inviting confidences. But Eleanora seemed so at peace – like that swallowtail flapping its wings over a clump of milk parsley – that words seemed intrusive. Her lips refused to form them.

Nora left Eleanora picking daisies for tomorrow's festival, still intending to search out the Quarry grave plot in The Flats. However, when the path proved too muddy, she arched back over Barrow Hill.

It wasn't until she had almost climbed to Henry Slater's Appian folly that she was forced to admit yesterday's Shadow had returned. She watched it slide like an oil spill under a row of yews, then dart through the copper door of the old editor's mausoleum.

Judging by its scratches, that tarnished door had recently been jimmied. Now it stood slightly ajar. Holding her breath, Nora laid her eye against the crack, then waited for it to adjust to the gloomy interior.

The Count lounged in black riding habit upon a mortuary slab, his sleek head pressed against the breasts of a marble angel, his skin as luminous as a glowworm's in the dismal light, looking one-dimensional – a shadow on a wall, a cardboard villain in an amateur theatrical. With his right hand he nursed a silver flask; with his left, he masturbated into Henry Slater's mortuary urn.

The tomb's marble walls ruffled like a reflection in water. Steadying herself, palms pressed against the cold pillars, Nora tiptoed away.

Agnes Wolfe perched behind the inn desk, twisted like a coat hanger over her ledgers. As Nora entered the lobby, she found herself wondering what had brought two such unlikely people as Agnes and Nicholas together. Sensing the woman's bitter isolation, she swerved toward the desk, wishing to say something friendly. "The flowers in my room are always so lovely, Mrs. Wolfe. I can see from my window that you grow them yourself."

Though the hotelier looked up crossly, her face turned unexpectedly mournful. "Flowers reward the effort, Miss Locke. With them, one experiences so few unpleasant surprises." She offered

Nora a silver tray bearing an envelope of thick vellum. "This came for you an hour ago." Her gaze followed Nora up the staircase, then crashed against the chandelier with its heavy burden of wax. "That girl forgot to trim those candles *again!*"

Once inside her room, Nora read the note addressed to her in a formal, flourishing hand:

> Dear Miss Locke,
>
> It is my hope that you will allow me the pleasure of escorting you to dinner this evening. I apologize for the late invitation but a change of plans takes me to London tomorrow for at least a week. Should I hear no protests from you via your stable hand, whom I have engaged on our behalf, I will attend you this evening at quarter of eight.
>
> Respectfully,
> John Slater

Nora fingered the creamy notepaper, embossed with the Slater crest: a torch encircled in laurel leaves. She should have been delighted. The editor was a knowledgeable and dynamic man; however, something restrained her. She paced from bed to window, trying to identify the squishy feeling in her stomach.

Hooves rattled across the stable yard. Glancing outside, Nora saw Nicholas Wolfe, in black riding jacket, boots, and jodhpurs, dismount from his snorting black mare. His face was flushed, his hair unruly, and every muscle exuded the glory of the ride. From her distressing rise in spirits, Nora diagnosed her problem: she'd been anticipating seeing him at dinner this evening.

Nora's mind filled with the soulful image of Agnes Wolfe, but it was her mother's voice that scolded: *"Muriel Gant, a cheap Woolworth's girl! She lived across that alley, right under my nose."*

Closing her blind, Nora tucked John Slater's invitation into the rim of her mirror, then informed her reflection: "Miss Locke will be delighted to attend."

But first. She undertook yet another Sherlock Holmesian search of her room: into every drawer of every table, desk and bureau, even lifting paper linings; through every pocket and purse of her wardrobe; under the cushions of the wing chairs; through every flap and fold of her suitcase. Still no passport.

As Nora dressed for the evening, her anticipation escalated. Since coming to Barrow she'd begun to feel that her brain had atrophied – at least, the left side. She'd always resented Lawrence's contention that educating the mind undermined natural instincts. It would be a relief to find a friend with whom to exercise her intellect.

By the time John Slater arrived at 7:40, Nora was dressed in a melon silk sheath with Empire waist and matching butterfly cape – one of the extroverted dresses that began to appear in her closet as her mood brightened.

Slater was a man for whom formal dress was as much an invitation to relax as blue jeans to a contemporary male. The expression on his lean face with its deep-set eyes and long nose, bracketed between bushy brows and a neat vandyke beard, seemed almost impish as he helped Nora into his buggy. "I hope you don't mind my being a touch old-fashioned. I can't abide hurtling through a splendid summer's evening at fifteen miles per hour, suffering gasoline fumes and fear of mechanical breakdown. In my view, technology should be confined to a man's workaday world."

As the chestnut filly looped over Barrow's crown with a cheerful clop-clop, he gestured toward men assembling a tent village on the Common, supervised by townsfolk leaning on walking sticks or twirling parasols. "That's for tomorrow's Flower Festival."

They halted to allow passage of a flock of sheep, temporarily ejected from the Common. "I was hoping to invite you to accompany me until my trip to London conflicted."

"Won't celebrating be difficult with half the town in mourning?"

The shepherd deferentially saluted Slater and received a democratic wave.

"Barrow people grieve hard and play hard. Particularly those from The Bottoms."

They had crested the hill and were sliding down the town's western slope into the sunset. Below them the Barrow River glided like a gilded serpent through glistering green meadows, ribbed with dark forests and limestone crags. As St. Michael's carillon chimed, Nora felt a rush of contentment heightened by awe: *if only time were to stop right now . . .*

The bells struck the hour . . . *one . . . two . . . eight . . . nine? . . . thirteen?*

"Our bell-pullers have turned leg-pullers!" John Slater chuckled. "Usually they take great pride in their skills, but tonight they're celebrating early. They're especially erratic at weddings. *High* Anglican, indeed!"

Nora recalled her day's uncompleted journey to the Quarry grave plot. "I'm looking for a church. It's a bit of an odd shape with a short tower and —"

"The Reform Church!" exclaimed Slater with a twitch of scorn. "It's located in The Bottoms."

"Reform of what?"

"Certainly not human nature!" He used his whip to shoo a fly vexing the ear of his filly. "Its leadership champions indulgences of the lower sort – wild dancing, bingo, gambling, religious fanaticism, even speaking in tongues and séances. It's a Spiritualist church."

Slater's patrician disdain, plus family loyalty, spurred Nora into a defence: "The British Society for Psychical Research is composed of some of Europe's most distinguished scientists. What makes you think your local group is entirely ignorant?"

"Because our mine-owners support it!" exclaimed John Slater. "It's an unholy alliance – wine, crosses and circuses – to keep their colliers down. If they were truly interested in their welfare, they'd end child labor and insist on Davy safety lamps. Instead, they scatter a few coins to reward their ignorance and discourage them from turning Bolshevik."

The editor halted his buggy for a landau with three female passengers. The way they ogled Nora confirmed that she was dating one of the town's most eligible bachelors.

"How did you come to adopt the cause of the working man?"

Slater squinted toward the horizon in a protracted silence, broken only by hoof beats. "My father was a man of large passions – some admirable, others causing himself and his family a good deal of anguish. When I inherited *The Barrow Times*, I was a stuffy conservative who, overnight, had acquired a liberal mantle I neither understood nor desired. The woman I chose as a helpmate had my father's political zeal without his lesser attributes. Unfortunately, a year ago she contracted typhoid whilst nursing children in The Bottoms in active dedication to her beliefs."

Slater's eyes filled with tears which he unselfconsciously dabbed with a large handkerchief. "I can assure you, Miss Locke, that if any truth lay in the Spiritualist message, I'd be the first to embrace it; however, I am confident my wife *does* live on through her good works. Have you heard of our Bootstrappers? It's a local group she founded to support the desires of working-class families to improve themselves – to pull themselves up by the bootstraps, so to speak. Though that name started as a joke, I daresay it has acquired a good deal of honor. At present, it's a private charity, though I'm working to establish new industry to support it."

He gestured toward a smudge in the lower corner of an otherwise idyllic landscape. "In another few years, Black Pit will be finished, and therein lies a blessing and a curse. Barrow – the whole Midlands – must be brought into the new technological age."

The Chalk and Cheese was a Tudor inn where fashionable guests were served in a courtyard on bare wood tables, yet its nine-course feast was the sort only the boldest modern chef would risk: ptarmigan and leek broth, *trout meunière*, artichokes with hollandaise, plover in a casserole, lamb cutlets with roast potatoes and beets, green salad and trifle. Each course was accompanied by its own wines and liqueurs, and its own entertainment: minstrels, morris dancers, even a dramatization from *A Midsummer Night's Dream.*

Afterwards, they trotted to Barrow, with the filly's hooves striking sparks from the flinty roadbed like the winged feet of Mercury. As they sat side by side stroked by moonlight, John Slater unsheathed his curiosity for the first time.

"So . . . you've winkled the soul right out of me without revealing a thing about yourself. I'm intrigued, of course. You remind me of a woman with her head stuck through one of those cutouts photographers use on midways. Why do I feel that you're a beautiful impostor?"

Nora had intended to serve up a polished version of her Exeter story, but John Slater was too shrewd for that. "Because I *am* an impostor."

"How did you know about the mine explosion and the cricket scores?"

Nora grimaced like a child caught in a sorry piece of mischief she now must confess to the headmaster. "I read them in your newspaper when I was still in Canada, eighty years after they were published. Of course, you believe me – every word!"

Looping his reins around his saddle horn, John Slater took Nora's hand. "The point is, you believe yourself, which interests me more than so-called objective truth. The biggest lies in history are the ones that everybody once believed: that the Earth was flat; that the Sun moved around the Earth; that you could save a person's soul by torturing him; that there's a place called Heaven where the elite play harps. I would prefer to put my faith in you, or Lewis Carroll, than in any of those prophets. As for the tricks of time" – he gestured to include the sky, drunk with stars – "if the new science is correct, simply to glance upward on a night like this is to gaze back millions of years." He concluded with a quirky smile, punctuated by his odd birthmark. "But now, would you please tell me more about the newspapers I have yet to publish and the history Europe has yet to experience?"

Nora reviewed some of the great stories of the epoch: auto and air travel, movies and television, Sputnik and the man on the moon, two world wars.

Somberly stroking his beard, John Slater inquired: "When does our war begin, the 'little' one in which only nine million are killed?"

"Almost exactly a year from now, and it lasts four years." Nora related what she could remember of the murder of Archduke Francis Ferdinand, heir to the Austro-Hungarian throne. "The assassin was a Bosnian nationalist. It became known as 'the shot heard 'round the world.'"

John Slater ruefully shook his head. "Don't tell that story to anyone but me. Almost everything else makes sense by comparison."

Once again they were passing the Common, now transformed into a colorful tent village. The editor glumly viewed the complex. "Now I'm even sorrier that I must go to London tomorrow."

Nora laid her hand on his arm. "May I ask a favor of you? I wish to return to Canada, but I don't have a passport."

"Ahh yes, I see the problem. I'll make inquiries."

When Nora unlocked her door, her bed was turned down and her gas lamp lit as usual. As she slipped on her freshly laundered nightgown, she glimpsed movement by the fireplace. Snatching up a letter-opener, she raised it like a dagger: "Come out from behind that chair, whoever you are."

A figure unfurled from the shadows. "It's just me, mum," whimpered Eleanora.

Nora cast down the letter-opener in relief. "What are you doing here?"

The frightened girl made a circular movement with her left hand, as if expecting a duster to materialize. "Just cleanin', mum."

"On all fours, in the dark?" Nora pointed to her other hand. "What's behind your back?"

"Now't, mum."

"Eleanora, please stop these games."

Sobbing, the maid collapsed to her knees. "I wasn't stealin', mum. I swear it. I just wanted to 'old it in me 'ands." She produced Nora's steamer ticket from behind her back. "Please take me with yer, mum."

"I'm truly sorry but that's out of the question."

The maid clawed at her skirt like a dying cat. "I'd cook an' I'd clean, mum. I'm ever so good at sewin'." She plucked at the patchwork quilt. "I made this, mum, every stitch. I'd work 'ard. I'd support meself." Eleanora buried her face in her pinafore. "Oh, I'm beggin' yer, mum, *please*."

"Have you and Daniel quarrelled?"

"No, mum. Now't like that." She wiped her tears with her skirt. "But 'e's not goin' ter want me now, mum. I'm in ever so much trouble. I've done a bad thing, I 'ave."

Without the extra layer of ruffles hiding Eleanora's waistline, Nora saw her problem. Outrage caught her off guard: how typical of Eleanora to blame herself, as if she were hosting the Immaculate Conception. "When will it be?"

"I canna say, mum, but soon. 'tis gettin' 'ard to lace up."

"Does Daniel know?"

The girl's eyes overflowed with liquid pain. "Oh no, mum!"

Tamping down anger, Nora pulled the maid from her knees, then set her in a wing chair. "You must get to a doctor. Maybe I could speak to John Slater and —"

Eleanora clutched her arm. "Promise yer won't say now't, mum."

"Do you know anyone who can help you?"

Eleanora shrank like a burrowing insect into the chair's cabbage roses. "No, mum. I'm on me own."

Nora settled in the facing chair. "Don't you have any relatives?"

"None who owns up to me. . . . Well, there's me sister, Flame."

"Flame's your sister?"

Eleanora peeked over the skirt of her pinafore. "She 'ates me, mum. She thinks I'm stupid, an' maybe I am. We've different natures."

Nora was still finding it hard to curb her outrage. "The father must be told."

"Oh, no, mum, I canna!"

"*Someone* has to look after you." She experienced a fierce, protective urge to feel the fetus's heartbeat, to assure herself it was all right. "He'll know soon enough, anyway."

The maid began to sob.

"Give him chance to prepare – to make the best of it."

Hope played over Eleanora's bleak face like the Northern Lights across a wintery sky. "Do yer think so, mum?"

"I'm sure of it."

A whisper: "Yes, mum."

Nora prowled her room, too keyed up to sleep, mindlessly refolding towels and fluffing pillows. Primal fury had seized her in its hairy jaws and would not let go. The beast seemed to possess the face of every man she'd ever known – *Daniel, Nicholas, David*. . . . These extreme feelings made no sense, but she could not alter them, and when the orange cat scratched at the shutters, she would not let it in.

10

Nora stands beside David at the helm of a great white ship with a prow that extends like butterfly wings. On the horizon, she sees an inky wave the size of a mountain. Awestruck, she watches it crest, then curl, then solidify to become a monstrous black tombstone.

Seizing the ship's wheel, Nora points the prow at the tombstone, then accelerates full speed ahead. As the marble mountain slides inexorably toward them, she turns her back to watch Eleanora, Daniel Slater and Flame decorate the ship's deck with garlands of spring flowers. They are laughing and singing. Nora and David join in.

Nora awoke gently, like a mermaid cast by rolling surf onto a pillow of sand. Peals of laughter ascended from the stable yard. Opening the shutters, she saw Flame, Eleanora, Daniel and the stable boy weaving daisy chains. At least that's what they were supposed to be doing. Instead, they were smacking each other with willow branches and giggling in that explosive, self-conscious way that she knew, from years of teaching Eng. Lang. and Lit. against the uproar of a spring day, signaled runaway hormones in the human animal. Inhaling a deep draft of the laughter-tinctured air, Nora playfully took her own pulse: perhaps her sap also was rising!

She studied Eleanora – heaving chest, flushed cheeks, bright blue eyes, panting butterfly lips, flying hair – as she swirled across the cobbles with the orange cat in her arms. Surely this couldn't be the same girl who only last night had begged to be taken to Canada! She stared at Eleanora's swollen waistline, deftly concealed in flounces and frills, then shifted to Daniel, galloping about in breeks and weskit, with a thick blond thatch falling into his eyes. His affection seemed so apparent in the brush of a hand, the flash of a smile, that Nora felt convinced that he and John Slater would, at the very least, take care of Eleanora according to the *noblesse oblige* codes of the day.

Nora spotted her steamer ticket still on her desk. Now that she possessed the potential to leave Barrow, her urgency to do seemed to have evaporated. She closed her eyes, trying to conjure up the red-haired figure in the train window, only to discover that her face had dissolved into the steam cloud that had engulfed her. Picking up her sketchpad, Nora attempted to draw David, Aunt Millie, Dolly Dolby, but her hand felt awkward and her eye uncertain.

She forced herself to face a once-untenable truth: for minutes, even for hours, she'd begun to forget she was one of time's displaced persons. In unguarded moments, she'd even begun to doubt: *am I a 1993 woman dreaming about prewar England, or am I a 1913 woman fantasizing about life at the end of the century?* Had the unthinkable happened: had her thoughts and desires taken root in Barrow, 1913?

To seal her alliance with her "real" future, Nora drew a two-week calendar, ending with July 8, when she was to sail. She stared at today's square – June 28 – and froze . . .

Impatiently, she turned her back: *no* anniversary! The accident with David would not take place for another fifty-seven years.

Choosing a filmy white dress with blouson top and gathered skirt, Nora checked her armoire for shoes. Where the oxbloods used to stand, she encountered a gap. After plunging in her hand to make sure, she laced on her gray kid boots.

❦

Breakfast was the usual groaning board of porridge, tripe, kidneys, kippers, eggs, toast, sweetbreads, brains and even pigs' feet. Pouring a cup of tea, Nora positioned her back to the greasy feast, with its entrails quietly congealing into lard.

Two people – a man and a woman – huddled in the gloomy bar, heads tilted together as if conspiring. As usual, the Count seemed to radiate a sinister glow from his beetle-black hair to his polished boots, inscribed with a silver "W." Between stacks of soiled plates, his head rose and fell with a scooping, gobbling motion that reminded Nora of heavy equipment working a construction site. Opposite him, equally absorbed, hunched Agnes Wolfe.

Repelled, Nora quietly replaced her cup, then tiptoed from the room. She was skirting the stable yard, headed toward The Bottoms, when a voice sang out: "Oh, come see!"

Eleanora and Flame were sprawled on the cobbles, laps heaped with flowers.

"Care to 'elp, mum?" asked Eleanora, holding up a daisy chain. "We still 'ave th' carriage ter do, an' our costumes."

As Eleanora scooted off with Daniel to fetch the carriage, Nora squatted beside Flame on the cobbles.

"Mind yer don't break their 'eads off!" ordered the maid, handing her an armload of daisies. "We've none to spare."

"What's your costume to be, Flame?"

"I'm goin' as a Suffragette." She preened. "They're th' ones that chain themselves to London lamp posts, but I suspect, as a traveling woman, you've 'eard all that?"

"I didn't know you were interested in politics."

"Well, me father put me off men real early. 'e was 'ard enough when 'e 'ad a wife, but ten times 'arder afterwards. I've been thinkin' o' skippin' off to London to get a little of me own back, but then I 'eard all them ladies wanted was th' vote. I'm wantin' a lot more out o' life than th' bloody vote, I can tell yer!"

Despite the tart phrases, a look of vulnerability had crept into the creases and corners of Flame's face. Nora thought about sounding her out over Eleanora's problem, but decided she had no right to break a confidence. "Have you heard of the group called the Bootstrappers?"

Flame screwed up her nose. "That I 'ave, but I don't trust Uppers who want to 'elp Bottomers! In their 'earts they blame us for our misery. They even blame us for our smell, though they're th' ones that 'ave th' profit o' it. Do you know what Uppers say when th' wind's blowin' up the 'ill? They say th' lady o' Barrow 'as lifted 'er skirts an' is breakin' wind! They call us th' little farters – I should know, for I've attended their schools an' I've 'eard their insults."

Flame had been snapping heads off carnations, and tossing them at the orange cat. "I'm th' sort who's goin' to be doin' things me own way. I'm anxious to use me mind like you, so I don't 'ave to work."

Nora suppressed a laugh: the old Flame had doubled back with the usual haymaker. "Eleanora said you taught little Tommy Ross his ABCs."

"That I did, an' a fat lot o' good it did th' lad!" She added mysteriously. "Fortunately, I'm as good at talkin' to th' dead as to th' livin'. 'tis another one o' me talents."

Nora's mind flashed to her conversation with John Slater about the weird goings-on down the hill. "I suppose you're referring to the Spiritualist church?"

"Well, first 'tis me Celtic blood singin' to me, though I'd 'ave to say 'twas th' church folk that put me onto it." Without warning, Flame scooped up Nora's palm. "Why, mum, yer 'ave th' longest lifeline I ever did see. It goes clear through to – oh, bugger off!"

The maid released Nora's hand to shoo the orange cat, which had grown bold with the return of Eleanora and the stable boy. Both were singing in loud voices that invited everyone to chime in:

Old Mrs. Fitch fell into a ditch
With her heels cocked up in the air.
The donkey took fright to see such a sight,
On the way to the Barrow Fair.

Hey, diddle, diddle, the man with the fiddle
Caught hiccups while riding his mare.
He took off his hat, and coughed up the cat,
On the way to the Barrow Fair.

A pair of slick riding boots clicked over the cobbles toward the singers. Glancing up, Nora saw a silver-tooled "W." Nicholas Wolfe was striding toward the stables, wearing a darkly distracted air like a highwayman his cloak. Spotting Nora, he reached for a smile as if for a silk hat.

"Miss Locke, I didn't think our small local festival would interest you. Surely I could amuse you much better than this?" Saluting her with his riding crop, he continued toward the stables. "I'm certainly going to try. You have my word on that."

When Nora turned back to her companions, she found a gap had opened between them. Conscious of having betrayed some female alliance for which she'd possessed only meager credentials, she attempted to bridge the silence by gushing: "That carriage looks magical! Like a bridal coach."

Rising from the cobbles, Flame circled the vehicle with hands clasped behind her back. "Oh, 'twon't be a bride that's celebrated 'ere," she proclaimed in her broadest Derbyshire accent. "'tis t'other end o' life that's a-comin'!" She stared at Nora, with eyes rolled into her head like Ping-Pong balls. "Crossin' an ocean canna help. 'tis th' Devil who'll be waitin' on t'other shore."

Clicking her eyes back into their proper position, Flame advised, in her usual voice: "Best wear plenty o' garlic!" Then, giggling, she skipped off into the inn, leaving Nora to wonder – as always – what part of Flame was a put-on and what part was all too real.

At noon the Flower Festival parade, spearheaded by the town's Volunteer Fire Brigade Bugle Band, left the railway station. Half an hour later it passed the Wolfe Inn Moon, leading what appeared to be every coach, carriage, wagon, pram and bike in Barrow, festooned with flowers.

Nicholas and Agnes headed the inn contingent in their carriage, followed by Flame in a Brünhilde helmet of red poppies, carrying a narcissus spear. Beside her was Tommy Ross's little red-haired sister, proudly holding her end of a banner, "WOMEN'S VOTES: Give Or We Take!"

Eleanora, trailing water reeds and lavender, was being wheeled by Daniel on his vine-entwined bicycle. Though she beckoned for Nora to join them, Nora held back, understanding that the fragile bond between herself and the others had been severed by Nicholas's attentions.

Admission to the festival grounds cost a ha'penny, with proceeds to the Benevolent Fund, and all children free. The whole town was here, from the top of Barrow Hill to The Bottoms – little boys in spanking sailor suits and urchins dirtier than the chimney sweep, ladies with lacy parasols and workers in caps and knotted kerchiefs. The Market Street organ-grinder and his gold-braided monkey now had competition from the hurdy-gurdy man with his dancing bear, an elephant that gave rides for thru'pence and a trio of acrobatic dogs. Musicians, magicians and jugglers performed wherever they could squeeze space: the button-coated "pearlies" danced to accordions; a soprano trilled "A May Morning" from a coffin-sized stage with velvet curtains; a Caruso pretender lip-synched an aria from *The Barber of Seville*; a top-hatted tramp, with a player piano on casters, pumped out tunes from *The Gondoliers*; the Leg o' Mutton barbershop quartet chorused:

If you knew Nellie
Like I knew Nellie
Sang the little bird
On Nellie's hat.

Was it just coincidence that Nora kept encountering Nicholas Wolfe – shooting arrows into bull's-eyes, lobbing balls into milk cans, ringing bells with mallets? Though their paths almost crossed several times, she always veered at the last moment. Was she unconsciously seeking him out, only to make a show of avoiding him?

Certainly, Nicholas wasn't to blame. Never had she seen anyone so concentrated on winning. Nothing existed for him except the narrow corridor between himself and the coveted prize, whether it be a silver trophy or a celluloid doll on a spangled cane.

Her first sighting of Eleanora and Daniel occurred at a Punch & Judy show, where she caught them laughing boisterously as they shared a currant-and-caraway Wakes cake. Worried by Eleanora's apparent state of denial, Nora followed them as they strolled arm in arm to the hand-cranked merry-go-round. While Daniel purchased tickets, she sidled up to Eleanora.

"Is everything all right with you today?"

The girl stared blank-eyed, as if lacking comprehension. Then, shifting her gaze toward Daniel, she nodded solemnly. "I told 'im, mum. 'e's takin' things in 'and. I'm goin' ter be taken care o', just like yer said."

Though it was hard to reconcile the girl's flat voice with her words, the sight of Daniel's unclouded face as he returned with the tickets reassured Nora.

The most daring fairgoers – the sort who didn't mind flying over roads at twenty miles per hour – collected at the Ferris wheel, the festival's newest attraction. Ladies willing to undergo the adventure were guaranteed free smelling salts; Lloyds of London, it was rumored, had only reluctantly agreed to insure its owners against accidents.

Nora decided to risk it.

"Does yer know yer'll be spinnin' like a waterwheel?" cautioned the ticket-seller as his youthful assistant helped her into a double seat, then waved for another passenger.

Flame bounded from the crowd, still wearing her poppy helmet. "What a piece o' luck, mum!" Grinning, she sat beside Nora. "Now yer can 'elp me with me pamphlets."

"Up and away!" shouted the ticket-seller.

The crowd cheered while Nora surveyed a swirling sea of boaters and bonnets, top hats and helmets, derbies and caps and beanies, even convincing herself that she was doing something daredevilish like bungee-jumping.

As the wheel made its downward sweep, Flame tossed a satchel of "VOTES FOR WOMEN" leaflets into the crowd and, when the wheel ascended again, onto the other riders.

"Stop that, now!" shouted the ruddy-faced ticket-seller. "We'll 'ave none o' that."

Flame rocked their seat; when Nora protested, she rocked harder.

A hysterical woman behind threatened to jump.

"Stop th' wheel!" shouted the woman's companion.

Instead of braking, the inexperienced operator shot it around faster. Other patrons became terrified, furious or ill.

"Fire!" shrieked an onlooker.

A call went out for the Barrow Volunteer Fire Brigade, which proved within minutes that they were better buglers than riot-fighters.

A constable bounded after Flame as she leapt over a guardrail, leaving Nora to deal with his stocky companion.

"That girl just jumped into the seat beside me, officer," protested Nora.

"That's a fact, Constable Ragley," assured the ticket-seller. "This 'ere lady is an innocent."

While up in the Ferris wheel, Nora had noticed a black tent among the candy-striped ones. Now the sounds of shouting and clapping lured her under its entrance banner, proclaiming "GOD IS WATCHING." Inside, a black-robed woman, raised on a dais so that she appeared to be eight feet tall, exhorted her flock. "What happens to Sinners?"

"THEY GO TO HELL!"

"What happens to those whom Jesus has saved?"

"THEY GO TO HEAVEN!"

"Tell me, tell me, tell me, about this Heaven."

"HALLELUJAH! HALLELUJAH! HALLELUJAH!"

Nora watched in fascination as the woman, head thrown back, flapped her robes like bat wings, in a transport of agony and/or ecstasy, while her flock shouted, clapped, swayed and stamped till the ground quaked and the tent quivered. As she urged her followers to greater heights of rapture, her hood fell to her shoulders, leaving Nora to wonder why she wasn't more shocked. Had she instinctively sensed that inside Agnes Wolfe's icy persona lurked this fire-breathing priestess?

Escaping out a side exit, Nora found herself on Freak Alley, where raspy-voiced barkers shouted the charms of a fat lady with "thighs that can strangle a bear," a sword-swallower with "a cast-iron throat," a calf with "seven, count 'em, SEVEN legs, and TWO 'eads." Tucked at the end of the row she found a red-and-gold gypsy caravan, where girls in flowered shawls and swirling skirts danced to concertinas pumped by men in corduroys and kerchiefs.

An old man with parched face and gummy smile enticed Nora. "Fortunes, only five pence."

She brushed past, stopped, returned. His smile grew sly. "Love, money, long life, only five pence."

As Nora mounted the caravan steps, he instructed: "Go in the right door."

Hearing a lascivious mix of male and female laughter, Nora glanced over her left shoulder. Through a gap in some orange curtains, she spied a heap of undergarments and a pair of black boots initialed "W."

Nora retreated down the caravan steps, stumbling against the old man. Thrusting a shilling into his hands, she fled into the jostling crowd, feeling as if she'd swallowed a grenade. *Nicholas or the Count?* She was shocked at the violence of her reaction.

The sun was sliding like a gold watch into God's vest pocket. Nora forced herself to get a grip on herself, to refocus on the sights and sounds of the fair: the barker promising eternal youth to all who would drink his elixir of sassafras and licorice; the "Science of Tomorrow" booth featuring jerky movies of King Edward VII's funeral.

A photographer by the exit gate was snapping souvenir pictures of couples with faces protruding through a bride-and-groom cutout. Remembering John Slater's teasing comment about her resembling one of these impersonators, Nora sardonically stuck her head inside the bridal veil.

"Give us a smile, m'lady," urged the photographer. "'ow d'yer expect to get a chap unless yer looks like yer wants 'im?"

As Nora retracted her head, a man's face appeared under the groom's top hat. He kissed Nora on the lips, thrusting his tongue down her throat in an acrid explosion of whiskey, cloves and nicotine.

"That's th' ticket," exclaimed the photographer, shooting their picture.

The Count grinned from under the groom's top hat. "Who could resist?"

Repelled, Nora dived into the crowd, putting as many bodies as possible between them; however, everything she'd once enjoyed now impeded her – the barkers hawking their last shows, the vendors clearing their stalls at bargain prices, the buskers milking the crowd for leftover change.

Half an hour later, she emerged at the same gate with the same photographer. As she hurried by, he shouted: "Bloody oath! It's nowt free with a pound o' tea, yer know."

By the time Nora left the Common, the moon was rising. All the traps-for-hire seemed taken. She noticed one parked under a gas lamp and raced for it.

Two people were inside, visible in profile, a man and a woman, apparently quarreling. Flinging her shawl over her head, Nora sprinted down the hill toward the Wolfe Inn Moon, crouched on its corner with its tower tilted toward the moon like a lone wolf howling.

11

The inky sea rises around the floundering white ship, whipped to a crested frenzy by a howling wind. Vast curls toss it toward the moon, hanging like a poached egg in the sky, then cast it down a deep trough, snapping it in two. Righting itself, the prow sails away, carrying Nora's mother and Flame, while the stern tosses like a cork in the roiling sea. Eleanora is wrenched from Daniel's arms, then pitched overboard into the coils of a giant whirlpool. Nora hears a loud sucking sound as the screaming girl disappears into its cavernous throat.

As the stern breaks up, Nora tumbles down the stairs with her ancestral suitcase. When she regains consciousness, the sea is calm, the sun is shining, and she is floating on the suitcase. Agnes Wolfe drifts past on the chandelier from the Wolfe Inn Moon, which she paddles with a silver crucifix.

Nicholas Wolfe drives across the water toward Nora in his wine roadster, with his ruby stickpin flashing like a distress signal. John Slater, in green touring car, speeds from the opposite direction. When they spot each other, they set their cars like fighting stags and accelerate to ram. Nora's suitcase dissolves, plunging her into the icy sea.

Opening her eyes, Nora observed the homemade calendar

attached to her bedstead: June 29. *So, the fateful date had come – and gone!* Scrambling out of bed, she determined to spend the day in The Bottoms searching out the Quarry grave plot, Grandpa Flowe, and "The Impact of Socioeconomic Conditions on the Work of D.H. Lawrence." Now that her stay in Barrow was finite, she had no time to waste.

After speeding through her morning rituals, Nora put on a navy skirt with white blouse and bolero jacket – just the thing to remind her that she was a working professor with a book and an ancestry to research.

Though it was nine when she reached the dining room, the lights were still out. No food burdened the wolves' head sideboard. The orange cat hunched in the shadows, balefully watching the kitchen door. As Nora bent to scratch its neck, that door swung open, admitting Agnes Wolfe with a tray of bread, cheese, fruit and cold cuts. Eyes averted, she announced: "No hot breakfast this morning."

Her defensive manner aroused Nora's curiosity. "Oh, is there some problem?"

Mrs. Wolfe lit a gas lamp. "One of our girls is gone."

Nora helped herself to cutlery. "Quit?"

The hotelier's eyes blazed like charcoal embers. "Gone!" She slammed the lid of a teapot. "Didn't come home from the fair."

So, the rebellious Flame had flown the coop, as she had boasted. "To London?"

Mrs. Wolfe shrugged her bony shoulders. "That's not for me to know or care."

Nora chuckled. "Last I saw she was galloping through the midway with a constable in pursuit."

Spinning, Mrs. Wolfe demanded: "Wasn't she with Daniel Slater?"

"You mean *Eleanora*?"

"Of course! They've run off."

"Eloped?"

"I suppose that's what you'd call it!" Kicking aside the cat, she slammed the kitchen door.

Nora pictured Eleanora and Daniel holding hands on the carousel in an advanced state of adoration. *Good for you!*

It was another flawless day. As Nora hiked toward The Bottoms, she heard St. Michael's carillon and remembered it was Sunday. By now the faithful would be settling their behinds into their pews for an hour's worship while the infidels would be sleeping off festival hangovers. It would be another two hours before anyone was interested in a stranger's prying questions.

Nora noticed a black-and-white swallowtail butterfly flap its wings over a clump of milk parsley, then fly purposefully toward the bog. Forking right instead of left, she followed it, away from The Bottoms.

Step by step, breath by breath, she immersed herself in the glories of the swamp, sorting through its rhapsody of sounds and shapes and colors, losing track of her scholarly intentions: that brown beauty with the red-striped delta-wings was a red admiral; that small emerald one, clinging to a spike of broom, was a hairstreak; that cheerful twitter burst from a swallow's throat, that drawn-out *tsweep* from a yellow-breasted wagtail, that bell-note from a great tit.

It was odd – almost spooky – the way Eleanora's luminous spirit seemed to haunt the place, like swamp gas that observers sometimes mistook for ghosts. Nora scrambled down the ditch, scraggly with scrub. She bowed then released a branch, watching its rusty "bark" splinter and then spiral, wondering where Eleanora and Daniel were at this moment – in a country inn sharing strawberries with coddled cream, galloping toward London in a coach-and-four?

Nora struck out for the Barrow River, lured by the exuberant shouts of two urchins with fishing rods. Climbing a stone stile, she followed the rush of water under a brooding canopy of beeches, accompanied by squirrels and a rabbit or two. The rill widened into a creek lined with alders, then into an old millpond with its mossy waterwheel now sprouting forget-me-nots. Sluffing off her boots and lisle stockings, Nora waded into the amber pool, its shoreline wild with arrowheads, ferns and lush grasses. When the water wet her knickers, she peeled them too, followed by her navy skirt, bolero and white blouse.

Nora plunged, feeling the silky liquid glide over her prickly flesh. She navigated through the pulpy stems of water lilies, attached like umbilical cords to buds floating overhead, then drifted sunny-side up beside a dragonfly with fluorescent wings, watching clouds scud across the translucent sky and the swift sallies of a flycatcher as it snatched its prey. *Oh, I want, I want, I want* . . . Nicholas Wolfe's face floated up like a deadhead from the silty depths of her unconscious.

Nora rolled over, staring into the amber water alive with minnows and frogs' eggs and the grasping fingers of submerged plants. Nicholas dwelled unabashedly in the world of the senses. When with him, Nora almost forgot she was trapped in a backwater of time. She almost forgot about past or future and lived in the eternal now. Eleanora also possessed this quality, offering herself as a gift to nature.

Nora saw a crayfish staring at her with Agnes Wolfe's jealous eyes: *"Muriel Gant, a cheap Woolworth's girl. She lived across that alley, right under my nose."*

Gulping brackish water, she sputtered to the surface, then stroked for shore, toward her bundle of petticoats with its sentinel pair of lace-ups. She spied something else: a shiny pair of riding boots poking through the ferns. A man with his face shadowed by a fedora was standing at water's edge. He had only to glance down or scuff his left foot to discover her bundle.

Nora dived again, swimming underwater as strongly as she could. She surfaced behind a hummock of sphagnum moss spiked with lyme grass. Her intruder posed in profile, gazing at the ripples caused by her departing *derrière*, the sun glinting from the silver "W" branding his boot. *Nicholas?* He turned his bloodless face toward her, whiskey bottle in hand. *The Count!* Squinting suspiciously in her direction, he caught the splash of a carp skidding on its tail, tossed his bottle – bull's-eye – into the concentric rings, then retreated into the alders.

Nora waited at least five minutes, with the gelatinous water congealing like aspic around her. Creeping back through arrowheads, she hurriedly dressed, then continued along the path on the assumption that the Count was headed to Barrow. Towering over a copse of lichen-scabbed ashes, she recognized the limestone crag resembling a bleached skull. A well-worn path led up through thorns and thistles. Nora made the short, steep climb, at first eager to distance herself from the Count, then compulsively drawn to the crag itself.

She stared at the grinning jaw of the skull, with its single loose tooth, struggling once again to remember what had frightened her here before, but the instant an image began to form, her mind went to black again. Extracting the rock, she retrieved Nicholas's torch and gasoline, then headed around the skull's jaw.

Something metallic glinted from the junipers by the cave's entrance. Nora investigated: a bicycle. She flashed back to the Count's shiny boots: those were not the footgear of a man who'd trekked across the fields from Barrow. A clammy sweat oozed through her pores as she imagined him down in the cave, crouched on a ledge, waiting . . .

Nora claimed the bicycle. Hitching up her skirt, she streaked down the slope, jouncing perilously over rocks and thistles. Once on The Flats, she abandoned the main roads, pedaling furiously along country lanes, deep into the forest.

Though Nora had intended to return directly to Barrow, she became seduced by the bliss of sailing with the wind in her face, senses attuned and fears forgotten. Gullies leapt with green frogs. Clumps of red clover hummed with bees. Dead logs clicked with crickets. Sedge nookeries chirped with grasshoppers. Swallows swooped and soared, trapping the sun in their elegant blue-gray plumage. Pheasants flushed from hawthorn thickets, hares bounded, mice scurried. The landscape was thrillingly, electrically alive with a plenitude Nora hadn't experienced since childhood. The Victorians had been right to blame bicycles for female eroticism – not because of the carnality of their chafing seats but because of their blessed freedom! In the slimy laneways of The Bottoms, with everything smeared in the same shade of mud, Nora had seen what Grandma Flora had escaped; now, swanning through the countryside, she understood what she had lost.

By the time Nora returned to Barrow, the sun hung like a gold sovereign in the western sky. She wheeled her borrowed bike into the Wolfe Inn Moon stables and was halfway across the yard when a hand clamped her shoulder.

"Miss Locke again, is it?" A stocky man with fleshy jowls and a ruddy complexion breathed garlic in her face. "Constable Stanley Ragley." He seized her elbow. "I dinna think ter meet so soon after th' fair."

The constable guided Nora into a book-lined parlor in a part of the inn she'd not yet visited. As she settled on a faded blue-velvet settee, an inner door burst opened, disgorging Flame. Her fists were clenched, her eyes swollen, and her red hair bristled like a wire brush. *So, not a bicycle thief. More about that silly business on the Ferris wheel?*

Constable Ragley ushered Nora through the same door into Agnes Wolfe's office, decorated with account books and religious artifacts. A tall, gray-haired man with bulging forehead, jutting chin and drooping mustache unfolded in herringbone sections from the desk. He gripped her hand.

"I'm Inspector Carnfield, Miss Locke. Please remain calm. It's all routine at this stage." He handed Nora a photo of Eleanora on the steps of the Wolfe Inn Moon. "Missing persons is how we're treating it. How we must treat it."

Nora gazed at the lovely face haloed with sable curls stuck through by a jaunty sprig of lavender while the inspector selected a pencil from a picket fence lined up across his desk. "Do you know this person?"

"Certainly. It's Eleanora, the maid from this inn."

"And when was the last time you saw the young lady in question?"

"Yesterday at the carousel, with Daniel Slater." Should she be helpful or evasive? "It was about five o'clock. They were obviously very much in love."

Carnfield stopped recording: "If you don't mind, Miss Locke, I'll draw the conclusions." He planted a row of plump dots like bombs across his page. "Did you speak to either of them?"

"Just to Eleanora." Nora remembered the dangerous shoals underlying their careful conversation. "I asked her if everything was going well and she said yes."

The inspector added fuses to his bombs. "Just yes?"

Was it customary for an officer of Carnfield's stature to chase down every eloping maid? "You don't wish me to speculate, do you?" *John Slater must be behind this!*

The inspector peered over Nora's shoulder. Constable Ragley stood in the doorway. Circling around Nora, he slapped a paper on the desk. Carnfield read the note once, ticked it twice, then challenged the constable. "You're quite sure about this?"

"I've checked it through, sir."

The inspector snapped his pencil in two – a nervy sound like the breaking of bones. Tilting way back, he inquired: "Miss Locke, would you care to explain how you came into possession of Daniel Slater's bicycle?"

Nora fell forward into the space the inspector had just vacated. "Daniel's?" She began to prattle. "I found it while hiking. It had been abandoned."

The inspector withdrew a knife from his pocket. "Where was this bicycle when you 'found' it?"

"Near the limestone crag with the cave. The one that looks like a skull – at least, I think it does."

Carnfield took his time sharpening his broken stake. "What hour would this be?"

Nora revised upward. "About two."

The inspector drew a clock with the hands at two, then checked the time against his own pocketwatch. "And it was fifteen past seven when you returned to this inn? I make that a journey of five hours and fifteen minutes."

"I finished my outing and then I had something to eat."

The inspector handed Nora pencil and paper. "Perhaps you would be so good as to draw a map showing us where the bicycle was 'abandoned.'"

Pressing hard to steady her fingers, Nora drew the limestone crag, the cave, the path and the juniper, which she marked with an X.

"Thank you, Miss Locke." The inspector held out his notebook for her to file the page, as if planning to dust it for fingerprints. "You've been very useful . . . in spite of yourself."

He unfolded his tall frame, like a sectional yardstick, from the desk. "That will be all for now – unless, of course, Daniel Slater wishes to press theft charges, which isn't too likely, given his condition."

Nora plopped back into her chair. "You know where Daniel is?"

The inspector leaned over the desk. "Ahh, but, of course, you were out bicycling all afternoon. Daniel Slater was found shortly after eleven this morning wandering around the fairgrounds in an apparent state of shock."

Nora clung to her seat as if to a raft in a squall. "But where was Eleanora?"

"That, Miss Locke, is precisely what we're trying to discover." The inspector gently tipped Nora's chair. "Young Slater had a bump on his head. Claimed not to recall the events of the last few hours."

Reluctantly, Nora arose. "Something terrible must have happened!"

The inspector ushered her to the door. "There are no 'must have's' in my work, Miss Locke. A missing person, no more and no less. This is a law-abiding community. A bit of poaching in spring. A certain seasonal drunkenness. The occasional assault and battery. In fact, the worst we get around here is" – a significant look at Nora – "bicycle theft."

Nora blocked the entrance, feeling ill. "Eleanora wouldn't just disappear."

Reaching behind her, Carnfield pushed open the door. "You seem to be a person who likes to jump to premature conclusions, Miss Locke . . . that two people who laugh together are in love, that a bicycle in a bush is a bicycle no one wants, that when a young girl doesn't come home at night it's foul play. In my business, it's important to hold all possibilities in the mind until one proves itself."

He plucked his herringbone cap from the desk. "Under the circumstances I'm sure you understand that you must not leave Barrow without notifying my department."

Nora climbed the hall stairs with her thoughts jumping like fleas. Why hadn't she told the inspector about seeing the Count near Daniel's bike? She raced to her side window. Carnfield was talking to a man in the stable yard. *I can catch him.* Nora recognized Nicholas, still in the riding clothes he'd worn to the festival, and hesitated: *I must extricate myself from this place, not dig myself in deeper.* She remembered Eleanora, clinging to her skirt, begging for help, then sped out the door and down the stairs.

The stable yard was empty, except for the orange cat, hunched forlornly in the center.

Nora prepared for bed, knowing that she wasn't going to sleep. After tossing for over an hour, she remembered that the waiting room commandeered by the police had contained a library. Taking her globe bed lamp, she tiptoed downstairs, through the darkened lobby into the reading room.

Here was a treasure trove of turn-of-the-century fiction: a half-dozen volumes by Galsworthy and H.G. Wells, along with popular schlock like *The Garden of Allah* by Robert Hichens, *Tess of the*

Storm Country by Grace Miller White, *A Husband by Proxy, The Key to Yesterday, The Gambler, The Sheik.*

Even in her agitated state, Nora quickened to the look and feel of the books as she ran her fingers along their spines, some prettily covered in violet-spattered wallpaper with ribbon page-markers – a quaint reminder of a time when books were savored then passed on to the next generation, not consumed in a few gulps and discarded.

Nora selected one at random – *A Midlands Girlhood* by Sara Thomas-Key. With speed-reading skills honed by a decade of marking essays, she skimmed the first few chapters: a girl with an embittered mother and a dead philandering father escapes her coming-of-age fears by collecting butterflies in a swamp.

She felt a queer twist in her gut: hadn't she seen this book before . . . *the year I was ill?*

Nora became conscious of quarreling voices.

First, Nicholas Wolfe: "How . . . threaten me?"

Then, Agnes Wolfe: ". . . earned the right!"

"I warn you . . . nothing . . ."

". . . idiot! In my house."

"In *my* house!"

". . . the gall of you!"

Now Agnes cried while Nicholas placated: ". . . see this through."

". . . your messes. How bad is it?"

". . . what you were in for . . ."

"Rot in hell!"

"Right beside you!"

As the voices crescendoed, Nora feared that the combatants might storm off in opposite directions, blocking her retreat. Dousing her lamp, she tried the back door. Its bolt snapped noisily. Closing it behind her, she tiptoed across the porch, then dashed around a yew hedge into Agnes Wolfe's garden, silvered by moonlight.

Nora halted, stunned by its opalescent beauty. The garden was as sensuous and seductive as its owner seemed straitlaced and forbidding. Flowers drifted, climbed, clumped, tangled, crept, clung. Nora inhaled the intoxicating bouquet of roses, carnations, lilies, wisteria, honeysuckle, with the colliery's taint fixing the scent like civet in perfume, rendering it more powerful and a little dangerous.

A chintz hammock hung between apple and pear trees, with a silky fringe that swayed in the wind. Sinking into it, Nora gazed up through rustling leaves. Though she could no longer hear the quarreling Wolfes, their anger had invaded her . . . *lying between starchy sheets, kicking her heels against the bars of the iron bedstead . . . rage that fed on itself, stoking and stroking, yet stopping one breath short of the thunderstorm that might disperse it.*

With a shock, Nora realized how jealous her mother had been of her, though both had repressed that knowledge from themselves and from each other . . . *a daughter's possibilities measured against the disappointments of her own unlived life.*

A door slammed, followed by the stamp of boots across the porch. Someone stood on the other side of the hedge. Nora heard the clearing of a throat, then smelled the acrid smoke of a cigar. Retreating farther into her hammock, she spun its fringe around herself like a cocoon, holding her breath to keep it from swaying.

A shadow stole around the hedge, eclipsing a lopsided moon bloodied by emulsions from the colliery. Nicholas Wolfe stood with his back to Nora, his fist against the apple tree, staring over the wall at sheep with fleece like buttered popcorn. Through the hammock's fringe, she saw the tautness of his body inside his frock coat as he prowled right and then left, pausing only to strike the apple tree.

Nicholas's hand caught the rope of the hammock. He yanked it, felt Nora's weight, paused, then turned. His eyes noted the abandoned lamp, then bore through her chintz wrapper. Nora burrowed deeper, hearing his breath mingle with the electric hum of frogs and crickets and grasshoppers, no longer able to stifle her own.

Silently, Nicholas began to undress – first his frock coat, which he hung on a branch, then his ruby stickpin, his silk tie and detachable collar. Staring into the hammock, he unscrewed his ruby cufflinks, unbuttoned his plum vest, then his shirt. He folded both garments, then peeled off his boots and socks. He unfastened his striped pants and his underwear, his fury channeling itself into a precise, methodical and ritualistic disrobing.

Nora watched as if in a trance, identifying with each piece of clothing as if fell. *Now his hands are on my flesh. Those are his palms caressing my breasts. Those are his fingers unbuttoning . . . me.*

As Nicholas unhooked the foot of the hammock with both hands, she felt its coarser fabric bite through her gown. She felt her heels, then her calves, touch the earth. She saw Nicholas move behind her, felt the release of the hammock over her head, then the lowering of her upper torso.

He knelt astride Nora, in full erection. She could hear his heart. She could hear her own. She counted their breaths, then found they had coalesced. *I've seduced myself and now he's going to rape me.*

She opened her mouth to protest but, instead, sucked in a powerful draft of whiskey, cloves and nicotine. As Nicholas unfastened her ruffled nightgown, a flash of sheet lightning illuminated a nest of sleeping birds while cindery clouds with fiery underbellies scudded like a wolf pack across the moon, devouring its face. Nora closed her eyes, feeling the lick of the feral moonlight on her lids, as he ripped her gown the rest of the way. Placing his hands upon her inner thighs, he pressed until she opened them.

Nora's eyelids popped open, as if worked by the same spring. She saw a cruel face ravened by lust, backlit by a red moon – the man in the moon, the Wolfe in the moon . . . *a black tombstone in the rain, my hand on the wheel.* With one fist she drove him away while the other clutched his chest hairs, pulling him closer . . . *my foot on the gas, full speed ahead.*

Nicholas's flesh prodded deep into her own, releasing an answering wellspring of lust. Wrapping her legs around him, she helped him to obliterate her.

12

Nora lay in bed, feeling drugged, feeling woozy. Bruises the color of dried blood bracketed her thighs. Her nightgown was ripped from waist to hem. She examined the jagged edges, half expecting them to bleed.

Nausea swept over her – fear and shame edging into self-loathing. Why this helpless, desperate feeling that some calamitous fate was sweeping like a black tidal wave toward her? She closed her eyes: *as if someone has died . . . myself?*

What had she expected – one of Lady Chatterley's erotic epiphanies? She realized that she had. While her mind had rejected Lawrence's phallic worship, some errant part of her psyche had clung to that fantasy of the rescuing "other" like her mother soaking up Harlequin Romances.

Swinging her feet onto the rug, Nora paused with her head hung like a broken dandelion. *Wolves, that was what I dreamt about. Wolves gorging on sheep . . . pregnant sheep. Wolves with men's faces. Waiting for the lambs to drop and then . . .* She could still hear their howling – but the sound wasn't only of wolves and it was no longer confined to her head.

She gazed out of the window. The sheep munched as usual – *like mashed potatoes on a bed of parsley, just asking to be eaten.* Two children sailed a kite, and an old man balanced a crate of geese on his handlebars as he pedaled to market. Everything was as it should be for a Monday morning in June 1913, except that the church bells were tolling – all of them, out of sync, charging the air like a dentist's drill. Nora distanced their disturbing reality: *probably some old gaffer – a pillar of the community – has toppled into his porridge, requiring Barrow's ringers to proclaim the town's respect.*

Turning from the window, she slashed yesterday's date from her calendar: *only nine more days!* As she replaced her black crayon on her night table, she noticed that her globe lamp was missing. An image of it lying beside the hammock flashed to mind.

She sprinted down the stairs, out the door, and around to the garden. The hammock was spread across the grass like an unmade bed, accompanied by her overturned lamp. Nora rehooked the hammock, then snatched up the lamp. She dashed back across the stable yard, remembering as her bare feet touched the cobbles that she was wearing only her torn nightgown.

Agnes Wolfe and Flame were in the lobby, their heads propped together like bulrushes broken in a storm. The older woman stiffened.

"No breakfast at all this morning," she announced in a cracked voice that struggled for control.

"They found 'er," blurted Flame.

"Eleanora? Thank god!"

Flame unleashed a wail.

"She's dead!" Nora slumped onto the stairs to keep from collapsing.

"You'd better go back to bed," ordered Agnes Wolfe, not unkindly. She thrust Nora's fallen lamp into her arms, noting her appearance. "Or *go to* bed."

Flame yanked the sleeve of Nora's nightgown. "All them wolves 'owling an' 'owling an' 'owling. Yer 'eard 'em, too, didn't yer?"

"No!" Nora snatched back her arm.

As she clambered up the stairs, Agnes called out: "The funeral's at five. You're invited, of course."

Nora halted under the chandelier, feeling a drip of hot wax. She demanded, already knowing the answer: "Where did they find the body?"

"In a cave." Flame's eyes rolled back, leaving only the whites. "Yer know th' one. 'tis shaped like a skull."

Nora fled to her bathroom and was ill in the toilet, retching so fiercely that she spewed up blood.

Afterwards, she drew her blinds, then wrapped herself in the patchwork quilt, rocking and grieving, grieving and rocking. She pressed her nostrils into its gingham backing, detecting the scent of lavender. All of a sudden the room seemed drenched with it. Hiding her head under the coverlet, she tossed in fitful sleep.

She rides the carousel with David, on the same white stallion, laughing and singing to the tune of The Merry Widow. *Without explanation, David pushes up a lever. The carousel swirls faster and faster, out of control. It grows dark. Their stallion breaks free, then gallops across the Common through torrents of black rain. She hears its pounding hooves and snorting breath; she feels its sweaty flanks heave between her bare legs. Nora and David plummet over the lip of Barrow Hill on their black stallion.*

At five, the funeral procession left the inn, with Eleanora's pine coffin wrapped in a patchwork quilt, drawn by a single black horse. Flame followed on foot, thickly veiled, shoulders hunched, and then the Wolfe Inn Moon carriage bearing Agnes and Nicholas. To her usual black dress Agnes had added a hat with skimmed-back netting – her impassive features were her veil. By contrast, Nicholas looked like a man on the knife-edge between sanity and insanity. His hair was dull and unkempt, his flesh the color and texture of a peeled grape.

Nora trailed the mourning party, still afraid to cast her lot with these people, but unable to separate herself. The procession was silent, except for muffled hooves and shuffling feet, deadened by low-lying fog that curled around their ankles. Curtains in windows swayed to reveal parts of faces. The whole event seemed like a macabre replay of Saturday's parade – Barrow's Festival of the Dead Flowers.

At the end of Edge Road the funeral party descended toward the Reform Church, as if into a noxious pit, with the sulfurous vapors now high enough to float heads free of bodies. Black Pit Square was so crowded with Bottoms folk that the undertaker had to clear a path for the coffin. Some merely jostled for a closer look, while others attached themselves to the procession. This was Barrow's first fatal crime in twenty years, since a Baldwin and a Bentley had shot it out over the theft of seven cabbages. Nora listened numbly to gossip in the slurred Derbyshire dialect, like porridge with a few lumpy consonants:

"Know wha' were a surprise to me? Tha' were th' young'un tha' come ter th' bad end, an' nowt tha' flame-'aired sister."

"Ay, but this 'ere's an 'igh-class crime with an 'igh-class gent."

"A crime o' passion!"

"They say th' body were 'orribly mutilated – all o' them middle parts missin'."

"Et by wolves?"

"Or else we 'ave a Ripper on our 'ands!"

"At least 'e's nowt roamin' free."

"Ay, if 'twere yer or me, they'd 'ave us strung by now."

"Thru'pence fer a farthing, tha' rich uncle o' 'is will 'ave 'im out fast as foam flees a pint in a 'igh wind."

"'e's a right 'andsome lad, an' polite as yer please. When we 'ad our accident down 'ere 'e was most obligin'."

"Well, them's th' ones yer 'ave to watch with yer girls. They charm th' pants right off 'em, then think th' Almighty 'isself won't touch 'em."

"Speakin' o' which, I've 'eard th' master o' th' 'ouse is likewise one fer th' ladies."

"Yer'd need a tickle or two on th' side with a wife 'oos 'ead is in th' church steeple."

"I'd say 'tother way misself. Beware o' th' man oozin' charm 'oos wife looks as old as 'is mither."

With its low-pitched slate roof, sooty bricks, and black-painted interior, the Reform Church seemed carved from a single clod of coal. After sliding into a pew with the folk from The Bottoms, Nora strained for a glimpse of Nicholas but found he was screened off with the other chief mourners. Caressing one of the silky pews that rippled in dark waves up to the altar, she felt the vibrations of the organ, mordant and deep-throated. Eight roughly tailored men from The Bottoms bore Eleanora's coffin to the altar, their legs working in unison like the appendages of a beetle. They were followed by Bottoms relatives and close friends, led by the rusty, bow-legged man whom Nora kept encountering.

A tall, black-hooded figure ascended to the pulpit. "We come to bury the body of our daughter and to commit her soul to the judgment of the Almighty. All too soon, by our earthly reckoning, has she passed from us, but in fit and proper time according to His Divine Will."

The preacher stretched his arms like the crucified Christ. "As to this evil deed itself, do not let acquiescence to God's plan blind us to the deviltry in men."

"OH, NO, NO, NO!"

"An eye for an eye and a tooth for a tooth!"

"AMEN, HALLELUJAH!"

Nora stared transfixed at the bluish face inside the preacher's cowl – the slick jet hair and broken, blood-streaked eyes. With her handkerchief pressed to her mouth, she fled the church.

For the next twenty minutes, Nora wandered from tombstone to tombstone, cloaked in a jaundiced fog that stung and itched and clung, reading inscriptions without absorbing them. She had to mouth the word "Quarry" a half-dozen times before its significance seeped in. She was standing before a granite boulder with that surname carved on one side and the names and dates of eight relatives on the other, including that of her great-grandmother, Jane Quarry. She traced the letters with her fingers, feeling reassured. Since these eight ancestors were indisputably dead, didn't that mean she must still be alive?

A shout from the church snagged her attention. The mourners were filing out bearing their trophy. Agnes Wolfe leaned on the arm of the preacher-Count while Flame clung to Pamela Birchwood. Had Nicholas taken ill or had she lost him in the fog?

Nora tracked the procession, still at a distance, compelled to see this wretched ceremony through to its bitter end. And bitter it was, for the group wound its way out of the tidy cemetery to a stony field where a new grave had been scraped. Why had Eleanora been banished to unhallowed ground? Did being murdered constitute a sin in this inverted religion, or had the Reformers discovered that their maid was no maiden?

Three other mourners stood halfway up the hill, well back from the official party – John and Daniel Slater, accompanied by Inspector Carnfield. Heads bare, the Slaters kept vigil with hands clasped behind their backs. It wasn't until Nora noticed that Inspector Carnfield carried two hats that she understood that Daniel's wrists were handcuffed.

By the time Nora returned to the inn, the lamplighter was reaching his pole to the lamp at the corner of Edge Road and Backwater Lane.

At first she thought the inn's lobby was deserted. Then she noticed Agnes Wolfe with her head smeared across her desk blotter, still wearing her funeral hat. With a shock Nora remembered her mother's corpse as Aunt Millie had discovered it – her black straw pushed to one side, her fingers clasping a pen.

Nora caught a whiff of whiskey as the hotelier extended her

head from her high black collar and blinked like a turtle emerging from hibernation. "It wasn't my fault, you know. I keep this place spotless and my accounts to the penny."

When Nora didn't respond, she scowled: "Oh, it's you." In a slurred, lugubrious voice, she advised: "Don't waste your sympathy."

She pointed to the chandelier with its candle stubs buried in melted wax. "That girl never did trim those candles. That girl was a slut!"

Shocked, Nora retorted: "Do you think I didn't know about Muriel Gant?"

"Her, too?" queried Agnes Wolfe, bleary-eyed. "So many! She was pregnant, you know."

Nora fled up the stairs, tripping over the orange cat, who scooted off, ears flattened. Once in her room, she thrashed about like a zoo animal.

Snatching a sheet of hotel stationery, she wrote:

> Dear John,
>
> I'm sick with devastation over what has happened. I know Daniel is innocent, as all fair-minded people must. . . .

The Count's face filled the dark screen on the back of Nora's eyeballs – in Rasputin robes behind the Reform pulpit, and then in the bushes by the millpond. With her head a blizzard of unsorted thoughts, she finished lamely:

> If I can be of any help, please call me.

Nora underlined the essential message: *please call me.* Hailing the stable boy, she tossed the note through her window, weighted with a crown.

She returned to pacing. Her nostrils filled with the scent of lavender. No matter how she twisted and turned, scrubbed and rubbed, she couldn't eradicate it from her hair, her clothes, the pores of her flesh. Closing her eyes, she conjured up Eleanora, with her apron pressed to her tear-stained face. Had the maid ever confessed that Daniel was the father of her child, or had that been Nora's invention?

Again, the Count's face filtered into consciousness. *Nightfall, just after the Flower Festival . . . a trap parked under a gas lamp with two silhouettes, quarreling . . . a man and a girl.*

Nora became aware of another odor – cigar smoke pluming through her window. Needing to confide, she hurtled downstairs, out of the inn, then across the stable yard.

Nicholas had just extinguished his cigar and was leaning against the apple tree, gazing over the moon-drenched Vale of Barrow. Seeing him in that incriminating spot halted Nora. As she turned to slink away, her impulse spent, she heard his footfall.

"Thank God!" In two strides he was embracing her. "I prayed you'd come."

As they stood under the moon-ripened apple tree, he stripped her body and then his own, not slowly and ritualistically as before, but as if hooks and buttons were masking tape and zippers. This time it was the act of sex that was slow and ritualized. She tasted his mouth, a now-familiar mix of cloves and nicotine, smelled his musty armpits, felt her chest heave and her limbs thrash, heard herself moan with his tongue in her mouth, responded to the swell of his sex against hers, felt him enter her, begin to drive her crazy. Yet, how could this be? How could she be groaning in Nicholas's arms when "she" was not looking *up* at him but *down*, suspended somewhere between the branches of the apple tree and a carnal moon *. . . a woman on a staircase, far below . . . a man crouched over her, sweat glistening from his balding head.*

Nora felt herself begin to fall, snatched at the shiny leaves of the apple tree, felt them slip through her fingers as she plunged to earth. She was once again inside her own skin, with her hands clutching at Nicholas's sweaty hair, his body over hers, his breath mingling with hers, knowing suddenly that, yes, these were her hands and her legs, and those were his wrapped around her. This was her face, *touch it.* Another face – Nicholas's – blanched by moonlight. She could feel the pebbles and twigs cut into her buttocks as she lay pinioned under him, hear insects whine, experience the prick of something tiny sucking blood from her calf.

Nicholas rolled away from her. He was weeping. "Oh God, forgive me. Eleanora was like a daughter to me." His eyes looked as if a beast had clawed them. "If I could wrap these fingers around Daniel Slater's throat I'd —"

Nora pressed her hand over his mouth. "I saw a man near the cave. Just before I found Daniel's bicycle. I saw the same man quarreling with Eleanora outside the Flower Festival."

He frowned: "Did you recognize him?"

"It was your brother."

Nicholas's frown rutted into a scowl. "You've seen him?"

"It must have been him."

His fingers dug into her shoulders. "How can you be certain?"

"You look so much alike." Nora described the man she called the Count, surprised at how finely etched his face appeared in her mind. "I'm not sure about after the festival. It *was* him by the pond, as I intend to make clear to Inspector Carnfield."

Nicholas shook her. "Don't mention this to anyone!"

Releasing her, he cajoled: "Forgive me, my darling, but this is a blood matter with me. Though my brother's a bastard, he's still my father's son." He stroked Nora's arms. "Let me question him first. Please do this for me. I've more to lose than anyone if he goes unchecked."

His voice turned as bitter as a peach pit. "I've covered up for him long enough. If I'm strong enough, we'll soon see a reckoning."

13

No dreams. Not an image, not a feeling. A blank slate.

Nora was used to gleaning a few seashells each morning from the ebb tide of her unconscious. First, she'd slept too heavily, then she'd been awakened by a woman's muffled sobbing. Though she'd listened for several minutes with ear pressed to a dozen places against the wall, the sound seemed without location, as if the hotel were weeping.

Next, the grate of heavy doors in the stable yard drew Nora to her side window. Through her shutters she observed Nicholas push his car out of the garage and halfway up Backwater Lane before starting the motor. Seconds later, Flame emerged from the stable, tugging a horse by its bridle. After two near-disastrous attempts to mount, she had trotted after Nicholas. All before dawn.

A cold buffet awaited Nora on the sideboard, including cold tea. No one had bothered to light the lamps. She selected a few morsels, which she attempted to feed to the soulful orange cat, but it too refused all nourishment.

❦

A crowd pressed around *The Barrow Times* – not the usual assortment of bankers and stockbrokers catching up on the latest news, but a mob. The rusty-mustached collier, who'd woven through Nora's Barrow life, was goading a *Times* spokesman with raised fist: "'ow is it we 'ears more about th' murder of me daughter Eleanora in th' pubs than in yer bleedin' newspaper?"

The frock-coated gent replied: "We print what the police allow us to print, sir."

Addressing his cronies rather than the spokesman, the collier demanded: "Where does it say in yer murderin' publisher's paper that th' youngun's feminine organs was ripped right out? Where does yer publisher admit 'is nephew's bike were found as close ter th' cave as damn is ter swearin'?"

The spokesman's reply was swamped in catcalls.

With vigorous finger jabs, the collier exhorted his friends: "Yer believe that, mates, an' yer'll believe this is gravy!" The "this" in question was a bucket of pig manure, now running like tears down the face of the sedate Times building.

Nora tried to propel herself to the brass door, but was repulsed by the surly crowd. In all other encounters with Bottoms folk, she'd experienced only their indifference. Now she felt their rage. Shaken, she retreated to the Wolfe Inn Moon.

A furtive glance toward the garage answered her first question: Nicholas had not yet returned though it was after three.

Flame limped back and forth behind the lobby desk like a wounded fox. She was wrapped in a vibrant gypsy shawl of poppies, nasturtiums and cornflowers, contrasting sharply with her pale face, crazy eyes and disheveled hair.

She did not acknowledge Nora until she had reached the first-floor landing, and then her voice seemed surly: "I almost forgot. Me sister left somethin' fer yer."

When Nora reached the desk, Flame set a pickle jar upon it. "This 'ad yer name on it. I guess she 'ad some kind o' premonition."

Nora picked up the jar. It was filled with crushed butterflies. She stared at the powdery mess, overcome with fury. "Did you do this?"

Flame's cheeks flared. "Well now, if yer think so, I guess I must 'ave, mustn't I? 'ow was I to know them things was so easy broke?" She grinned – more like a grimace: "By th' way, that's me jar when yer wantin' to return it."

One hand twisted the fringe of her gypsy shawl while the other played with her necklace.

"That's Eleanora's!"

Flame clasped the silver heart. "Well, she 'asn't much use fer it now, 'as she?"

Outraged, Nora climbed the stairs.

"Ooo, by the way, these letters come fer yer." Flame held out a silver plate with two envelopes. "My, but aren't yer th' popular one?"

Nora picked up her messages as if they might be letter bombs. Both were in identical, unmarked envelopes, suggesting Flame had read and resealed them.

Back in her bedroom, she tore into the first note.

Dear Nora,

I'm touched more than I can express that you would write to me, offering your friendship and support for Daniel and myself. Needless to say, I am committed to proving my nephew's innocence. It is not possible that he would hurt anyone, and especially not a girl whose family was once in service to the Slaters.

Of course, these heartaches fill the forefront of my life; yet, as regards that other matter, my initial inquiries in London lead me to believe that I will have a passport for you within the month.

Meantime, let me confess that I have thought often about you in the days since our last meeting. If your feelings for me have advanced as far as friendship, please permit me to advise you: you are living in a house of shadows, as this recent tragic event has proven. If you but agree, I will send my carriage to you before nightfall for the purpose of relocating you in the home of my aunt, who lives in a commodious residence on Church Street, attended only by her servants.

I have, of course, already spoken of your circumstances to this lady of great good humor and goodwill. She looks forward to receiving you with all assurances of hospitality.

Warm regards,
John Slater

Nora opened the second note.

Dear One,

I had to leave on urgent business, but, God willing, we will be together again before this long day's end. I have information along the lines that I promised to provide. Please meet me at the railway station at ten this evening. Leave by the garden gate and take the brow path to the station, being <u>absolutely certain</u> you are not followed. It's <u>imperative</u> that you tell <u>no one</u>. Destroy this missive.

Your servant,
N.

Nora lay the two notes side-by-side on her patchwork quilt: the gentleman or the tiger? She picked up one, changed her mind, put it down. Closing her eyes, she lay a palm over each, then made her decision: *both.*

Dear John,

Thank you for your concern, which good sense tells me I, too, must share. I will be ready, with bags packed, in the lobby of the Wolfe Inn Moon tomorrow at noon, if your kind offer still stands.

Gratefully,
Nora

After sealing the note, she hailed the stable boy. Then she memorized Nicholas's message and shredded it as directed.

❦

For the rest of the afternoon Nora focused on her rendezvous, blotting out every other reality: she bathed, washed her hair, oiled her skin, forced herself to nap, laid out her dress – the white muslin that she'd worn to the Flower Festival, embellished with lace and a sash. She piled her hair up, tried it down, then decided on the upward swirl, more suitable to her chronological age. Her gaze brushed the pickle jar with its pathetic burden of broken wings like shards of stained glass. Damn Flame! She attempted to stash the hideous collection in her suitcase, but found it missing. She stared at the rack where the case should be: if I think about that, I'll go crazy.

Like a natural sundial, the shadow of Barrow Hill was sliding across The Flats toward the horizon. The last peddlers were trooping home from market along the brow path, dragging their wagons and carts and buggies. A boy toted a brace of pigeons while another hauled potatoes.

The back door slammed. Agnes Wolfe was cutting roses for tomorrow's tables. Nora watched the capable hands linger over each exquisite bloom, stroking and selecting. As the hotelier picked black "smuts" from the ruffled faces of her creamy roses, Nora remembered how her mother had rewashed lines of bed sheets because of cinders from Hamilton's steel mills, and how her bitterness over a husband's infidelity had poisoned her life.

Impatiently drawing away from the shutters, Nora decided: *No, you will not control me.*

Her ivory boots were not in their usual place. In fact – she flung open both armoire doors – all her shoes were missing. She groped across the floor. All but one pair. Nora picked up the right, then the left. Their cleated heels gleamed in the light from the window. Patches of charring showed through their oxblood gloss.

In panic, she ransacked her room, peering under her bed, yanking out drawers, even opening hat boxes. Gritting her teeth, she slipped on the oxblood shoes, feeling repelled. They fit like Cinderella's.

Another slam – the noisy bracket ending Agnes's garden visit. Wrapping herself in a hooded black cloak, Nora was inspecting the garden for an early departure when she spied a man shadowed by bushes. He ignited a cigar, spurting a tendril of flame up its shaft. *Nicholas?* He swiveled. The half-brothers did look alike.

The Count lay down in the hammock, rocking languidly, with smoke rising. The grate of rope against the tree mimicked rusty bedsprings.

How conspicuous were Nicholas and I?

At last he disappeared inside. Nora was closing her shutters when she thought she heard the gate click. Again she checked. No phantoms skulked about the greenery.

It was 9:30. She tiptoed to the head of the stairs. No one occupied the desk. Dashing down and out, she skirted the stable yard, then swooped through the garden.

Beyond the gate she crouched behind a poplar screen to check that she hadn't been followed, then hugged the brow as instructed.

Once clear of the inn with its moat of poisoned emotions, Nora experienced a surge of blissful relief, thankful to be leaving tomorrow.

Below was a row of miners' houses clinging precariously to the hill – perhaps the Bootstrappers the Slaters were helping to climb up from The Bottoms. She noted their special signs of industry – a carefully mended white tablecloth hanging from a line, clumps of cutting flowers amidst the bean and tomato plants, a youth bent over his textbooks after a shift down the mine. She recalled, all of a sudden, that the Quarry monument had recorded only Great-grandmother Jane's death. Did that mean Great-grandfather Quarry might still be alive? Perhaps he was in one of these houses, reading *The Barrow Times* or drinking a pint before retiring. Tomorrow, when she was safely ensconced in John Slater's aunt's house, she would investigate.

Nora's pace slackened: who was this crazy woman, racing along a slippery path, with a murderer on the loose? She should be back at the inn right now packing.

So conflicted was Nora that she didn't notice the figure huddled behind a crumbling wall until it sprang. With feet astride and arms akimbo, Flame blocked her path, still wrapped in the gypsy shawl.

When Nora angled to pass, she shifted, too.

"You're in my way," complained Nora.

"I'm doing you a favor."

"Step aside, please."

Flame proudly tossed her coppery head. "You're a fool."

"Get out of my way."

The girl had entirely dropped her dialect. "I know whom you're meeting."

"You read my note."

"Of course, I did."

Again Nora tried to pass; again Flame shifted.

"You're jealous," accused Nora. "You used to be his lover."

"Oh, did I now? If so, I had the company of half the women in Barrow."

"Did Agnes Wolfe put you up to this?"

"Oh, gawd you're thick."

Flame advanced, forcing her into a mucky ditch. "Can't you see who your friends are?"

"After the hateful mess you made of those butterflies?"

Flame's voice snagged in her throat. "That was *her* doing – Mrs. Wolfe's."

Nora eyed Eleanora's locket around Flame's neck. "What a convenient liar! Get out of my way."

Flame cleared the path. "Bugger off then, arsehole!"

A full moon drenched the vale in a ghostly, incandescent light. To her left were the colliery and chemical works, overhung by smoldering clouds. Below was the train station, frosted like a gingerbread house with glittering sugar-panes. As Nora descended, St. Michael's bonged the hour . . . *eight* . . . *nine* . . . *ten.* She searched the station parking lot but did not see Nicholas's wine roadster. Again, she might have turned back, but for Flame's opposition perversely spurring her on.

Nora was mounting the station steps into the shadowy embrace of its gingerbread towers when a sinister possibility seized her. Had Nicholas really written the note? Was it coincidence that the Count had appeared in the garden as she was leaving, or had he been taunting her?

A hand gripped Nora's forearm. When she tried to scream, another clamped her mouth. Together they half-lifted, half-dragged her into a trap concealed in the brush, black-hooded like a cobra.

It wasn't until they were galloping through a forest of beeches, with their branches clasped in a gothic arch, that Nicholas relaxed his guard. "Are you sure you weren't followed?"

When Nora nodded curtly, he belatedly embraced her, taking time to soothe her. They seemed to be paralleling the Barrow River, through alders screening the abandoned mill, with the horse's hooves muffled in mud.

Nicholas halted the trap. Overhead loomed the limestone skull, awash in moonlight. Nora clutched his sleeve. "We can't stop here!"

"What's the matter, my darling?" Again he kissed her, this time more gently. "I know I've been neglecting you. All that will come later, but first . . . we *must* stop here. I need your help, your strength. Oh God, you're all that's kept me going." He slithered his warm hands up and down her arms, ironing out the shivers. "I've something important to show you, just as I promised. You must trust me."

Feeling fated, Nora allowed him to lift her from the trap and then to guide her toward the limestone crag. She watched, trance-like, as he yanked the stone tooth from the grinning skull, then retrieved his torch, gasoline and matches. Still split from her emotions, she observed as he soaked the torch, then replaced the gasoline and the rock, relieved to note that he was, indeed, dressed for dinner in frock coat, plum vest and striped pants.

He caressed Nora's hand. "Come, darling, be brave. . . . I know the identity of Eleanora's murderer, but I need your help. The evidence is unmistakable. Trust me."

Nora let him draw her into the skull's ear cavity. He ignited the torch, then poked it into the tunnel, flooding the passage with friendly light. "Remember . . . a steep grade, then a ladder. I'm right here with you."

The tunnel felt slimy, as if a prehistoric slug had just crawled through. While dodging one brackish rivulet, Nora caught another down her back.

Nicholas paused. Again, an encouraging smile. "Here's the drop off."

Clasping Nora's waist, he swung her down. Now they were in the twenty-foot dome where a couple of decades of miners had lain on their backs, plucking black diamonds from the rock. Nicholas shone his torch toward the low arch opposite. "That's our way." Though he all but pushed Nora through, his words were reassuring. "Just one step then you can stand."

Nora scarcely noticed the soaring blue-green cathedral dripping in stalagmites and stalactites. Nicholas pressed her cold palms against his chest. "Nothing bad will happen to you as long as you're with me. I promise." Though his voice had a hollow ring, she sensed that he was somehow telling her the truth.

He shone his light onto the archway, concealed amidst the encrustations of what he once identified as the witch's garden. "You'll have to tunnel a bit – maybe five yards."

The third cave. Unexplored territory. Again Nicholas urged Nora through first. This new space felt stuffy and claustrophobic. In the flare of torchlight, she saw that they occupied a small, irregular crypt scrawled with graffiti. Her companion stood between her and the exit, his cufflinks glowing like ruby eyes. Wedging his torch, he peeled off his black frock coat. Spreading it over a bench created by a cold sweep of limestone, he beckoned Nora to sit beside him.

"My poor darling, as pretty as a bride in your lovely white dress. You must wonder what all this is about. I'm sorry for your distress, but when you see the evidence, you'll understand that I couldn't work this out in any other way."

She sat down on his frock coat, as directed. "You know who killed Eleanora?"

"It's the person you guessed."

"Your brother!"

"This is the surest way to get him to show himself."

"He's coming here?" Nora gripped Nicholas's vest. "I don't understand."

He tried to kiss her, but she pushed him away.

"Eleanora's death was an accident." He stroked Nora's hair. "Her condition was too advanced for the medical procedure that was tried."

"An abortion?"

Nicholas continued to stroke Nora's hair. "My sister is a skilled midwife. She did her best."

Nora was incredulous. "Your brother? Your sister?"

"No." His voice was icy. "Just my sister and myself."

Nicholas slid his hands down Nora's neck till they rested on her watch pendant. "I'm truly sorry, my darling. I'm very fond of you, but you must take some responsibility, too." He lifted the pendant from her neck, then slid it into his pocket. "No one sees 'my brother' who doesn't secretly know him already. He's your invention, too."

As he encircled Nora's neck with his fingers, his words slowly began to sink in. With lips almost too dry for speech, she attempted to bargain. "You'll be found out. Flame knows. She warned me."

His fingers played with her neck cords. "Flame's my property, too, though she sometimes forgets it." His smile was broad, his eyes bleak, blank and very yellow. "You left me no choice, as Eleanora left me no choice." His face turned mournful. "A Wolfe kills only out of necessity."

Nora felt the tendons in her neck begin to contract. Beads of sweat rimmed Nicholas's forehead, then trickled down his cheeks.

With an explosion of fury, Nora yanked free. Scrambling farther into the cave, she climbed to a ledge. Her foot trod air. She tumbled.

Nora lies on stone, dazed and disoriented; her left ankle is throbbing, her oxblood shoe missing.

Nicholas crouches on the ledge above, eyes aglow in firelight. With an easy pounce, he lands by her side and once again encircles her throat with his hands.

Nora feels a stoppage of blood around his fingers and the bulging of her eyes. His eyes are protruding too, while his tongue lolls inside his mouth like a fish flopping in a boat. She knows he is mirroring her, beginning to enjoy her death, for she has become all women joined to him in an act of intimacy deeper than sex.

Something else. The more ecstatic Nicholas becomes, the more luminously his flesh glows and the more grotesquely his features alter. His body exudes a pungent smell – the whole cave reeks of it. Rolling on his haunches, Count Nicholas flings back his head and, with his voice penetrating ever deeper into the chasms of the cavern, he howls.

THE SPIRAL

14

Can't breathe, choking . . . cold, so cold. No point in struggling. So this is death, this floating and this falling. A cave of stalagmites and stalactites like jaws dripping blood . . . howling. Something in the cave . . . lurking, evil – a wolf gorging on a girl with bloated belly and vacant eyes.

Nora stares into its fanged face, rutted with lust, haloed in moonlight. Seizing the steering wheel, she smashes one cleated oxblood loafer onto the gas pedal, gouging through flesh. A full-throttled lurch of acceleration . . . metal crumpling like cellophane against iron spikes. Head shatters into glass – blood, its sweet, warm gushing smell. A long, shuddering silence – head aching, left foot throbbing. Sudden noise – sirens, so noisy! The swish of tires and sweep of misty headlights like tearful yellow eyes. Ambulance, people shouting . . . stretchers . . . the smell of antiseptic . . . calm, professional voices. David? Where's David? DA-VID!

Blinding white light . . . an angel in white? A hand . . . reaching out of the light . . . warm, holding mine. A woman in an electric halo, peering through wallpaper clouds. Mother? *My arm resting on a patchwork quilt. Fingers . . . feel them, feel with them. My face.* Feel it. That other face . . .

"Mother?" *Am I late for school?* "Is that you, Mother?" *Is there an exam today? David . . . where's David?* "Is David all right?"

"Yes. He's fine, Nora. Everyone's fine. We've just been worried about you, dear."

"Mother —"

"It's me, Nora."

. . . the angel with outspread wings.

"It's Aunt Millie."

Foreground separates from background. Familiar objects waver, then grow substantial . . . a toy trunk made from orange crates, a mirrored vanity. *No posters, no banners . . . no photographs of David?*

"Land sakes, but you gave us a scare!"

Nora is lying in her attic bedroom.

"You've had a nasty fall." Her "angel" smooths her starchy white apron. "The cab driver thought you were a goner. He could see you through the window of the door. He fetched me, and of course I called the doctor."

The calendar tied to her iron bed says July 2, with each preceding day crossed off since the accident. *Eleven days?*

Though Nora desperately wants to know all of this, she's still having trouble concentrating. Her mind is pregnant with strange sounds, smells, images . . . nothing that makes sense: *clattering hooves . . . a black trap with a single black horse . . . the moon oozing blood . . . a cave.*

Nora focuses on Aunt Millie's mouth to keep it from sliding over her face like a bar of pink soap. She watches the lips pucker and part, hears words.

"You'd eat. You'd sleep. You'd draw – all sorts of drawings. Your eyes would be open but you just weren't here."

. . . an old-fashioned bicycle . . . a red-fringed shawl . . . crushed butterflies . . . an overpowering scent of lavender.

"The doctor said it must be shock. He didn't want to move you if it could be avoided. He figured being with your own things might bring you back sooner."

. . . eight pine coffins . . . a tolling bell.

"I've been sleeping in your mum's room, just in case."

Nora patted her head, found no bandages. *Eleven days!* "Did I say anything?"

"Sometimes you'd talk a blue streak." Aunt Millie scratched through her unruly white hair with a knitting needle. "Your accent was so thick you could cut it with a knife – just like your grandma's. Sometimes – I don't mind telling you – it was a mite unnerving."

"What did I say?"

Sighing, Aunt Millie gestured toward the cage perched on Nora's toy trunk. "You'll have to ask Billy Boy. He and Flora used to chatter like that all the time."

At the sound of his name, the parrot opened his yellow eyes, tossed back his green head and howled: "OoooOOooooooOOOooo."

Sweat bled through Nora's scalp.

"Kind of weird, isn't it? That's something he picked up years ago when Mr. Baxter and I took him camping. Mr. Baxter thought it was real cute. So did your grandma, but it sure got my dander up." She stood. "We'd better toddle off and let you rest."

Nora clasped the older woman's hand. Tears spilled from her eyes.

"Now, now . . . I was glad to do it. All that nurse's training, and nowhere to use it anymore. Besides" – Aunt Millie dabbed her own eyes – "your mum would have done the same for me. Has done, many a time." She picked up Billy's cage. "When I had my gallbladder out, she was over every day with soup and flowers."

Aunt Millie paused by the light switch over the attic stairs. "By the way . . . the young Sullivan boy you were asking about? He did send you a postcard." She turned out the light. "It's in the drawer of your night table when you're feeling up to it."

Nora waited till the footsteps had receded down the stairs, then turned on a bedside lamp.

The postcard, displaying the skyline of Toronto, read: "Sitting at Pearson Airport thinking about you. Let's get together when both of us get back home. As ever, David."

❦

Dolly Dolby visited a few days later with a box of chocolates. "You look chipper – considering." She settled in a wicker chair hauled up from Grandma Flora's tearoom. "I'm not quite sure what I expected." She shucked the cellophane from the candy box. "I took a few prospects around while you were conked, but so far no nibbles."

Nora gingerly touched her head. Though she'd asked for this meeting, she was finding it hard to concentrate. "Did I mention lowering the house price before I went to black?"

Dolly passed the chocolates, then helped herself. "Nope."

"Just as well. I sublet my own house in London until Christmas." A strange light played about Dolly's head. Nora had noticed this same iridescence around Aunt Millie. "I've nowhere else to stay."

Dolly peeled the foil from her chocolate. "You know, it still gives me the willies thinking of you, lying conked out at the foot of that staircase, with the rest of us sure you were drinking tea with the Queen in England!"

Nora tried not to stare at the real-estate agent's head as Dolly reached for another chocolate.

"The thing is . . . don't stay here too long," advised Dolly.

Was she seeing auras, or was this just a trick of the light and scrambled neurons? "Is the real-estate market finally hotting up?"

"That's not what I meant." Dolly shifted uneasily. "I know this house has settled down. I can feel that." She popped her chocolate. "But then, it has what it wants."

Nora crushed hers in its foil wrap. "What?"

Dolly wiped her sticky hands on a Kleenex. "You!" She pushed away the box. "I should've brought perfume."

Nora spread her drawings, preserved by Aunt Millie in a shirt box, across her patchwork quilt: *a sooty-faced boy in choir surplice . . . a clock featuring a Grim Reaper with a scythe . . . an antique touring car . . . a roadster . . . a peaked and turreted railway station trimmed in iron licorice . . . a windowless black church like a lump of coal.*

Thanks to her extensive turn-of-the century research, Nora was able to date the Lanchester touring car and other arcane bric-a-brac at 1913. That implicated the ancestral suitcase. Question: *In the case of Nora Locke now before the courts, m'lord, can we trace her historical hysteria to years of immersion in early-twentieth-century literature, plus the psychic impact of this battered suitcase, Exhibit A, with its random assortment of personal mementos? Did the accident on the staircase stop her mind in time, causing it to recycle her last thoughts like an automatic washer stuck on 'SPIN'?*"

Nora dumped the contents of the suitcase onto her patchwork quilt: sepia portraits of ancestors in starched collars and stiff petticoats; a once-vibrant gypsy shawl; a cotton chemise, a pair of knickers and a hobble harness; a heart-shaped silver locket; a copy of *The Barrow Times* for June 23, 1913; a barely legible envelope, addressed to Mrs. F. Flowe, containing clippings about a mining accident.

She identified the choir boy as a victim of the mining disaster, which probably accounted for his sooty face. The old-fashioned railway station also seemed inspired by a news photo of the mayor of Barrow welcoming a dignitary, while the ungainly church had been copied from a building-fund pamphlet for Barrow's Reform Church.

Nora examined the Canadian Pacific Steamlines ticket, purchased at Thomas Cook & Sons on High Street in Barrow: Tuesday, July 8, 1913, *The Empress of Ireland*, Deck A, Suite 100. The pawn tickets were for a pair of ruby cufflinks, a man's ruby ring, a man's gold pocketwatch and a lady's gold-and-pearl watch pendant. Weren't these luxuries a little posh for a seventeen-year-old miner's widow with an infant daughter?

Nora repacked the old suitcase, essentially pleased with her findings. "*And so, m'lord, my client, in a state of shock following a neurological accident, has fixated upon and randomly reproduced items on her mind at the time of the mishap, reinforced by years of literary research. This is a condition known as cryptomnesia, meaning the conscious regurgitation of material unconsciously acquired, first as a child with possible access to the ancestral suitcase, then as an adult who had recently skimmed its contents, and thirdly through knowledge absorbed as an over-researched D.H. Lawrence scholar. I rest my case, confirming sanity."*

Nora had assumed that her obsession with the past would now cease; however, after a twenty-four-hour hiatus, she again began sketching – stray images like debris that drifts to the surface from a shipwrecked dream: *a candle chandelier . . . a mausoleum with Corinthian columns . . . a woman's hat swathed in veiling like a bee-keeper's helmet . . . an Empire-waisted gown with butterfly cape.*

Though unable to remember her dreams, Nora had the feeling that her sketches were the spillover of a nocturnal mind in foment; therefore, she took to setting her mother's alarm clock to jolt her from sleep in mid-plot. After writing copious notes, she would slide back into oblivion, then awaken to a blank page, informing her that she'd only dreamed that she had awakened, or that she'd only dreamed that she'd written or . . . *other?*

Nora's passion turned to portraiture . . . surreal faces so particular and quirky that she felt sure they were snapped by a camera hidden in her unconscious mind: *a beautiful girl with black wings hovering over a spike of purple flowers . . . a granite-faced woman wound in crosses and chains like the ghost of Marley . . . a centaur in boots and jodhpurs with two heads – one dark and curly, the other sleek . . . a bull-chested workman with cap and mustache, sitting on a boulder . . . an angular-faced woman – probably Grandma Flora – with a red hedgehog bizarrely balanced on her head.*

Several times during July, Nora dialed David's office, only to hang up before his phone could ring, feeling like an adolescent playing telephone games. Then, one day toward the end of the month, she noticed that the old suitcase's silver pendant, which she'd taken to wearing, possessed a hairline crack. Prying open its heart with fine wire, she found a few strands of blond hair and a photo of a boy with an infectious grin – *David?* Hardly, but very like – or did all clean-cut teenage boys look alike to a middle-aged woman?

Nora dialed David once again. After four rings, a recorded secretary informed her: "The office of David Sullivan will be closed until Labor Day. For questions pertaining to legal matters, please leave a detailed message at the sound of the tone, and someone will return your call as soon as possible."

Could lawyers afford a two-month holiday in today's competitive market? Curiously, Nora dialed David's home number. A taut female voice, which she only belatedly recognized as belonging to Alison, reported: "Mr. Sullivan is no longer living at this residence." The uninflected voice pitched one notch higher: "David . . . Mr. Sullivan . . . is traveling in Europe and cannot be reached."

Before Nora was obliged to identify herself, a loud click cut the connection, leaving her to wallow in a giddy mix of excitement, disappointment, fear, relief. The relief won out. She wasn't ready yet, and neither, most likely, was David.

Since Nora's friends assumed she was on sabbatical in England, no one phoned, and Nora discovered she preferred it that way. Encouraged by Aunt Millie and her doctor, she adopted a low-key, apparently normal lifestyle.

In truth, Nora had awakened from her spartan world of practical needs sensibly met into a multilayered, kaleidoscopic universe in which colors had smells, sounds had taste and even rainbows had texture. The squish of moss under a bare foot, or the shimmer of a perfectly executed spiderweb, could send shivers through her soul, while music – whether Mozart on a mouth organ or a robin's chirrup – made her heart weep.

Just as significantly: her migraines had entirely disappeared. With the relief she'd felt as a child when the dentist finally hung up his drill, she knew they would never return. Her head felt airy – massaged by gentle fingers of wind.

Before her accident on the stairs, Nora had been a desultory gardener – petunias in window boxes, clumps of impatiens, and a boy to mow the grass. Now she labored in her mother's backyard, attempting to achieve a particular look and even a special fragrance – a drift here and a tangle there, a clump here and a cling or a climb over there. As for the perfume, again it was a blend – a distinctive potpourri she carried maddeningly in her scent glands. Roses, of course, but what else? Lilies, honeysuckle . . . *lavender?* And what was that spicy fixative? After one misadventure, in which she pursued a promising aroma past a short-tempered Rottweiler on a long leash, she unexpectedly discovered the elusive smell in her mother's spice cupboard . . . *cloves!*

Toward the beginning of August, Nora became fixated on stringing a hammock between the apple and pear trees in her mother's backyard. However, her trips to various hardware and department stores failed to produce the right kind. Of hemp, of plastic, of sailcloth, of denim, of canvas, they lacked the allure of the one hanging in the back garden of her mind.

During a Saturday stroll along Hamilton's King Street, Nora spotted exactly the hammock she wanted in a shop specializing in stage props. Fringed, flowered and faded, it looked like prewar summers in Muskoka, to be accompanied by wicker furniture, tinny Victrolas and lemonade. Nora purchased it without bothering to ask the price, and next day it floated with the cabbage moths in her mother's garden.

Most evenings, at sunset, Nora rocked in her hammock, watching the western sky glow pink, catch fire, smoulder to charcoal, then die. One night she awoke after dark, swaying gently in her now-silver cradle, gazing up into the face of a lopsided moon. What had awakened her so abruptly? Certainly not the darting flight paths of fireflies like distant flying saucers. *Voices . . . quarreling voices. A whine and a growl, male and female, twisting, tangling, tightening into a juggernaut.*

"How . . . threaten me?"

". . . earned the right!"

"I warn you . . . nothing . . ."

"The gall of you! What must the neighbors think?"

. . . lying between starchy sheets, kicking her heels against the iron bedstead with the sound invading her pores.

Now her mother sobs while her father placates: ". . . see this through."

". . . your messes. How bad is it?"

". . . what you were in for . . ."

"Rot in hell!"

"Right beside you!"

Hands over her ears, Nora flees the house, down the yard, in her ruffled nightgown. She huddles on the swing that her father hung in the apple tree, twisting the rope into a corkscrew, along with her face between her braids, trying to keep from screaming.

A screen door slams, followed by the stamp of boots onto the stoop. Her father, slickered in moonlight, is puffing a cigar with smoke streaming out of his nose, his mouth, his ears, like an engine about to explode. He prowls the stoop, his body taut inside his Sunday suit – right, left, then back again – pausing only to strike the post of her mother's clothesline.

With a grunt, he stumbles down the steps, then staggers through the yard, trailing sparks like a black comet, his panting breath electrified by the hum of crickets, his shoes leaving graves in the dewy lawn.

Planting her bare feet in the same slippery grass, Nora pushes her rump against the swing seat, straining deeper into the shadow of the garage, holding her breath. She hears the grate of the gate as it opens, then the creak and click as it closes.

Her father swaggers across the alley. Halfway, he pauses, crouched, to gaze back over his shoulder, his Sunday hair slick with oil, his eyes glowing yellow, his phosphorescent face rutted by lust – the man in the moon, the wolf in the moon.

As Nora pumps higher in her swing, a light blazes in an upstairs window across the alley, then quickly extinguishes itself.

"Muriel Gant, a cheap Woolworth's girl . . . across that alley, right under my nose."

Nora stares at that window buttered in moonlight, imagining her father disrobing in the opposite way she watches him dress for church – first his black jacket, which he drapes over a chair back, then his stick-pin and matching ruby cufflinks that she chose for him last Christmas. Next comes his gray tie, his plum vest, white shirt and trousers, unbuttoning and folding as her mother insists, along with black socks and the shiny boots Nora polishes for quarters. She knows the rest from the clothes her mother hangs on the line – the white undershirt, the red-checked boxer shorts with elastic band and frontal slit . . .

Leaning back in her swing, Nora sails up into the rustling green-taffeta petticoats of the apple tree, with her own white gown billowing around her thighs, then higher still into the smoldering clouds from Hamilton's smokestacks, feeling the feral lick of moonlight on her lids, hearing the rhythmic groan of the rope against the limbs of her apple tree, smelling the stink of whiskey and cigars through the bouquet of Sunlight soap and shaving lotion that tastes like cloves. A flash of sheet lightning illuminates a nest of sleeping birds while the cindery clouds scud like a wolf pack across the moon, devouring its face.

The screen door slams – a thunderclap! Nora spies her mother hunched on the stoop in her good black dress. She peers down the yard, across the alley, with neck cords stretched like the high strings on a harp. After checking the neighbors both ways, she cowls her scarf around her head, then marches down the yard, elbows churning like eggbeaters. She makes it as far as the gate across the alley, opens it, closes it, opens, closes, then spins, rushing back in defeat to her own yard.

She is sobbing, thin chest heaving, only yards from Nora, still straining backward into the shadows with her legs as stiff as stilts and her hands pressed between her thighs, not even daring to strike the mosquitoes sucking blood from her exposed flesh.

Ellen Locke's spine straightens like the mast of a sloop that has weathered a nasty squall. She rewinds her scarf in a lanyard around her throat, secures her hair inside its net, and then, all shipshape, sails into her garden. She kneels in the grass before her creamy roses, glowing like silver cabbages and, unmindful of the wetness oozing up her skirt, removes the cinder smuts from their petals before making love to each radiant bloom, stroking and selecting.

"Next I heard the police had fished their bodies out of the Burlington canal. Of course, they were all liquored up. That was to be expected. Muriel Gant was pregnant, you know."

As August floated like a milkweed tuft toward September, Nora rocked mindlessly in her hammock with her drawings in drifts around her.

Sometimes Aunt Millie would join her. Hooking Billy Boy's cage in the pear tree, her elderly neighbor exclaimed: "My, but it's nice to see you taking up your art again. Your mum was always so sorry when you stopped. She blamed herself, you know, for making you draw things as they were supposed to look instead of how you imagined them."

Though Aunt Millie's conversation often seemed a part of nature like a buzzing bee, this line of talk snagged Nora's attention. "No tombstones with faces, or monsters in caves!"

"To tell the truth, I think some of your early drawings frightened her. They were too much like the nightmarish creations your grandmother painted just before she died . . . not the sort of images you'd think to be in anyone's head, let alone a child's."

Aunt Millie picked up the sketch Nora had just completed. "You certainly made a heap of those when you were ill that first time as well. Some were very good, as I recall."

"I don't remember that at all. What did I draw?"

"Some about the car accident with the Sullivan boy – that's to be expected – but many were like you're doing now." She held up Nora's sketch of strollers at a country fair. "I remember being struck by the fact that everyone was always in old-fashioned dress – at least, old-fashioned to you, though my mother wore hats like these and so did your grandmother."

Nora handed Aunt Millie a portrait of the angular-faced girl she thought to be her grandmother.

"Oh, that's Flora to the life!" Aunt Millie adjusted her drugstore bifocals. "Of course, you've drawn her much younger than when I knew her, and I don't remember that hat."

Nora laughed. "It's a hedgehog. I don't know why I stuck it on her head."

"But that's what Flora used to call Billy Boy – her little hedgehog."

"'edge'og," corrected Billy Boy. "'edge'og."

"Your grandma could turn her Derby accent on and off like a tap. She did it to tease him."

After assuring herself the tea was strong enough, Aunt Millie poured two cups and handed one to Nora. "My word, I always strain my tea, but today I clean forgot!" She tipped her cup so that a cluster of leaves appeared over the liquid. "I wonder what your grandma would make of that?"

Nora gazed into the cup. "Looks like a baby bootie, Aunt Millie."

"Well, I've made my share of those, the good Lord knows!" She dumped a bag of booties, which she knit by the dozen for church bazaars.

Nora poured her own tea back into the pot, leaving islands and isthmuses of leaves, then overturned her cup and spun it three times on its saucer. She pointed with her little finger to a tea-leaf constellation. "See? A skull and crossbones."

Aunt Millie shuddered. "There were two things Flora always said she'd never do – read her own fortune and go back overseas, not even to her father's deathbed. All she'd ever say was, 'The Devil set me packing and it's the Devil who'll be waiting for me on the other shore.'" Aunt Millie paired up her booties, decorated with lamb faces. "Your mother said you had the gift. You used to hang over our shoulders and point things out. . . . Not that that was the sort of thing she encouraged."

Aunt Millie discovered she had one pink bootie without a mate, and began to cast on pink stitches. "There certainly was a stack of those drawings from that first time. I wonder what became of them?"

"The bleedin' book!" hollered Billy Boy.

Aunt Millie admonished him with her knitting needle. "No swearing, Billy Boy."

Nora handed the older woman one of her sketches of the butterfly girl. "Do you recognize this person?"

Aunt Millie peered through her bifocals. "Why, she looks rather like you."

"You're joking!" Nora reclaimed the drawing. "I don't see that at all."

"People seldom do when it comes to their own faces. She's you with a bit of meat on your bones – what you might call the upholstered model."

Nora played with the heart necklace from the old suitcase. "But she's so beautiful!"

Aunt Millie smiled. "Ellen worked so hard to keep you from getting a swelled head that I think she overdid it. When she put you into those drab little shirtwaists with your hair so tight you could barely open your eyes, I sometimes had to bite my tongue to keep from giving her a piece of it. It's done my heart good to see you blossoming. If it took a fall on the noggin, then I'm all for it."

Nora sifted her fingers through her hair, enjoying its gloss and heft as it tumbled to her shoulders, hearing her mother chide – "*No woman over thirty should wear her hair below her ears*" – but no longer reacting.

"Now, that little cherry sundress you're wearing – it's so becoming."

"But mother made this for me."

"Really? It's more like Flora would have done. That woman surely had a passel of talents, and didn't she enjoy showing them off!"

Billy threw back his yellow beak: "OOOoooOOooOoooo . . ."

Again Aunt Millie admonished him. "This talk of Flora gets him excited." She picked up Nora's drawing of the stiff-necked woman wound in crosses and chains. "Many's the time I've seen your mum with an expression like that, though the features aren't the same. I like this softer one where the mouth's not so —"

"OOOooOOooOoOoooo . . ."

"Now stop that, Billy!"

"OoOOo —"

Aunt Millie jumped up, spilling her flock of lamb booties. "When he gets like this there's no stopping him." She yanked the cage from the tree. "Had me up half last night with his howling. Lucky I have my lambs to work on." She trod up the yard, indignantly swinging the cage, with Nora carrying her wooly flock. "It's a darn sight better than counting sheep, I suppose."

"The bleedin' book. OOOooOOooOoOoooo."

Billy Boy's howling still shivered through Nora's bones as she entered the living room to watch the late news. That damned bird had been a red-and-green fly on the wall for fifty-five years of her family's life in this house. He'd listened to her ravings through two illnesses with his pea-brain recording every third phrase – a snip-and-paste Watergate to be regurgitated in off-guard moments. She remembered the single point of discord between Aunt Millie's household and her own – the day Ginger proudly padded through the front door with Billy Boy hanging greenly from his jaws. If only cats lived seventy years instead of parrots!

Attempting to curl in the arm of her mother's plastic-coated chesterfield was like trying to knead a nest in rocks. Nora pressed the TV's remote control, watched the screen burst into color, then fade to black. About half the time it worked – just enough to keep her from calling a repairman. *Rats!* What did people do before TV? She reminded herself that she was a professor of Eng. Lang. and Lit. *Ahh, yes.* She poked through her mother's bookcase: a set of forties' encyclopedias, assorted inspirational books, biblical bestsellers like *The Robe*, several more shelves of Harlequin paperbacks and a dozen wallpaper-covered novels by the likes of Emily Loring and Gene Stratton-Porter, the Romance writers of yesteryear.

Nora slid her fingers over their wallpaper covers, reading the titles hand-printed on their spines. She stopped at *A Midlands Girlhood* by Sara Thomas-Key. Hadn't she read this one herself, perhaps the year she was ill?

She skimmed the first chapter – all about an embittered mother, a philandering father and a girl who escaped her blossoming sexuality by collecting butterflies. Not hard to understand its appeal to her adolescent self, despite Mrs. Thomas-Key's outdated prose, as overstuffed as a Victorian loveseat.

As Nora refiled the book, its wallpaper cover all but disintegrated in her hands. Tucked in its pockets she found four drawings. She spread them over the living-room floor – an old woodcut of a wolf howling at the moon, engraved WOLFE INN MOON; a limestone outcropping, resembling a skull; her butterfly girl with broken wings, cradling a bleeding lamb; her centaur with two heads – one a carnivore with snarling fangs and the other an idealized portrait of David.

At first light, Nora left home by way of the alley, pausing to pick two creamy roses flushed with dawn. She boarded a Delaware bus, then transferred uptown to the #8 York bus. At Dundurn Park she debarked, crossed York Boulevard, then entered Hamilton Cemetery by its central iron gate.

The pulpy floral mound had been removed from her mother's grave and the ground resodded – a seamless restoration like those Ellen Locke used to accomplish with broken china. Purchased years in advance of its need, her parents' joint tombstone consisted, ironically, of marble pillows, side by side, as if in a double bed. "His" half was inscribed "LOVE'S LABOR'S LOST" which, as a child, Nora had thought wonderfully romantic, even though she didn't know what it meant. She still didn't, in context, since her mother was not given to wry jests.

As Nora placed a rose on Harry Locke's pillow, she tried to snatch his identity from the jaws of her own sentimentality and her mother's bitterness. Like two equally matched bulldogs in a tug-of-war, they had clamped teeth on opposite sleeves of his memory, unwilling to give in or to let go. Now she tried to redraw his portrait in her heart and mind, shaded by the "secrets" she had recently allowed herself to remember, acknowledging that while her father was alive his sexuality and drunkenness had often dominated their house – dirty words scrawled on the walls, a musky scent drenching the air, a beast that pawed and paced and prowled until it could escape down the street or across the alley. His meteoric death, with its long vapor trail of shame and blame, had torn a crater in her memory, which she had hidden behind rainbow fantasies.

Nora laid her other rose on the facing pillow, remembering the equally blank notepaper – "THINGS TO DO IN THE EVENT OF MY DEMISE" – which her mother had left on her desk, wondering how Ellen Locke might have inscribed both. Kneeling with palms against the pillow, Nora meditated on the publicly cheerful woman who seldom missed church, who divided her time between worthy causes and a dusty bookkeeper's job, who coaxed prize roses out of stony ground and left a trail of Harlequin Romances like pebbles leading into a forest.

With her index finger, Nora printed "SAFE IN THE ARMS OF JESUS" across her mother's pillow. Yes. Unrequited yearning for the idealized bridegroom – the Savior of the New Testament, filtered through the Romance novels of Emily Loring, Gene Stratton-Porter and their heirs – had been the passion fueling her mother's life of duty. All the rest – the endless cooking of meals and bleaching of sheets – had been her way of serving time . . . a diligent Martha rushing through mundane chores so she, too, could slip across the alley and down the street to His house to attend His altar.

Nora remembered her father once bellowing: "Why don't you take your bed to church and stay there?" The cuckold husband had got it exactly right.

Nora also realized that her mother had done her best for her. The same eraser that had rubbed out Harry Locke's halo now eliminated Ellen Locke's thorns. She had protected her daughter against the thing she feared most – the appetites and passions of men – unfortunately, sometimes screening out the appetites and passions of life. While both Grandma Flora and Harry Locke had surged full speed ahead, Ellen Locke had seen fit to apply the brakes, creating a buffer zone between Nora and some perilous past that she still did not entirely understand.

Though Nora had run out of roses, she had one more stop in this place of busy memories. Starting at the center gate, she ran her fingers along the iron fence till she found a bend in the bars, still visible despite regular coats of black paint. Sitting crosslegged on the cemetery grass, in spandex shorts and "Save the Wolf" T-shirt, she laid her head into the dent and closed her eyes, willing herself back to . . . *June 28, 1970.*

The smells and sounds came first – *the lush, verdant scent of wet foliage in a balmy night, the steamy sweetness of warm asphalt, the swish of speeding tires and the rhythmic beat of a windshield wiper* . . . something else . . . *quarreling* . . . her parents' voices, a whine and a growl, permanently tearing and spitting inside her head, but not just those . . . *mine and David's.* Not just one quarrel, but many, like waves in a turbulent sea, with each breaking before the other has receded.

"If you loved me you would . . ."

"If you loved me you wouldn't . . ."

Cajoling, then badgering and bullying, with the threat of his summer's-end departure for university already added to the weigh-scale against her. After a father's death, she knew the despair of loss!

They turned onto York Boulevard, headed toward Snake Road . . . *the smell of liquor, laced with Old Spice – just like* HIM*! She hates the stink of whiskey and tobacco, and those slurred and shmarmy tongue-kisses.*

He lays his hand – five hot fingers – on her thigh, claiming territory, then grins over his shoulder, already tasting triumph, with lust eating like acid through the boyish smile, awash in moonlight: FREEZE-FRAME.

Nora seizes the wheel, slams her foot over his on the gas pedal, preferring – in that split-second of decision – anything to recognizing, in the carnal needs of her former sandbox companion, her father's "other" face.

"Next I heard the police had fished their bodies out of the Burlington canal. Of course, they were all liquored up. That was to be expected. That slut was pregnant, you know!"

Leaving the cemetery, Nora caught a homeward bus. As she covertly observed the other passengers inside their private bubbles, she realized that she'd seldom drawn a face "straight" or – as her mother complained – "the way it really looks." Always she had editorialized with butterfly wings or locks and chains, refusing to let anyone speak for him- or herself in case that person said a dangerous thing. She thought of David, his adolescent clamorings forever frozen in moonlight . . . *another face to be snatched from the jaws of saintliness and bestiality, to be humanized.*

Nora scooped up the mail as she entered her mother's house. By now, most of it was junk. She sorted through this batch: a notice from the Red Cross about their next blood drive; a letter congratulating her mother for having won a trial membership at Amazons' Gymnasium; a reminder from the Leading Light Foundation that her subscription had expired; a bill from Greenhouse Nurseries for reseeding, which Nora knew had been paid – *nice try, guys*; a letter for a Mr. Bob Goodwin on which Nora scrawled "Unknown." She was poised to do the same to the next when her heart began to thud.

Slitting the envelope, Nora read:

Dear Mrs. Flora Flowe,

I hope that your transatlantic voyage was a comfortable one and that you have arrived safely in your new country, your new city and your new home.

I am a Canadian teacher related to you through a branch of the family that moved to Exeter. Recently I arrived in Barrow only to find you had departed by train for Liverpool . . .

For weeks Nora had tried to convince herself that her memories of another time and place were fantasies, but unlike a dreamscape that fades, these had grown more vivid with each passing day.

Her thumb played with the stamp on the letter – King George v. Without the mutilations of age and squirrel droppings, the handwriting on the envelope looked terrifyingly familiar. The note was signed "Nora Locke." It contained newspaper clippings which, unfolded, read: "MINING DISASTER KILLS EIGHT."

Reaching for the phone, Nora dialed her travel agent.

15

Aunt Millie worried that Nora wasn't yet well enough for transatlantic travel, but Dolly Dolby had a buyer for the house and was relieved to see her go. "I'll drive you to the airport to make sure you get there."

However, the day before Nora's departure, Dolly's mother in Vancouver had a stroke, so Nora was once again alone in her natal home, awaiting a taxi to Pearson airport.

She did a last-minute check of her luggage: photos and mementos from the ancestral suitcase; a selection of her drawings; a travel flashlight to explore the area's limestone caves if she should have the opportunity; and her D.H. Lawrence manuscript.

It felt unbearably heavy. Nora leafed through it: *too many charts and graphs. Congratulations, Dr. Locke. You've turned a paper on one of Britain's sexiest writers into a treatise on coal-mining!*

The doorbell rang – her cab.

"Just the one bag?"

"Yes. This leather one."

The youthful driver in his McMaster University T-shirt reached for the handle. Nora seemed disinclined to release it. "It's a new one."

"Yes . . . expensive." He waited patiently.

Why couldn't she give up the damned bag? She rationalized: "It contains my research notes."

Even after handing over the case, Nora watched while the driver placed it in his trunk.

"Do you want me to wrap it in a blanket?"

"No, that won't be necessary." But she couldn't stop thinking about her suitcase.

"This is my second try for Manchester," she announced as the cab pulled away from the house.

The driver was trying to listen to a Blue Jays' game on a transistor played low in the front seat.

"Last time I tripped downstairs and landed on my head," she continued.

Resignedly, he switched off his radio. "Something like that happened to a customer of my dad's a month or so ago. She ended up with a concussion. I'm very nervous about head injuries."

"So am I . . . now. Mine sometimes still buzzes as if it were full of neural bees."

The driver swung right, onto Bay Street. "I saw a television show about a Dutch guy who fell from a ladder onto his head. After the accident, he claimed he could tell the future."

"You know, I think I saw that same show!"

"There was an American guy, too – real famous. My dad was talking about him just last night. Edgar – "

"Cayce."

"He had an accident – "

" – a baseball hit him." Nora laughed. "We must watch all the same schlock." She studied the licensing photo of the cab's owner – a dark, balding man with a Velcro mustache. "Or else I've met your dad."

"Yeah, it's his cab." The driver's head swiveled like the demonic child's in *The Exorcist.* "You don't tell the future, do you?"

"Not a chance." *Only the past.*

As the cab turned north onto Highway 403, Nora checked the time. "Damn!"

He slowed. "Forget something?"

"My watch, but it's okay." She rubbed her wrist. "I can buy another." But she couldn't stop chafing her wrist.

For the next thirty minutes Nora dozed while the driver split his attention between the traffic and the Blue Jays' game. As he glided into the terminal he inquired: "Do you want help with your bag?"

"No, thanks." She was most emphatic. "I'll look after this myself."

No delays, no problem with her ticket. As Nora fastened her seat belt, a gangly youth stowed his coat in the overhead bin. *Something about the way he shot his bony wrists from his sleeves.*

"Don't I know you from somewhere?" she blurted.

"I don't think so." He settled in the aisle seat. "The name's Hampton."

"Howie?"

"Gosh, maybe you *do* know me."

Nora made a joke of it. "Just a lucky guess. So many people with 'H' names choose first ones to match. Howard Hughes. Howard Hawkes. Hubert Humphrey."

"Hey, I've noticed that, too. Hugh Hefner. Hal Holbrook. Holly Hunter. Helen Hunt."

"Attention, please."

Howie listened transfixed to the flight attendant's instructions, then clutched his armrests and turtled his head into his collar. "I've taken a couple of pills. This is just my second plane flight. If I don't fall asleep before takeoff, I may get sick." Then he donned his ear-phones, closed his eyes, held his breath and passed out almost before the pilot raised the landing gear.

He slept till breakfast, then awakened like a man experiencing the resurrection. "Wow, look at those clouds." He scooped up a forkful of powdered egg. "This food is wonderful. Imagine eating breakfast in the sky. Isn't this whole adventure just amazing?"

As it transpired, Howie was employed by the Registry Office in Thunder Bay, where he processed death certificates. "Probably that doesn't sound too exciting but it got me interested in genealogical research."

"I knew I'd heard that name." Nora pulled a pamphlet from her purse. *How to Trace Your Family Tree* by Howard A. Hampton. "Is this you?"

"But that's uncanny! I only printed a few of those."

"I found it on a bus in Hamilton – at least I think I did."

Howie held the pamphlet as reverently as if it were a moon rock. "Peculiar things like this are always happening to me."

Nora thought of her identical suitcases. "Carl Jung called that synchronicity."

"You mean, there's a word for this?"

"According to Jung, the pile-up of coincidences means your unconscious is about to erupt into consciousness." Nora felt goose-bumps shiver up her arms: "Better watch out!"

Howie's buoyant spirit carried her all the way to the luggage carousel at Manchester airport. By now most passengers from her flight had sprinted away with their bags. One set of golf clubs had passed her a dozen times and no more cases were sliding down the chute. An invisible hand switched off the rolling carpet. An attendant began clearing the ramp for the next flight.

"Excuse me, but I think I've lost my bag."

He scrutinized Nora's ticket upside down and without shifting his eyes, then burst into a gap-toothed grin. "More bags. Another place." He pointed to a bench. "You sit. I fix."

Minutes passed. Nora was panicking all over again when the handler reappeared wheeling a shiny cart. On it he carried a single bag.

Her beautiful new suitcase!

THE CAVE

16

After the thrill of soaring fells, rippling hedgerows, verges gilded with goldenrod and towering upthrusts of limestone, Barrow's yellow-brick train station proved a letdown.

Nora approached its lone ticket-seller in his glass cage reading a tattoo catalogue. "What happened to the old Victorian building?"

He squinted at her from under bushy brows and a shaved head. "You've asked me that before, now 'aven't you, lady?" Flapping his tattooed arms as if to prove they concealed nothing, he responded: "I 'aven't got it, now 'ave I?"

Perplexed, Nora withdrew. *The natives are not friendly.*

No taxis awaited in the station's parking lot. After climbing a dusty hill, she turned right on Station Road between humdrum rows of red-brick shops, chockablock with polyester blouses and matronly shoes. As she was about to inquire for accommodations at a corner video store, she spotted a promising, red-brick inn down the side street. Though its single listing turret made it look like a schooner about to sink into a cobbled sea, a newly painted sign read "BED & BREAKFAST. THELMA BRIGHT."

As Nora approached, toting her heavy suitcase, she grew apprehensive. The place seemed like Rip Van Winkle caught in the middle of a century's sleep. She was withdrawing when an orange and white cat stretched its forelegs on the cobbles, then ambled through its red-pillared entrance. Nora followed.

She stood in a faded lobby with Victorian furniture poking out of foliage like temple ruins through jungle. No one was at the ebony desk. She peered up the worn burgundy staircase – no sound, no motion. Even the air felt empty. Again, she was retreating when she heard the brisk *tap tap* of heels across tiles. An elderly woman in blue-gingham house dress, with rows of white sausage curls, emerged from the shrubbery.

"Don't go, luv!" She took two more steps, then gaped at Nora through an incongruous pair of pink harlequin glasses suspended on knotted twine. "Sorry, luv. For a moment I thought you were somebody else."

Nora remembered the ticket-seller's rudeness and commented wryly: "If I'm being impersonated, I hope it's by someone who pays her bills." She deposited her suitcase. "What are your rates for a single?"

"Sixteen a night with bath and breakfast."

Nora stifled the nonsensical urge to ask, *shillings or pounds?* "I'll take it."

"Bless you!" Mrs. Bright pulled a ballpoint pen and a blue-lined scribbler labeled "REGISTER" from under the desk. "Number Two has our prettiest view. My, that bag looks heavy." Though probably in her eighties, she attempted to wrest it from Nora.

"No, please. I'll carry it."

Nora halted on the landing, feeling her left foot go numb. She stared up at a wagon-wheel chandelier set with candles and suspended on an iron chain.

"Just walk around it, luv," advised Mrs. Bright. "You've got to expect a place like this to have a little history."

Nora's room was more charming than she dared expect, given the tapestry jungle below: a brass four-poster with a patchwork quilt overhung with a coronation picture of Queen Elizabeth II; a cast-iron fireplace bracketed by chintz wing chairs; assorted Victorian lamps on tables with barley-sugar legs; a mahogany high-boy, armoire and vanity set against densely flowered wallpaper; a Queen Anne desk with needlepoint chair; a dark-stained floor scattered with rag rugs.

The orange cat lay curled in the center of the patchwork quilt.

"Shoo!" exclaimed Mrs. Bright, standing hands-on-hips as it scooted out the window. "I'll swear that thing's been here as long as I have – either that, or one just like it. Ma kept saying 'Cheerio' to the first one, hoping it would take the hint and sashay off, but it ended up thinking that was its name, and from then on never missed dinner."

The window looked out onto an old stable converted into a concession stand and a park with children's swings. Absurdly, Nora had anticipated something pastoral, like sheep.

"Shall we expect you for dinner then?"

"Probably not. I'll be wandering about the town and . . ." Her hostess seemed so disappointed, Nora promised: "Tomorrow though."

"Meals can be any time you want, and we eat dinner in the garden on sunny days." Mrs. Bright drew two keys from an apron pocket. "The small one's for the front door, the big one's yours. . . . Cheerio."

Nora unfastened her suitcase, intending to shake out a few clothes; however, she was distracted by a chattering magpie outside her bathroom window. He was quarreling with the orange cat, now perched on an old stone wall, teasing and being teased.

The bathroom fixtures looked like museum pieces. Though the toilet took a long time to clear its throat, it gushed up, then sucked down without mishap. Nora washed with lavender-scented soap, fluffed her shoulder-length hair, then headed downstairs.

Once again, she had the oddest feeling as she stepped under the chandelier – as if a piece of air were missing. Taking her hostess's advice, she swerved around it.

❦

According to the street signs, Thelma Bright's B & B was at the corner of Backwater Lane and Edge Road. A sharp dogleg right took Nora into Market Street, another cobbled passageway lined with red-brick shops. Though most were turn-of-the-century, their false fronts gave them the gaudy, nondescript appearance of stores in any modern town. A discreet sign on a steeply pitched, red-brick building advertised: "BARROW TOWN LIBRARY." Smelling maps, Nora entered.

The librarian seemed so familiar Nora caught herself staring. Then she realized her strawberry hair and Kewpie-doll features, scrunched in the center of a full face, reminded her of Dolly Dolby.

Glancing up, the woman smiled. "You look like you might be interested in our local-history section."

Taking Nora to an alcove, she pulled down a faded green book. "You may enjoy this one. *Barrow: Our Heritage, 1800–1913.*"

Without opening it, Nora exclaimed: "It's perfect."

"I'll make out a visitor's card."

Nora checked the author. "Is this the John Slater who was editor of *The Barrow Times*?"

The librarian beamed. "He was my great-grandfather." She printed her own name – "PAMELA SLATER" – across a bookmark. "If I can be of help."

"I'd love to find where my grandmother lived before she emigrated."

Pamela Slater handed her a pamphlet from a desk display. "Try the county office at Matlock, sixty miles up the road. They've got the Derbyshire census records back to 1840. What family name are you looking for?"

"Quarry."

The librarian's smile turned rueful. "Never ask a Slater about a Quarry."

"And Flowe."

The corners of her mouth dipped deeper. "Or a Flowe!" Picking up a book, she retreated into the stacks.

By good fortune, one of John Slater's 1913 photos was shot from the library steps, allowing Nora to view the street as it must have appeared the year Grandmother Flora emigrated. Though "Miss Jepson's Millinery" was now a stationery shop, "Thomas Ball & Sons" was still a chemist's, "Alcott the Wheelwright" had become a hardware store, "Wilson's Dry Goods" was a variety shop with a Vietnamese proprietor, and the handsome "Picture Palace" now advertised Monday-night bingo and meetings of the Barrow Friendly Society.

As she strolled the cobbled street, Nora imagined a jumble of bicycles and dog-carts and pony-traps and antique cars. She could almost hear clomping hooves and jingling harnesses and tooting horns and the cries of hawkers: "Thread an' twine, thick an' fine!" She could see shop windows displaying lace-up boots and derbies and saddles and kerosene lamps. And the smells, *ahh, the smells* – fresh-cut sandalwood and beeswax and vinegar and leather and peppermints. Sometimes it seemed she need only twist her head to catch the flutter of a long skirt, the strut of a frock coat, the sheen of a high hat.

Nora rounded a corner, then halted, feeling dizzy: a woman in old-fashioned, ankle-length traveling suit, with red hair tucked under a straw boater, waved to her with a copy of *The Barrow Times*.

Collapsing against a gas lamp, Nora realized she was staring at a life-size cutout, bearing a banner that urged: "Come with me to Barrow's Full Moon Festival, August 27–29. Celebrate eighty years of history!"

Turning her back on the lady, Nora reoriented herself with John Slater's map. She was in Market Place, now a conclave of boutiques, with several also advertising the upcoming festival. "Jenny's Lingerie" featured knickers, starched crinolines, hand-embroidered camisoles and a hobble-skirt leg-harness. "Millie's Millinery" displayed a jade turban with an ostrich plume, a tulle wedding cake topped with nesting bluebirds, a motoring bonnet swathed with veiling like a beekeeper's helmet.

Zigzagging across the square into Market Park, Nora was strangely relieved to see two children in denim playing with a plastic submarine and a teenager skateboarding. She emerged onto High Street, lined with banks, brokerage firms and insurance companies, still with their Georgian dignity intact. Where Slater's map had situated a pawn shop, she found an antique store called "Déjà Vu." In a musty purple-velvet box, between an old bugle and a soiled ostrich fan, Nora spotted a gold pendant watch encircled in seed pearls.

I must have that.

The proprietor was a puffy-faced, heavy-lidded man whose toupé had twisted like a teacosy on his bald pate. He sprang to life at the sight of Nora's too-eager face as she pointed out the watch.

"My, but you have an eye!" Fishing it out with a hook, he burnished it on his worsted sleeve. "This is the finest piece in the shop."

Liar, liar, pants on fire. "How much?"

"That beautiful little watch, Madame?" He ironed its dirty velvet backing with thick, spatulate fingers. "This exquisite gem is £150."

"Out of the question."

"It's very old." Turning it over, he revealed the delicate engraving of a butterfly. "It belonged to the original shopkeeper. It's one of a kind."

Nora picked up the watch. She could not put it down.

"For you, Madame, I'll throw in this lovely box." Prying the watch from Nora's hand, he slipped it back into its tatty purple coffin. "Though money is something we can't hold on to, using it to purchase a piece of eternity makes up the loss."

Leaving the shop, Nora trashed the moldy box in the nearest dust bin. The watch's hands were folded at twelve o'clock like the wings of a black butterfly. It wasn't even ticking! As she wound and reset it, the clock on *The Barrow Times* building across the street began to bong. Nora looked up at its Grim Reaper, striking a bell with his scythe, and was startled to recognize one of her drawings, precise in every detail.

Had she seen other photos of Barrow besides those still in the ancestral suitcase? *Other photos, yes!* A simple explanation and a plausible one. A spilled cup of coffee, a piece of toast jam-side down, squirrels gnawing in the eaves, and yet another precious souvenir is lost to posterity.

More photos in the suitcase. Why hadn't she thought of that before? How treacherous the human desire for Mystery!

Yet Nora did not experience the relief she expected. From the moment she'd debarked in Barrow, apprehension had undermined her sightseeing pleasures – a fated sense that nothing had been random. At the station, this uneasiness had nipped like a stray mutt at her heels; it had tracked her to Thelma Bright's B & B, then pestered her inside the library. It caught her scent again on Market Street, tore at her hem while she stared at the poster woman, then howled as she fondled the oval watch in "Déjà Vu." She was not given to impulse purchases, and she wasn't fond of jewelry. She didn't understand what had happened to her then, or what was happening now as she gazed at the Times building's revolving door, fighting a shrieking urge to push through it.

I must see John Slater.

Surely he was dead by now! Her feet refused a direct command: *not* back, only forward.

People were forking around her as she stood rooted to the sidewalk, terrified to the point of fainting . . . terrified to pass through the brass door of the Times building to its bird-cage elevator as she now so vividly pictured it . . . terrified to confirm the geometric, blue-and-white pattern of the third-floor tiling, or the portrait of *Times* founder Henry Slater, with signet finger across his vest.

Determinedly, Nora shifted her focus to the *Times* bulletin board.

Under "TODAY'S NEWS," she read: "SUMMIT LEADERS LUKEWARM TO BOSNIA PLAN." "JAPAN PRESSES TO REDUCE G7 AID TO RUSSIA." "MATES TELLS MAJOR: BACK ME OR SACK ME." "U.S. MOURNS NIXON'S LOYAL FIRST LADY."

Her eye caught the name of the publisher: *Daniel Slater*. Wasn't that the reporter who wrote the 1913 mine-explosion story? He must be over ninety for sure!

While Nora calculated, her feet drew her through the revolving door into the Times lobby, vaulted like a cathedral.

What would a man in his nineties be doing in a newspaper office? By now the title of "publisher" must be honorary. Even if she found him propped up with canes and pinstripes, what could he tell her about a collier's daughter who emigrated in 1913?

She remembered the librarian's odd response to her grandmother's name. *I have to warn him . . . a murder . . . someone is going to be murdered . . . warn him . . .*

The elevator, *like a brass bird cage*, stood open and empty. With her feet still leading, Nora entered, slammed the door, spun the wheel. She emerged onto the third-floor hall, *with its blue-and-white geometric tiling*, then paused at the toe of founder Henry Slater, *with his signet finger laid across his vest.*

Beside him, in an identical gilt frame, stood another frock-coated gent whom Nora identified as John Slater even before consulting the brass plaque. As she gazed up into his stern but quizzical face, his painted brows seemed to converge over his nose while the mole punctuating his mouth twitched in exclamation: "*Miss Locke, you must curb this desire for drama.*"

Breaking away, Nora sailed through a paneled double-door, passed a woman at a switchboard, then through another paneled door into another antechamber. She yanked on a third brass knob, all but colliding with an elderly secretary.

"What are you doing in here?" demanded the tiny woman, prancing like a scrappy Chihuahua.

"Daniel Slater?"

"You must leave at once!"

Nora tried to explain, to herself as well as to the secretary. "I must see him . . . warn him."

"You have no right to be here."

". . . a murder . . . warn him."

The elderly woman advanced with fists raised like little brown walnuts. "Mr. Daniel Slater died half an hour ago, and I can assure you, Miss Whomever-you-are, that it wasn't murder. The old gentleman was ninety-six. He'd been doing poorly for – " She condensed into an even denser ball of fury. "If you're one of those blinkin' reporters come to dig up all those nasty lies – "

The certainty propelling Nora dissolved. "I'm sorry . . . I'm really very sorry." Stepping back, she pivoted, then bolted – through three doors, down two flights of stairs, almost knocking over a blue-uniformed teenager in pursuit of his elevator.

She continued along High Street at top speed. Ahead she could see the Norman tower of St. Michael's *just as she had drawn it*, even to its gate featuring Crusaders' shields.

Nora retreated to Market Park. Claiming a sunny bench, she stared unabashedly at the clerks and secretaries on their coffee break, delighting in the modern tackiness of their clothes – the wash-'n'-wear shirts and thigh-high skirts, the jellybean shoes and fluorescent sunglasses. She congratulated the taste of the mother who had outfitted her children in the latest Disneywear, and admired the crash helmets, spandex tights, assorted limb guards and high-tech maneuvers of Barrow's rollerbladers.

Gripping John Slater's history in her hands to steady them, Nora studied his maps in search of the mining district.

The Bottoms was still accessed from the southern tip of Edge Road; however, where Slater's cartographer had drawn a crude path, Nora found flagstone steps decorated by butter churns planted with marigolds. Black Pit Square had become Olde Black Pit Square, featuring a turn-of-the-century blacksmith shop with a forge that gleamed like the family silver. An apple-cheeked chimney sweep posed under a gas lamp. Souvenir shops displayed miners' picks made in Taiwan, and a gum-chewing teenager hawked £5 tickets to Black Pit No. 8 Colliery, a "genuine reproduction" visible as a wooden finger protruding through a golf-green sward.

Where were the heaps of raw sewage and the outdoor privies? Where were the chicken coops and pigsties? Why did she smell caramel corn and sausages instead of soot and excrement? Nora chided herself for reverse snobbery: sanitized reconstruction was the way of the world. Olde Black Pit Square was to its historical counterpart what Madame Tussaud's effigies of Churchill and Princess Di were to theirs. Did she really want to look down and see her Roots sandals sinking in sheep dip?

Though Nora searched for the Reform Church, marked by an X on John Slater's map, the unnamed jumble of cul-de-sacs proved too difficult to negotiate. She did, however, find The Bottoms school – not the depressing brick box that she had expected, but a charming Georgian building that would have looked at home on High Street. It was called the Pamela Birchwood Primary School and its cornerstone read:

DEDICATED ON THE EIGHTH DAY OF SEPTEMBER, 1919
by JOHN & PAMELA SLATER
So That Eyes May See
Ears May Hear
Tongues May Speak
Minds May Know
Hearts May Love
And Souls May Sing.

Claiming one of the playground swings, Nora pumped herself up into the cloudless blue sky. "*When I first moved to Barrow, oh, the difference I was going to make. I would tutor a few promising girls from The Bottoms, and they would tutor other Bottoms children. Of course, I was naive then, and filled with my mission.*"

Nora's expensive watch now proclaimed seven o'clock. Returning to Olde Black Pit Square, she settled on the Leg o' Mutton pub for dinner. Like the rest of Ye Olde Bottoms, it featured genuine fakery – stick-'em-on Tudor timbers, spittoons blooming with chrysanthemums, seats made from beer barrels, and sturdy dust-capped waitresses who balanced twin trays like barbells. She ordered fish and chips from a menu that began with *pasta e fungi* and ended with Häagen-Dazs.

A ditty ran through her head:

Old Mrs. Fitch fell into a ditch
With her heels cocked up in the air.
The donkey took fright to see such a sight,
On the way to the Barrow Fair.
Hey, diddle, diddle, the man with the fiddle
Caught hiccups while riding his mare.
He took off his hat, and coughed up the cat,
On the way to the Barrow Fair.

Nora tapped the catchy rhythm on the table, wondering where it had come from. Perhaps it was recorded in the dints and cracks of the walls, like notes punctured in the rolls of a player piano. Perhaps —

Nora cuffed her ears. *Admit it!* She'd been hearing voices ever since she arrived in Barrow. She had a skull full of them, like a regular bloody Joan of Arc! Half the time she even knew what people would say before they opened their mouths – an echo preceding the sound. Nothing erudite or even particularly useful, more like –

If you knew Nellie,
Like I knew Nellie,
Sang the little bird
On Nellie's hat.

A hand touched Nora's arm. "Are we really so bad, then, luv?" A young man in braces and striped shirt was grinning at her – a member of the Leg o' Mutton's barbershop quartet.

Removing her hands from her ears, Nora laughed in relief. "I must have jetty lag . . . I mean jet lag."

Outside she hailed a cab. Fifteen minutes later she entered her room at Thelma Bright's B & B to find her lamp lit, her bed turned and her nightgown garnished with a sprig of dried lavender. Nora's eyes flew to her suitcase – open and empty.

Like a person possessed, she dashed from bureau to armoire to vanity, dumping their contents and examining buttons, collars, zippers, seams. She threw an armload of underwear into the air, baffled by what had come over her. Did she think Thelma Bright had stolen one of her pleats?

Nora collapsed, exhausted, on the bed. After throwing her navy pantsuit onto the pile, she stashed her passport under her pillow, then slept like a stone.

17

Nora awoke to a beautiful day and complete disarray. Clothes were spewed across her floor from dressers with their mouths hanging open. Hastily tidying, she put on her cherry-print sundress, then went down to breakfast, stepping around the chandelier the way some people avoid ladders.

Though Nora had requested breakfast at eight, the dining room was locked. As she stood on tiptoe, peering through smoked glass, she heard Thelma Bright's sprightly tread on the stairs behind her.

"I thought I saw you come down here, luv. We've never used this cellar room. Ma thought it far too showy." Mrs. Bright ushered her up to a homey parlor set with four gate-leg tables and bordered with a plate rail.

Nora paused on the threshold . . . *shelves of books, a faded blue-velvet settee.* "Didn't this used to be a library?"

Mrs. Bright peered around her in surprise. "Why, I guess it did, but that's going back a long way, luv." She served Nora a glass of orange juice. "May I ask how you knew?"

Nora rubbed her forehead. "Just a hunch."

"You must have inherited the Celtic strain. When I was a tyke, people in these parts were always having premonitions and no one thought anything about it. Now if you talk like that too much, folks think you're daft." She lifted the corners of her apron like a curtsying child. "I hope you didn't mind my unpacking your suitcase. I knew you'd be ever so tired. Our up-and-down streets take it out of a body."

Guiltily, Nora reassured her hostess. "Thanks. I *was* tired after tramping through The Bottoms."

Mrs. Bright exchanged her empty juice glass for coffee. "Some say The Bottoms is the tops these days. Ever so posh!"

When her hostess retired to the kitchen, Nora checked the contents of her shoulder bag: her money and passport (retrieved from under her pillow), a Derbyshire map, a Matlock bus schedule and an envelope of sketches. She was brooding over her drawing of the Wolfe Inn Moon sign when Mrs. Bright served a plate of eggs, bangers, fried mushrooms and tomatoes. Nora showed her the sketch.

"Have you ever seen anything like this?"

Thelma Bright donned her startling pink, harlequin glasses. "Can't say as I have. It's not in Barrow. People around these parts are mighty proud of their signs and that looks like an old one. . . . Wolfe, let me see. There's a Mr. Woolfley two streets over. Other than that the only wolves I ever knew were the kind that ate sheep. We used to have a saying, 'When wolves howl, pregnant virgins die.' Something like that." She returned Nora's sketch. "Sorry I can't help you, luv. Ma was the one for knowing and remembering. She'd be here with me one minute buttering toast, then back fifty years making Pa his pit lunch as if time were a revolving door and she were spinning through it. Got so I didn't know whether *I* was coming or going!"

Nora laughed in sympathy. "I've felt that way sometimes myself."

"Me, I'm more for the living, and doesn't it keep me running with our Friendly Society and what-have-you!"

❦

Since the bus to Matlock didn't leave until noon, Nora crossed the inn's old stable yard to where she guessed she might find a path down to The Flats. On her left was the yellow-brick railway station with its sunstruck tracks; on her right, a bog of reeds and bulrushes. Nora forked right, through a tangle of lyme and sedge, still blanketed in morning haze, trying to ignore the swish of cars on the M1, the oil scum on stagnant waters, the occasional slimy boot.

She touched a waxy green chrysalis hidden among the milkweed pods, hearing a lilting voice in her ear: "*What I really come fer are th' butterflies.*"

As Nora picked a few sprigs of lavender, she remembered the summer she and David had spent hunting caterpillars – fat green roly-polies, brown fuzzies, striped and tufted clowns – trying to reconcile that joyful innocence with their later estrangement. Given their mutual hangover of guilt, small wonder both had tried a little harder to avoid each other than to connect.

The same sweet voice whispered in her ear: "*Come . . .*"

Nora stepped into a misty ditch, scraggly with scrub, then bowed a branch and let it explode in a coppery cloud of moths.

"Oh, I'm beggin' yer, mum, please. I'm in ever so much trouble."

Nora tramped toward The Bottoms along a winding bog path. Despite a clear sky, oppression threatened her, aided by fog that slithered up from gullies to snake around her ankles.

"They say th' body were 'orribly mutilated."

"Et by wolves?"

"Or else we 'ave a Ripper on our 'ands!"

"Beware o' th' man oozin' charm 'oos wife looks as old as 'is mither."

From The Flats she identified the sooty tower of the Reform Church, and trekked toward it.

"We come to bury the body of our daughter and to commit her soul to the judgment of the Almighty. All too soon, by our earthly reckoning, has she passed from us, but in fit and proper time according to His Divine Will. . . . An eye for an eye and a tooth for a tooth."

Veering from the building, Nora forked into the cemetery.

Minutes later, she found herself standing before a boulder inscribed "QUARRY." She remembered her sketch of the bowlegged workman, with cap and mustache, sitting on a rock like this, as she curiously circled it.

Carved on its back were the names and dates of nine dead relatives. The latest was:

JEREMIAH QUARRY
1870–1943
"Bitter Is the Struggle"

Was this Great-grandfather Quarry, whose deathbed Grandma Flora had refused to visit?

"Th' Devil sent me packin', and 'tis th' Devil who'll be waitin' fer me on t'other shore."

Closer to the church, Nora located a plot of Flowes marked by an ebony crucifix and isolated from lesser graves by a wrought-iron border. According to the headstones, the latest burial was 1901. Where was the grave of Grandfather Flowe, killed down a mine in 1913? This did not look like a family of colliers.

Though Nora was anxious to catch her Matlock bus, she found herself marching through the cemetery toward its back gate. Behind a yew screen she discovered a stony field with a single grave marked by a graceful lamb on a marble plinth.

ELEANORA
June 6, 1898–June 28, 1913
"A Moth to Flame"
D.S.

Those dates electrified her – her birthday and the date of her accident! Eleanora, too, was fifteen. Even that name – *Ellen-Nora* – had resonance for her. What could possibly be the meaning of these coincidences, reverberating through time?

Kneeling, Nora laid her hands on Eleanora's lamb, feeling its heart beat, sensing a connection to her beautiful butterfly girl. She scattered her wild lavender as tears gushed down her cheeks from some subterranean spring.

"D.S." . . . *Daniel Slater?* "A Moth to Flame" suggested tragedy.

Nora's gaze shifted back to the provocative dates on Eleanora's gravestone. *Why did I assume the burden of this unknown girl's life?*

It was almost twelve. As Nora hurried toward the gate, her shoe struck a metal extrusion, pitching her into some briar roses. Picking her way through thorns, she found a bronze plaque, icy to the touch:

A.F.
1867–1913

Why were these two people banished from the cemetery? What, if anything, connected them?

Nora had to sprint to catch her bus. She was still struggling to control her breath and collect her thoughts as the little red Trent vehicle chugged up Barrow Hill. By the time it reached the crown, the driver was staring at her, as if awaiting an answer.

Assuming she was hard-of-hearing, he shouted again: "That's for our Full Moon Festival." He pointed to workmen erecting a midway on a cricket field which, according to John Slater's map, had once been a Common.

"I saw a couple of posters downtown."

"The wife's been bakin' all week." He raised his voice another notch. "This year they've got the bungee-jumping."

From the lovely Derwent River to its limestone bluffs and hilltop ruin, the town of Matlock was as picturesque as Barrow struggled to be. After climbing a vertical grid of streets more challenging than Barrow Hill, Nora arrived panting and perspiring at the county records office. Fortunately, a microfiche machine became available through a cancellation, and soon she was scrolling through Barrow census records from 1840 to 1890: who lived in every house on every street; the relationship of each tenant to the head of the house, along with his or her age, occupation, place of birth.

Through her door-to-door search of The Bottoms in 1890, Nora located her great-grandparents, Jane and Jeremiah Quarry, married but still without children. She traced the family back through four other censuses and three residences, all numberless homes on nameless streets in The Bottoms. The men were miners or laborers; the women, seamstresses, lace-makers, stocking-makers or domestics.

She found no Flowes and no Wolfe Inn Moon, either in The Bottoms or up the hill – at least not before 1890, which was Britain's latest census to be made public. However, in *The Directory of Derbyshire Businesses, 1910*, she stumbled upon a listing for the Full Moon Inn at 42 Edge Road. Thelma Bright's B & B was No. 1, suggesting this other hotel was located at the opposite end, where the street dipped toward The Bottoms.

Nora caught the 4:00 bus back to Barrow and, by 5:30, was striding along Edge Road with John Slater's map in her fist. She found a brick bungalow at No. 41, but only scrub and a drop-off where No. 42 should have been.

A man with a potato face mounted on parsnip shoulders was hoeing his vegetable patch. Nora called to him over his hawthorn hedge: "Excuse me, but was there ever a hotel next to your house?"

Shoving his cap back from his craggy face, he stared at the scrub-lot as if deciding for the first time. "Canna say as 'twas."

"Back in 1913?"

He tugged his cap down his brow. "Canna say I ever 'eard tell o' one." Dropping his hoe, he ambled over to the hedge, hooked his thumbs under his braces and leaned into the conversation. "Tha' twere me great-granddaddy's wood lot till th' First War, when they cut down th' trees fer to timber th' trenches."

Nora showed him the Wolfe Inn Moon sign. "Have you ever seen anything like this?"

He unhooked his thumbs, then leaned back. "Canna say as I 'ave." He scratched his thick chest then cleaned his ear with an index finger. "Only 'otel on this 'ere street is 'tother end."

"Thelma Bright's Bed & Breakfast?"

"Used to be a proper 'otel till they 'ad their troubles. Locals still don't like it much." Again, he repeated his gestures in reverse: cleaned his ear, then scratched his chest, hooked his thumbs into his braces and leaned back. He eyed her notebook and pen. "You aren't one of those TV people, are you?"

"I'm an academic researcher. For a university."

"Me great-granddaddy was th' constable." He waited expectantly for Nora to write that down. When she didn't, he continued more emphatically: "Th' mister run off with 'is maid."

"You mean the owner of the hotel?"

"When 'e niver come back 'is missus locked 'erself inside, then 'anged 'erself. Ragley was the name."

"Of the innkeeper?"

"Me great-granddaddy, the constable. 'e cut 'er down – "

" – from the chandelier!" Nora felt a visceral chill.

"Well, now, s'possin' 'twere."

"Was 'Wolfe' the name of the hotel owners?"

"Canna say if 'twas or 'twasn't. The family died out afore I was born." When Nora still didn't write anything down, he tipped his cap. "Well, this won't 'elp me cabbages to grow, now will it, ducks?"

Thelma Bright's backyard caught Nora by surprise. Here was the glorious, giddy English garden-of-the-imagination she'd spent a couple of months at home trying to create. Flowers climbed, clumped, crept and clung – lupines and delphiniums, daisies and cornflowers, roses and peonies – all wind-tossed with a generous helping of summer greens, like a fragrant salad served up in an old stone bowl.

With the tantalizing scent filling her nostrils, Nora strolled around a yew hedge. Stretched between an apple tree and a pear was an elderly chintz hammock like the one she'd discovered at the shop on King Street. She lay down, wrapped its fringe around her, folded her hands across her chest, and began to rock, overcome by such intense erotic urges that she feared her body would dissolve into the fabric.

"I see you've found our little rock-a-bye."

Nora jerked upright, hand to throat.

Thelma Bright stood awkwardly, in frilly apron and oven mitts, with a steaming plate of roast beef, Yorkshire pudding, boiled cabbage and beets. "Sorry, I saw you come back here and thought you were at table."

Nora guiltily scrambled out of the hammock. "I guess I dozed off."

She followed her hostess to a nook entwined with roses where a table had been set for one. Cheerio the cat perched on the single chair, wearing its white bib as if awaiting service.

"Blamed cat!" Mrs. Bright shooed it with a napkin, which she then unfurled on Nora's lap. "You'd think it owned the place," she groused. "I've tried not to overcook the meat, luv. I know how you young folk like it with the juice still running. My generation . . . we were trained to dry everything out like shoe leather. Mind, don't burn yourself."

Though Nora was anxious to question her hostess, she waited until the first course was cleared before inquiring: "Would you care to join me for dessert, Mrs. Bright?"

The elderly woman flushed with pleasure. "Well, now, I guess I jolly well would if you've a mind for it." Again, she lifted the corners of her skirt like a curtsying child. "Of course, you'll have to call me 'Thelma.'" She transferred two generous pieces of apple pie from a hot plate. "I've never had a Canadian guest before. We're too far north, too far inland and not pretty enough for the main run of tourists. More's the pity that they don't come and see for themselves, like you've done."

Nora accepted a cup of tea. "How long have you had this hotel, Mrs. . . . Thelma?"

"Not till partway into the First War. Ma had the idea of putting up the soldiers and their families, who were running around the country. By then, you see, this place had stood empty for over a year, so we got a good price. Pa had already got the T.B. from the coal dust in his throat, and our little Tommy had got killed down the mines so that —"

Nora dropped her fork. "The explosion of 1913!"

Mrs. Bright gaped. "Fancy your knowing a thing like that. Eight dead, and my little brother lying among them." She forced a smile. "Those Black Pit tours down into the mines are real informative, aren't they?"

Nora studied her hostess's freckled face encircled in white curls, lightly spun with copper . . . *a child standing on tiptoe to kiss her brother's cheek.* "Thelma Ross."

Mrs. Bright shyly touched her flushed face. "It's been ever so long since I've heard that name."

Reaching for her shoulder bag, Nora withdrew her sketch of a sooty-cheeked boy in choir surplice. "I saw his photo in an old paper."

Mrs. Bright's hazel eyes pouched with tears as she tried to brush the paper thatch from her brother's eyes. "You know, I can see the tyke even now, though of course I wasn't any bigger than a flea myself." With her little finger she gently tried to clean her brother's cheek. "And wasn't he a sight when he came home with his empty lunch pail! You know, they only got twenty minutes to eat, and that underground."

"Would you like this drawing, Thelma?"

"I surely would. Many a year ago a friend drew one like that for me. I still have it tucked away." She wiped her eyes on a Kleenex from her apron pocket. "That'll be enough of that! If you don't mind me asking, did you happen to find those innkeepers you were looking for . . . the Wolfe people?"

Nora's fingers tightened around her envelope of drawings. "Have you heard of Forty-two Edge Road?"

Mrs. Bright's eyes strayed to the portrait of her brother as she picked up her teacup "Why, there isn't any. Only to Forty-one – the Ragley place."

"I found the Quarrys in The Bottoms, even saw the family grave plot, but when it comes to —"

"Oh, my stars!" Thelma Bright put down her cup, but missed the saucer. "You're a Quarry."

Nora caught the cup as it was overturning. "Flora was my grandmother."

"Oh, my stars! After all these years." Mrs. Bright pressed both hands to her chest. "Just let me catch my breath . . . so many shocks all at once. I had that funny feeling when I saw you that day in the lobby. Remember how I gawked as if you were a ghost? Just goes to show – trust your first instincts." She studied Nora's face. "You have Flame Quarry's blue eyes."

Nora felt a constriction in her chest. "Flame?"

"Well, that's what we always called her. Flora Quarry. She taught Tommy and me our ABCs. Folks always said she had the fiery temper that went with the hair, and I guess that was one side of her, but she could be patient as a lamb, and that was the side she showed to us." Thelma Bright fingered her own once-vivid curls. "I guess you could say I used to know a thing about temper myself, but life has a way of ironing out the peaks and valleys."

Holding her breath, Nora laid her sketch of the black-haired butterfly girl on the table. Mrs. Bright fumbled for her pink harlequin glasses. "Oh, doesn't it all come back!" She touched the girl's hair. "Mercy, mercy me. I remember Eleanora's black curls . . . how tangled they'd be with burrs and dandelion fluff after we played in the swamp. Two sisters, yet as different as a rose and its thorn."

Nora felt something hard give way in her chest, as if a dam might be about to burst. "I didn't know Grandma Flora had a sister."

Mrs. Bright nursed her tea like hot soup on a cold day. "Eleanora was more what you might say placid, and didn't she attract the young men like bees to honey! That Slater boy . . . such a tragedy." Carefully placing her cup in its saucer, she blew her nose on her Kleenex. "First our Tommy gone and then your Eleanora. They arrested poor Daniel Slater, but of course they didn't have enough evidence to convict him. He never married, you know . . . so devoted." She gazed mistily at Nora. "Flame Quarry's granddaughter! Many's the time I wondered what happened to her on the other side of that ocean."

Nora smiled. "She opened a tearoom and told fortunes."

"That sounds like Flame! She promised to write, but, well . . ."

"She just had the one daughter – my mother. She died of a heart attack an hour before I was born."

"Well, then, you missed a treat. Flame was surely someone who liked her funnin'!" Mrs. Bright's amiable face puckered in thought. "Now, Flame and Nicholas . . . that was a real strange combination."

"Nicholas? My grandfather?" Nora placed her portrait of the two-headed centaur on the table.

Frowning, Mrs. Bright placed her freckled hand over one face and then the other. "Well, I guess it is. . . . I was only young then, but I've seen my share of pictures. You know how it is with folk telling stories in front of children. Sometimes they spell out d-a-m-n as if they think you've never heard the word, and at others they act like you were born without ears." She squinted at the drawing. "Mind you . . . it isn't one face or the other, but a bit of both. Of course he wasn't so handsome. This is more like a movie star – probably how he fancied he looked, given the stir he caused among the ladies." Mrs. Bright applied herself to her pie. "When he and Flame ran off, people were pretty judgmental – not like today when folk more or less have their freedom."

Nora numbly tried to eat her pie. "I thought Grandpa Flowe was killed down a mine."

"Nicholas Flowe down a mine?" Mrs. Bright's voice rose indignantly. "Hauling coal was the job of little boys like our Tommy, or

Pa with his throat rotted out, not swells with ruby stickpins! What Flame saw in Nicholas Flowe is hard to imagine, but if they found their happiness across an ocean then —"

"Grandpa Flowe didn't come to Canada."

Mrs. Bright smoothed her napkin. "Well, if he didn't, he certainly made a fine show of pretending to!" She folded it into ever-smaller triangles. "Ma had a postcard from Flame in Liverpool, sassy as you please. I came across it just a week ago in my postcard scrapbook." Closing her eyes, she recited in a child's voice: "'Sorry to leave without good-byes. Tonight Nicholas and I sail for Canada on *The Empress of Ireland* – Deck A, ever so posh! Promise to write real soon. Kisses and hugs to Thelma, I'll miss her lots and lots."

Mrs. Bright opened her eyes. "Fancy keeping a thing like that all these years. I suppose it was the 'Kisses to Thelma' part. You could say I had a crush on Flame Quarry. Of course, I had my anger about her running off – there'd already been far too much leave-taking in my life for my liking. Oh dear, oh dear, what a pity I kept that old card so long and then threw it out."

Nora conjured up the photo of her grandmother docking at Quebec City with her infant in her arms. "It was only Grandma Flora who emigrated to Canada, along with my mother as a baby."

"There was no baby, luv . . . not on these shores. Though what Flame and Nicholas got themselves up to on another continent would be another story."

"Grandma Flora arrived in Canada with a baby but not with Grandpa Flowe," insisted Nora, pushing aside her pie. "That baby was my mother."

Mrs. Bright shook her head. "That doesn't fit with what I've been told, luv, but pieces do get jumbled through the years." She narrowed her eyes as if peering through a time warp. "Rumor had it that Eleanora was in the family way when she went missing, but Flame – now she was a different kettle of fish! Folks around here figured Flame was too smart to get involved with any man without first being sure of her prospects, which was why it was such a shock when she ran off with Nicholas. You see, Nicholas had a wife . . . Agnes Flowe, poor soul."

A.F. . . . a black-haired woman bound in chains. "I saw her grave outside the cemetery!"

Mrs. Bright made a steeple with her index fingers. "Some religions are pretty fussy about 'by her own hand,' and especially the Reform Church, with its views on wandering souls and hauntings and such." She scraped her already-clean plate with her fork. "Ma thought this hotel was such a bargain, but it's not a happy place, and don't I feel that sometimes!" She shook the empty teapot. "My my, it's a long time since I've sat at table to the last cup. Here it is, almost eight-thirty, and I've still got my pies to bake for tomorrow. I suspect you've heard about our Full Moon Festival? You'll enjoy the parade. It's all about how things used to be in Barrow when – "

Mrs. Bright plunked down the teapot. "What a ninny I am! Lots Forty-one and Forty-two – that's what this hotel used to be when the streets were numbered from the colliery. Then the center shifted to Market Place and our stables became a park. Forty-one and Forty-two – that's what the numbers still say under the plaque the town nailed to our door. You see, this was the original Slater mansion and —"

"The Slaters lived here?"

"Old Henry's father built it. When he died, John kept the land and made Nicholas take the house. There was real bitterness between them, luv. Nicholas claimed the only reason John was so keen on his having this place was because it would cost more to fix than it was worth."

Nora's hands gripped her drawings. "But why did Grandpa Nicholas inherit from Henry Slater?"

Mrs. Bright began brushing crumbs from the table. "Well, now, 'that gypsy bastard' was how folk around here talked about Nicholas. He and John Slater were half-brothers, luv. Henry Slater was Nicholas's father. It was all supposed to be hush hush, but that's the way it is in small towns – everyone pretends, like children playing house, that walls exist when everyone knows they don't. Nicholas worked for Henry Slater – you might say he kept him around as a pet. I supposed that's what made Nicholas so wild, being close to the dinner table but getting only the scraps."

Mrs. Bright retrieved Nora's uneaten pie. "I know you're not up to this, luv. That doesn't hurt my feelings. Too many other things to digest all at once. I feel the same way."

"But what happened to Grandpa Flowe?"

The older woman shrugged. "Who's to say? Whatever happens to someone who knows no rules but his own." She sighed, suddenly wearying of her tale. "That's the problem when you're the youngest in the family. You expect your elders to carry all the history. When they die off, you're the only one left to hold the memories, and isn't it a job sometimes!"

She patted Nora's hand. "We'll talk again tomorrow, luv."

Nora barely remembered climbing the stairs. She barely remembered washing her face or switching out the light. A *tsunami* from deep inside had crashed against a restraining wall, sweeping images and perceptions into her conscious mind. She was still feverishly trying to sort and order when St. Michael's tower struck twelve. After allowing the sound to settle in the cool night air, she fished her flashlight from her purse and tiptoed down to the lobby. She groped under the ebony desk till she found a ring of oversized iron keys, then snuck down the basement stairs.

The third key opened the iron-ribbed door.

Holding her breath, Nora swung her disc of light around the gold-and-burgundy dining room, discovering plump and dimpled Victorian chairs drawn up to white-linen tables set with cranberry glass and silver; globe gas lamps with brass fittings; crimson damask wallpaper patterned with Turkish scrollwork; mahogany sideboards bearing silver bowls.

Despite the dust and decay, Nora couldn't help imagining women in *décolletage* gowns, men in frock coats and jeweled stickpins, waitresses in crisp black and white uniforms with caps perched like sailboats on their waves.

"I say I'm the captain, but my wife runs a tight ship."

Attached to the dining room was a pub with everything as it must have been the night the bartender made his last call – the curve of a marble counter, a row of brass spigots, shelves of glasses and beer mugs. It was uncanny, like exploring the *Titanic* after disaster had struck – in this case, the future. Nora examined a mug stamped with the inn's silhouette against a full moon. Repeated washings had worn the pattern so that its peaked tower looked like a lone wolf howling.

"When the moon is full, Wolfe eats Wolfe. One version tells of a Wolfe who slew and ate his brother, then swore the body had been devoured by wolves."

With moistened finger, Nora printed "FLOWE" in the mirror of a sideboard carved with wolves' heads. Scrambling the letters, she produced "WOLFE."

"Another claims that a scullery maid killed her master at full moon, then ate him to feed the little Wolfe she was carrying."

The dust and mold were choking Nora. Muffling her nose in the sleeve of her nightgown, she retraced her footprints back to the lobby.

She should have returned to bed, grateful to have escaped the ghosts of time past, but one other room still tempted her. Stealing through the breakfast nook, formerly a library, she confronted an oak door concealed behind a wallpaper screen. It opened with her fourth key.

Inside, Nora found an old-fashioned office decorated with religious artifacts, ledgers and account books. All were written and initialed in the same spidery hand – "A.F"

Claiming a swivel chair at a walnut desk, Nora rifled drawers and pigeonholes. In a legal folder, she found a file of powdery

Barrow Times clippings, reporting on the disappearance and murder of Eleanora Quarry. Even as she skimmed their content, she understood that they were not so much providing information as confirming what she already knew.

Reincarnation? Nora turned over that possibility like a many-sided jewelbox, searching for a hidden spring. Though she did possess "memory" of this other time and place, it wasn't from the view of any one ancestor. It was more like a jerky period movie, independently shot from a camera set on her own shoulder, with many frames still missing. If she had actually traveled back in time, or even if she'd replayed a tape of genetic memories as if it were a home video, how to explain its aberrant mixture of fact and fantasy?

Nora wondered if, instead, she might have journeyed into some Lucid Zone of heightened experience, in which past and present were superimposed in a way that resonated with the truth of both. Events in this zone would be akin to computer portraits, created by overlaying a hundred faces to create one, capturing the reality of all – essence of face. Its insights, in comparison with ordinary experience, would be like photos taken by the Hubble Space Telescope, beyond the interference of Earth's obscuring atmosphere, yet still limited by the interpreter's skill in assessing and utilizing them.

Daylight was beginning to creep through breaks in the dirty windowpanes. In the few minutes left, Nora refocused on the news clippings. According to *The Barrow Times*, Flora Quarry had attended Eleanora's funeral as a chief mourner; therefore, she couldn't have left Barrow on June 23, 1913, as Nora had assumed.

Swiveling, she confronted a shelf of dusty hotel registries from 1892 to 1914. She chose 1913, then flipped to June 23. The familiar signature on an otherwise blank page confirmed who had put the June 23 "souvenir" issue of *The Barrow Times* into the ancestral suitcase and why that date was significant: *not to commemorate*

Grandma Flora's departure from Barrow, but to mark the arrival of a woman named Nora Locke.

Nora closed her eyes, letting these implications sink in. Had the red-haired woman, waving to her from the train window, been a necessary illusion to prevent her from identifying Grandma Flora and interacting with her in a way that might botch the historic record, thus preventing her own birth?

18

Nora sits on her mother's lumpy chesterfield, with Ginger on her lap, trying to watch TV *but producing only snow and static. In disgust, she throws down the remote control. Suddenly, the screen switches to a channel she has never seen before. As she stares at the ghostly, multi-layered images, she realizes that she is watching all the channels at once, with their characters and plots superimposed.*

A girl is rocking in a hammock in the outstretched arms of an apple–pear tree. The luscious fruit gleams phosphorescent in the light of a full moon. The fragrance of the garden is intoxicating – roses, honeysuckle, lilies, with a spicy underscent.

Dislodging her cat, Nora creeps closer to the TV *screen, eager to inhale the garden's giddy fragrance.*

The girl reaches up her arm and plucks the fruit. As she presses it to her lips, with the juices rivuleting down from her mouth, a shadow steals between her and the moon . . . something shaggy . . . shameful. Her nostrils flood with a pungent, gamy odor . . . frightening, fascinating. She sees a wolf with ruby eyes.

The beast peels the girl's arms from her chest as easily as tearing off the wings of a butterfly. With one hairy paw clamped over her mouth, he mounts her – his penis preceding him like a poisoned toadstool, his lank hair smothering her.

The wolves are howling with fanged voices. They gorge on the moon, tearing gouts of flesh from its underbelly, as tasty as a newly dropped lamb. The moon bleats in helplessness and pain, with tears of blood scoring its wounded face.

Ginger leaps through the TV screen. Nora follows. She is in a cave of stalagmites and stalactites as sharp as teeth. The butterfly girl lies on a limestone altar. She has swallowed a piece of the moon. Her belly waxes like the full moon rising.

The wolf is here, and a gypsy midwife. The wolf raises, then lowers, his dagger. The girl's belly bursts like a ripe melon, spilling its blood fruit. Pain spirals outward, turning her flesh into a single, supersaturated wound. She screams from the soles of her feet to the tips of her hair, one ululating, never-ending howl, echoing through all the mouths of this cavern, the next and the next, rippling backward and forward through time. Her last breath turns into a black butterfly.

Gypsy hands rescue the blood fruit. They wrap it in a red-fringed shawl, then spirit it from the cave.

Now the wolf is crying. He sits like a child beside the mutilated girl with his knees pulled up to his chest, howling.

Flame is crying. She tries to sew crushed and broken butterfly wings into a patchwork quilt, while Ginger paces on a ledge overhead, growing larger and wilder at each step, her yellow eyes blazing in the torchlight.

With a fanged snarl, the large cat pounces.

Nora surfaced slowly, her body in a sweat, convulsed with undigested emotions. She could hear her name, echoing as if through dank cellars: Nora . . . Nora . . . Nora . . .

Noise, so much noise . . . people shouting. *David? Where's David?* She felt her head, found no bandages.

That other voice again. "Nora!"

Mother? Am I late for school? The patchwork quilt in her fists seemed to possess a scrap from every outfit she'd ever worn. *So hot.* She cast it from her, dislodging an orange cat from its nest on her belly.

Footsteps were coming up the stairs. *Is there an exam today?*

"It's me, Nora."

Aunt Millie?

Someone was knocking. "Nora . . . are you awake, luv?"

Sunlight filtered through shutters. Foreground separated from background: a fireplace bracketed by wing chairs, a desk set against densely flowered wallpaper, a coronation picture of Queen Elizabeth II.

That disembodied voice again. "You're going to miss the parade."

Nora peered through her window: a children's playground, an old stable converted into a concession stand.

"Thank you, Mrs. Bright."

Still mesmerized by her dream, she reached for her bathrobe and slippers, then shuffled downstairs, hearing band music.

Thelma Bright, in old-fashioned blue-gingham dirndl and dust cap, beckoned from the inn's archway. "It's our Fire Brigade Buglers. They've won ever so many prizes."

Though the buglers were indisputably lively as they high-stepped in their red and gold uniforms, Nora couldn't seem to scour the blood and anguish of last night's dream from her brain.

A cardboard lady, the height of a two-story building, glided behind the buglers, waving a *Barrow Times* dated 1913, and trailing a banner proclaiming "MANY MOONS AGO."

Various businesses had sponsored floats celebrating their stake in Barrow's history: a row of papier-mâché storefronts depicted Market Street as it had been eighty years ago, with "Thomas Ball & Sons Chemists," "Miss Jepson's Millinery," "Alcott the Wheelwright" and the "Picture Palace." The staff of Thomas Cook & Sons, in celluloid collars, frock coats and striped pants, threw streamers from a white steamship with prow extended like butterfly wings; the fuzzy-headed proprietor of the old "Time Past" pawnshop, an amiable cross between Gepetto and Einstein, again perched amidst his clocks and fiddles; little girls in middies and pleated skirts received instruction from a prim, honey-haired schoolmistress in high-necked shirtwaist and pince-nez; a bearded gent with a distinctive mole like a punctuation mark rallied the editorial board of *The Barrow Times*; the potato-faced Ragley, whom Nora had met yesterday, posed as a constable in front of the old Barrow police station; gypsies in colorful shawls and scarves pumped concertinas atop a red and gold caravan; black-faced miners worked their stalls while relatives wept at No. 8 pit head in a re-creation of the 1913 explosion; a red-haired girl in a poppy-ladened hat threw flyers from a Suffragette float: "WOMEN'S VOTES: Give Or We Take."

The citizens of Barrow, decked out in prewar costumes, clapped and shouted while Nora stared in wonderment: was it the past that she had been hallucinating, or this future? As in the ancient Gnostic symbol, linear time had curled like a snake and begun devouring its own tail.

"Mercy me, my pies!" exclaimed Mrs. Bright, gathering up her skirts and heading toward her kitchen.

The house smelled of flaky pastry oozing peach juice. Calling through the kitchen doorway, Nora assured her hostess: "No need to make anything for me. I'll just help myself to coffee and toast."

Mrs. Bright bustled into the breakfast room, wiping her hands on a peach-stained towel. "Are you sure, luv? I don't mind telling you that would be a godsend. I'm already late for the Friendly Society bake booth."

Nursing coffee in a paper cup, Nora returned to her room. With the band music still in her ears, she donned spandex shorts and her "Save the Wolf" T-shirt.

Her Nikes were nowhere to be found. Ransacking her armoire, she found a pair of cleat-heeled oxblood shoes, hand-crafted from the finest of calfskin. They fit perfectly. When Nora tried to peel them off, they seemed stuck to her feet like a second skin.

Impulsively, she donned the other foreign item in her armoire – a long-skirted white muslin dress, which she assumed Mrs. Bright had intended for her as a costume. She added the silver locket and a sprig of lavender. *When in Barrow . . .*

It cost £7 to enter the fairgrounds – once a Common for sheep, later a cricket field. Musicians, magicians, acrobats and jugglers performed wherever they could squeeze space. An organ-grinder with a fez-wearing monkey posed for pictures. A pony offered rides to the children. A trio of dogs performed tricks for a clown. "Pearlies" jigged to an accordion. The Leg o' Mutton barbershop quartet crooned "If Those Lips Could Only Speak."

A photographer in a brown derby and red braces winked at Nora. "'oo d'yer fancy?" He gestured toward his gallery of prewar cutouts, supplemented by Princess Di and Elvis.

Nora stuck her head through the veil of an old-fashioned bride escorted by a frock-coated groom.

"Now give us a smile," urged the photographer. "'ow d'yer expect to get a chap unless yer looks like yer wants 'im?"

She tried to withdraw her head before he could snap his picture.

"Easy, lady! Yer bloody well ripping me bride to bits!"

Extricating herself, Nora strode away.

"Bloody oath! It's nowt free with a pound of tea, yer know."

Reluctantly, she purchased the Polaroid, then watched as its images materialized – her own face agape in the bridal veil and, under the groom's top hat, a swirl of light and shadow that resembled a grinning skull.

Ahead Nora saw a Ferris wheel looking like an abandoned water wheel amidst the fair's gaudier attractions.

"'twon't even ruffle yer hair," urged the ticket-seller. "If you faint from fright, it's money back, guaranteed."

As Nora installed herself in a double seat, the red-haired girl in poppy hat from the Suffragette float squeezed in beside her. "Might as well. They're all going the same place, now aren't they?"

"Up and away!" confirmed the operator.

The wheel ascended to the strains of *The Merry Widow*. Below bobbed a sea of bald pates and permed hair in L'Oréal shades of gold to blue-black. Beyond that, the Barrow River snoozed like an amber serpent across the Vale of Barrow, with its head nestled against a limestone outcropping that resembled a prehistoric skull. Nora began rocking her seat, at first gently, then gaining force.

"'ere, you. Stop that!" growled the operator as the wheel made its second sweep.

Grinning, her seatmate rocked harder.

"Stop the wheel!" shrieked a woman in the seat behind.

"Fire!" shouted Nora's companion. She handed Nora a leaflet, then tossed the rest into the air.

PSYCHIC READINGS!
Past & Future
£5.

The operator applied the brakes. As he yanked Nora from her seat, her giggling companion bolted over a guardrail and disappeared into the crowd.

"I could 'ave you arrested!" stormed the operator.

"That unruly girl just threw herself into the seat beside me," deadpanned Nora. "It was frightening."

"Don't let me catch you back 'ere again – a woman of your age!"

Nora slunk off into the crowd.

While airborne, she had noticed a black tent amid the candy-striped ones. Over its entrance was a gold-and-black banner: "GOD IS WATCHING." Lured by shouts and clapping, she entered. A pair of black-cowled preachers swayed like hooded cobras over a frenzied collection of mice.

"What happens to Sinners?" demanded the woman.

"THEY GO TO HELL!" shouted the crowd.

"Are you going to Heaven?" queried the man.

"YES, YES, YES, WE'RE GOING TO HEAVEN!"

"Tell me, tell me, tell me about this Heaven."

"HALLELUJAH! HALLELUJAH! HALLELUJAH!"

The two preachers clapped and stamped and chanted. The crowd joined in, slowly and rhythmically, then gaining in fervor. Nora felt the ground quiver and quake through the soles of her oxblood shoes. With the sweat sieving from her body, she began to stamp. The cowled figures raised their arms, exhorting their followers to higher levels of adoration. Breaking free, Nora shoved toward the exit.

Now she was in a place called Freak Alley, where raspy-voiced barkers touted the charms of a fat lady with "thighs that can strangle a bear," a sword-swallower with "a cast-iron throat," a calf with "seven count 'em, SEVEN legs, and TWO 'eads." Tucked at the end of the row she found a red-and-gold caravan where girls in flowered shawls gyrated to scratchy tunes blared over loudspeakers.

A tobacco-skinned old man, who looked as if he had been twisted out of used pipe cleaners, beckoned. "Fortunes, only five pounds." Grinning to reveal gums blackened from chewing licorice, he thrust a leaflet into her hands, identical to the one she'd received on the Ferris wheel.

"Go in the right door."

Nora opened the left one by mistake. Her Ferris-wheel companion, naked except for her rakish poppy hat, waved back. She was mounted on a man wearing only black riding boots.

Nora slammed that door, yanked open the one opposite. A crone in an orange turban, fastened by a ruby stickpin, dozed in a bamboo fan chair with her flesh cascading like inner tubes around her. At the tinkle of the doorbell, she beckoned to Nora with an arm from which wrinkled flesh flapped like a crumpled sheet on a line. As Nora claimed the stool opposite, she dealt Tarot cards onto a bamboo table, clicking her tongue against a single front tooth. Her flesh seemed mummified. She could have been three hundred years old!

"You'll get a letter with money in it. You'll take a trip across water. You'll meet a dark and handsome man – very thin he is, someone you've known before."

As the crone thumped down her cards accompanied by her clichés, Nora stared mesmerized into her turban's winking ruby eye. Clasping an arm, she demanded in a voice that seemed to echo through wet caverns: "What happened to Eleanora Quarry?"

The crone's wrist bone twisted like a chicken's neck inside its loose skin. Slumping, she hyperventilated alarmingly, tongue clicking against her single tooth, exuding the scent of licorice.

"Confusion . . . darkness . . . black . . . black . . . black. Beware, beware, the August moon. Wolves that howl, the open womb." Her eyes rolled into her head, leaving two dirty mushrooms. "One dead instead of two. The moon was fuller than we knew. One soul for the other, that choice made by the mother. A pact between earth and heaven. Flames without fire! One eye paid for two, one red for two blue."

Nora released the crone's arm. Her head snapped forward and back so rapidly her neck seemed broken. Her eyelids fluttered open. "What did I say?"

The bell behind Nora tinkled. "Oh, you're so lucky!" enthused the barker, rubbing his hands in the doorway. "She's in spirit. Many folk have paid twenty guineas for that, but we'll only charge you —"

Pressing a £10 note into his outstretched hand, Nora fled the caravan and the fair.

She wasn't sure when she began to hear the tolling bell. Somewhere around *The Barrow Times* building the sound invaded her skull as if it belonged there. Ahead she could see a funeral procession just leaving St. Michael's Church, bearing an oak casket covered in white roses. She recognized the librarian, Pamela Slater, and the elderly secretary who had banished her. She trailed the mourners at a discreet distance as they threaded their way to the Slater plot for a brief ceremony.

As the grave-diggers indulged in a last smoke before filling the hole they had so recently gouged, Nora ascended to the now-deserted Slater obelisk. Winding the heart necklace around a sprig of lavender, she tossed it onto Daniel Slater's casket, weeping silently.

Nora climbed to the apex of Barrow Hill. The scratched, dented and jimmied copper door of Henry Slater's overstated mausoleum submitted easily to pressure, like a strongbox tired of keeping its secrets. In its gloomy interior Nora saw a marble angel with broken wings, a mortuary slab that seemed to have been used for picnics and – padlocked in a decorative cage – the remains of Henry Slater. *Great-grandfather Henry Slater*, she reminded herself, whose dual nature had perpetuated itself through his sons.

As Nora gathered up petrified orange peels and cigarette butts, she pondered the Western prejudice that viewed each life as a story complete in itself. When you really thought about it, the space bracketed by birth and death seemed more like a clause in a sentence in a paragraph in a chapter in a book in a library. Each of us was born into this world carrying a suitcase containing a record of the lives we had already led, echoing back millions of years. Perhaps it was our task as humans to solve various problems in consciousness, resonating from generation to generation until an answer could be found and genetically encoded. A contemporary family was at least as different psychically as physically from a Cro-Magnon one. Despite some evidence to the contrary – including the stink of human urine inside Henry Slater's final resting place – a strong case could be made that life on this planet was evolving toward greater consciousness.

Seeking out a dumpster, Nora deposited her trash, then continued her journey down into The Flats.

She climbed a stone stile into a brooding stand of oaks and beeches, following the gurgle of water. The rill widened into a creek lined with alders, then into a pond with a water wheel, all but obliterated by decades of sphagnum moss. Kicking off her oxblood shoes, she waded into the amber pool, its shoreline wild with arrowheads, ferns and lush grasses. When water soaked her white muslin dress, she peeled that off, along with her bra and briefs.

Nora plunged, feeling the silty liquid glide over her prickly flesh. She navigated through the pulpy stems of water lilies attached like umbilical cords to the waxy flowers floating overhead. When a submerged log turned into the grinning visage under her cardboard groom's top hat, she surfaced, determined to wipe that macabre image from her mind.

Emerging behind a hummock of sphagnum moss spiked with lyme grass, Nora crawled into the mud flats, then smeared her flesh with clay, feeling the intimate contours of her breasts, her thighs, her hips, her calves, inside their slicker of primordial ooze, no longer seeking herself in the embrace or face of another, knowing that no one else could give herself to herself or make her whole – that task was hers alone.

Nora patted mud over her face, then lay on her back, flapping her arms to create a mud angel. She strung garlands of water lilies around her neck, weaving them through her hair, bringing her body to consciousness through the recognition of her mind, and allowing her mind to root itself through her body, inhabiting her own skin with every cell of her mind while her body rejoiced in the psychic dance of life.

Old Mrs. Fitch fell into a ditch
With her heels cocked up in the air.
The donkey took fright to see such a sight
On the way to the Barrow Fair . . .

Breaking from the mud flats, Nora plunged into Barrow River, thrilling to the icy bite of the current as it scoured the clay from her flesh. She rolled over onto her back, watching clouds scud across the incandescent sky and surrendering herself to air and water, feeling herself stretch from shore to shore and then from horizon to horizon, from the fiery eye of the sun to the fire in the belly of the earth. She contemplated the striated rocks and multiringed trees, understanding that our sense of linear time was only a once-serviceable illusion, like the theory that the world was flat.

Back on shore, she shook herself on all fours, then dressed layer by layer.

Towering over a copse of ashes scabbed with lichen, Nora glimpsed the limestone skull she'd spotted from the Ferris wheel. Though the sun had not yet set, the full moon hung like a plucked eyeball over the dark hollow forming the skull's left socket. Curiously, she labored up the short, steep path choked with thorns and thistles, to the protruding jaw, then stood on the rise, surveying. Where she'd expected meadows embroidered in wildflowers, ponds regal with bulrushes, forests woven into a sun-drenched tapestry of green, she saw only trucks, gravel pits, rutted mud, barbed-wire fences.

A gold-on-black sign proclaimed:

SLATER QUARRY FIELDS

PRIVATE PROPERTY

WARNING:

Trespassers Will Be Prosecuted.

"Have you heard of our Bootstrappers? It's a local group, founded by my wife, to support the desires of working-class families to improve themselves – to pull themselves up by the bootstraps, so to speak. . . . Barrow must be brought into the new technological age."

"When I was a boy, that was my favorite place for sparrowing. My sister and I used to sneak in there of a winter's night with a net on a pole, and in no time we'd have a dozen I could sell for thru'pence."

Life was a muddle. Good intentions often produced negative results, while selfish ones might prove wise. Nora weighed this gravel pit against the new Bottoms school: was the deal worth it? That question was a specious one: instinct and intellect, the natural and the cultivated, were not themselves opposed, except in divided people. All one could do, when confronted with this present atrocity, was to hold onto one's own integration and to take the leap of faith, grounded in that certainty.

The limestone crag resembling a skull remained intact, except for one missing tooth. Inside its cavity, Nora found a rusty gasoline can and the stub of a torch, reminding her of the flashlight in her shoulder bag.

She walked around the skull to the ear canal, guarded by a wood door strung with barbed wire that hung like Halloween curtains. Drawing it aside, Nora shoved open the rotting door. Her beam illuminated a carving on its splintered inner surface: the faint outline of a wolf howling at the moon.

"We can't stop here!"

"Come, darling, be brave. I need your help, your strength. Oh God, you're all that's kept me going."

Nora groped her way down the steep tunnel, watching it expand and contract under the play of light and shadow. Her left oxblood shoe found a drop-off spanned by a ladder with six rungs. After descending, she swept her beam overhead, illuminating a roughly hewn, twenty-foot dome.

Opposite her was a three-foot arch. Again, Nora hesitated.

"I've something important to show you, just as I promised. I know the answer to the mystery. The evidence is unmistakable. . . . Trust me."

Ducking through, she discovered a soaring blue-green cathedral dripping with stalagmites and stalactites in patterns mystical and magical. She slid her light like a phosphorescent paintbrush over the ceiling, then groped around the cavern, exploring each pocket of shadow.

Inside an icy cluster of fangs, Nora encountered a tunnel.

"My sister found this place. We used to hide out here. It was our secret."

Claustrophobia made the tunnel seem narrower than it was. As she crawled through, she imagined how a salmon might feel if it knew it were swimming upstream to spawn and die.

"My poor darling, as pretty as a bride in your lovely white dress. You must wonder what all this is about. I'm sorry for your distress, but when you see the evidence, you'll understand that I couldn't work this out in any other way."

The passageway broadened and deepened. As Nora again swung her light, her left foot stepped off a ledge. Losing her balance, she tumbled over.

Nora lies on stone, dazed and disoriented, in a cave rancorous with death. The heavy air, possessing no mixture of moisture or light or sound, compacts in her lungs, choking off breath. Her ankle throbs. Her left shoe is missing, along with the flashlight.

Nora's fingers scuttle like crabs over the porous rock, exploring. Gradually, she allows herself to understand that she is not alone in the cave. She holds a hand . . . *a skeletal hand.*

Groaning, Nora unhitches flesh from bone. Her frantic fingers discover her flashlight. She clicks, producing a pale yellow funnel.

Nora forces herself to examine the other occupant of the cave, beginning at . . . decaying shoes with button tops, bits of striped cloth clinging to shank-bone. She slides her beam upward to the face – a mummified gentleman, grimacing as best as he can through patches of brown skin, dressed for death in frock coat and plum waistcoat.

The horror . . . that first time in the cave!

Nora notes the corpse's missing assets: a vest without a pocket-watch, a silk shirt without cufflinks, a gray cravat without a stick-pin . . . a severed ring finger.

A yard from the crushed skull, she finds a cleat-heeled oxblood shoe. She slips it on – identical to the one she's just lost, except for its patina of eighty years.

Now in a place beyond terror, Nora lies on the rock in her filmy white dress, holding her bridegroom's hand . . .

Beads of sweat rim his forehead, then trickle down his cheeks. The reek of nicotine and cloves and whiskey clogs her lungs as her neck ten-

dons contract under the pressure of his thumbs. She experiences a stoppage of blood and the bulging of her eyes as she passes in and out of consciousness.

"A Wolfe kills only out of necessity. You must take some responsibility, too. No one sees 'my brother' who doesn't secretly know him already. He's your invention, too."

Something else, something new – at least, to her – the next instalment, recorded eighty years ago in the dry air of the cave:

As the breath slowly expels from Nora's lungs, the air seems to catch fire over her strangler's shoulder. A girl crouches on a ledge, her hair licked to flame by the torchlight. She arcs back a hand, bearing a cleat-heeled shoe she found on the ledge. As she pounces, she strikes, avenging herself for a sister's death.

Working nervelessly, she strips the still-warm corpse of its booty, including a ruby stickpin to be bartered for her sister's child, ripped too early from the womb but already possessed of a will-to-survive far stronger than its mother. She has climbed a hill, and now she will sail an ocean, for back in a hotel room a steamer ticket awaits, The Empress of Ireland, *Suite 100, Deck A, July 8, 1913 – the legacy of a traveler who no longer needs it, along with a new leather suitcase!*

Nora opens her eyes, releases the corpse's hand. Though she now knows the end of his story, she is still in the dark about the larger Mystery: who, or what, has summoned her to this place of violence and confrontation? These restless bones of Grandfather Nicholas Flowe, demanding burial? The guilty ghost of Great-aunt Flora needing expiation? The sorrowing spirit of Grandmother Eleanora seeking solace? None? All?

Scraping soil from the porous rock, Nora sprinkles it onto the remains of Nicholas Flowe who, as family legend recorded, had indeed lost his life down a mine. Then, using her gold-and-pearl watch with its hands folded at twelve as if in prayer, she petitions for his soul, calling upon their entire ancestral flock to bear witness, to bring forth their own sins of commission and omission, to cleanse and be cleansed, to bless and be blessed.

Nora swings her pale beam overhead. The cave's irregular surface is pocked like skin with every square inch inscribed with erotica from savage to space age. People, animals, people and animals, half-people and half-animals, monsters, demons, angels, astronauts. Some drawings seem sacred, some profane. Clambering to her feet, she stretches forth her hand, drawn to their terrible primal power.

Her light falters, then fades to black, leaving only a metallic click, echoing in the silence as she worries its switch. Once again it is dark in the cave, and very, very quiet. She has come to the end of biography, though not of questions.

Where, geographically, is her body now? Is it in a limestone cave in the Midlands of Britain, or does it lie on the staircase of her natal home? Is she having a near-death experience or a near-life one? If she is not on a staircase or in a cave, is she already curled in a womb? Any second now will its walls begin to contract, pushing her bald head into another life, like a blood moon rising? In this century, or another? On this planet, or another?

Nora weeps, surrendering to the perpetual moment. The mouths on the wall also begin to grieve and then to howl. The cave is a single wailing wound.

A hand clasps her. Her companion's bony fingers encircle her wrist. His hand bursts into flame, torching hers. The fire spurts up her arm, consuming her. She sees other figures in the flames – men attacking each other with clubs, with spears, with swords, with guns; women devouring their young; eyes being torn from sockets, breasts slashed off, children raped, animals skinned alive; chemicals dumped into streams, cities bombed, smoke spewed from chimneys, forests leveled with giant saws. The pain is so intense that she passes into apocalyptic shock – beyond agony, revulsion, even judgment. As she stares deeper into the flames she feels herself in the presence of a power so overwhelming that all she can experience is awe. Despite its potential for destruction, she knows it is Creative Force, for nothing can be destroyed that hasn't first been created.

The walls of the cave grow silent except to beat. Deep within what might be her own heart she hears chanting; the air trembles with its bouquet of subtle and exquisite odors. As she listens, the music deepens, soars and swells in intimacy, scope and profundity. Grief gives way to reverence and then to joy. Each note is a rainbow of love; each inhale of the cave's ether, an invocation into the Mystery. She struggles to name this Mystery but the closest she can come is Meaning or Purpose. She has never felt so insignificant and yet so all-encompassing. She is a single radiant note in a melody sung in perfect harmony. She is that note and she is that harmony.

She is infused with the spirit of hope. She knows that everything is in order, though she has caught only a fleeting glimpse of that order – shadows of shadows of shadows flickering across cave walls. She knows that all is One within the cave. She knows that she, along with the other muddlers bearing the same genetic zip code, are to be given another chance. The sets and costumes may change and their roles may be reshuffled, but the journey continues and it is a single journey. They are parts of a whole as inseparable as drops in an ocean, to be inhaled into the sun before being shed once more as tears into the ocean.

Again the cave falls silent. Nora is ready. Soon, very soon, she will open her eyes, count to three, then crawl toward the mouth of the cave.

One

Two

Three . . .